CW01628118

SHADOW CRIMES

A gripping crime thriller full of twists

MICHAEL HAMBLING

JOFFE BOOKS

Published 2018 by Joffe Books, London.

www.joffebooks.com

© Michael Hambling

This book is a work of fiction. Names, characters, businesses, organizations, places and events are either the product of the author's imagination or are used fictitiously. Any resemblance to actual persons, living or dead, events or locales is entirely coincidental. The spelling is British English.

All rights reserved. No part of this publication may be reproduced, stored in retrieval system, copied in any form or by any means, electronic, mechanical, photocopying, recording or otherwise transmitted without written permission from the publisher. You must not circulate this book in any format.

ISBN- 978-1-78931-045-0

To the people of my home city of Salisbury.

We've experienced difficult times this year, due to the reckless use of a nerve agent that killed one woman and put the lives of others at risk. Throughout this lengthy and dangerous episode, the people of Salisbury went about their business in an atmosphere of calm and cheerfulness, beneath that glorious spire.

I love Salisbury. I love its people, its cathedral, its streets of medieval buildings, its schools, its parks, its pubs, and I am proud to have been a resident for nearly forty years. This book is for you, Salisbury.

Chapter 1: Friction

Saturday, Midday

A few minutes after midday on a cold January Saturday, Lydia Pillay stood outside a shabby pub near Dorchester's railway station. She was wearing grey skinny-fit trousers, ankle boots and a leather bomber jacket, jet-black like her cropped hair. She looked around as if she were expecting to meet someone, tapping a foot impatiently, glancing at her watch and tugging at the gold stud earrings that glinted above her red silk scarf. Evidently whoever she was waiting for was late. After one final look at her watch, she turned and opened the door of the bar, hesitating for a second as her eyes adjusted to the low light.

The pub seemed busy, more so than she'd anticipated. A large group of men clustered near the bar, all clutching pints of lager or glasses of spirits. This wasn't what she'd expected. She made her way to the bar and ordered a glass of apple juice, took off her gloves and stood waiting for her drink. Around her, the chatter suddenly ceased and she was aware of being observed closely. These weren't ordinary drinkers in for a quick lunchtime snifter. They might well be a range of sizes and shapes, but they had several characteristics in common. All had shaved heads, menacing tattoos and an intimidating manner. She noticed that the bar staff looked worried, as if they didn't quite know how to cope with this threatening group. She picked up her glass, retreated to a small table against the far wall and sat down, taking a magazine out of her shoulder bag. She looked up. One of the men had followed her, his stocky form hunched forward in a menacing way. His tone was threatening.

'We don't want you in here. Fuck off back to where you belong, you Paki bitch.' He seemed to seethe with anger, his fleshy face red, eyes slitted. He'd jabbed a finger at her as he spoke but now this hand was clenched into a fist. A nearly empty pint glass of lager was in the other.

'I was born here in the UK and that makes me as British as you. And, if you must know, my parents are from India, not Pakistan. Not that that would be of much interest to you, would it?' She was aware that two other men had walked across to stand behind the first. Both wore the same uniform of denim jeans, T-shirt and tattoos on their arms. One was tall, thin and wary-looking, the other short and pugnacious.

'Fucking right. I couldn't give a shit where your grubby family comes from. Just piss off back there. That's once you've fucked off out of this bar, 'cause we don't want you in here, polluting our clean air with your stink.'

She pulled a slim wallet out of her pocket, opened it and placed it face up on the table in front of her, not taking her eyes off the man's face.

'Detective Sergeant Lydia Pillay. Dorset police.'

She sensed someone approach from behind, but she didn't want to take her eyes off the man. Was there some uncertainty in the way his eyes flickered?

'Hello, boss. I was delayed by a few minutes. Alright?' The reassuring voice came from behind her.

The taller man put a warning hand on his colleague's shoulder as if to calm him, but said nothing.

'I think your timing's okay on this occasion, Jimmy,' she said to the person who'd quietly approached from behind, still with her eyes on the intimidating man standing opposite. 'You've just broken the law, Mr Whoever You Are. But you know that, don't you? I bet you even know the exact charges I could bring against you. But I've got other things to worry about right now, so just get out of my sight and take all your friends with you. If any of you are still here in ten minutes' time, we'll lift the lot of you.'

The man turned away, muttering obscenities under his breath, and returned to the group at the bar, who had largely fallen silent as the scene unfolded. He jerked his thumb towards the door and the group slowly followed him out.

She waited until the tall thin man bringing up the rear had left, and then turned to the person who had joined her.

'Where the hell's Andrea Ford?' she hissed. 'She should have been here fifteen minutes ago.'

Detective Constable Jimmy Melsom shrugged. 'I know. She phoned in a short while ago to say she couldn't make it. I knew that meant you'd be here on your own, so I moved as quick as I could. Sorry I wasn't here earlier.'

'It's not your fault, Jimmy. I'm glad you came, but what's going on in Ford's head? Why did she phone you instead of me? And why were that lot of thugs here? It was meant to be a low-key meet-up with this informer of hers. So why did it go so badly wrong? I don't even know what he looks like, so I can't tell whether he was here or not. One thing, though. If he witnessed that little scene, he'll have scarpered by now.' She sighed. 'Tell the bar staff we'll be back in a few minutes, will you? We'll take a quick look around the area to check that this lot aren't raising mayhem somewhere else. Then we'd better head back to the office.'

The group of men seemed to have split up. The two detectives spotted a few of them in a pub closer to the town centre, but they no longer stood out from the crowd. Instead they were quietly sitting around a table studying the sports pages of some of the tabloid newspapers on display in the bar. The leading trio were nowhere to be seen, so Lydia and Jimmy returned to the scene of the confrontation.

The duty manager was keen to talk. 'No idea who that lot were,' he said, running his hand through his mousey hair. 'I know we're not exactly an upmarket kind of place, but it's not often we get a crowd as bolshie as them. They were arguing about everything. I could see trouble brewing, so it was a relief when you turned up and got them to go. We had a few regulars leaving because they felt threatened.'

'So, you've no idea who they were or why they were here?' Lydia asked. He shook his head. 'They were looking for trouble, I can tell you that.' He paused for a moment. 'I think they were waiting for someone. Maybe you?'

This shocked Lydia. 'What makes you say that?'

'The ringleader, that heavily built aggressive bloke, kept his eye on the door all the time, and he was on the phone a lot. He reacted as soon as you walked in. You must have seen how they all went quiet when you came up to the bar. I didn't realise you were a cop. Maybe they didn't either.'

Lydia thought for a moment. 'Did you hear any of them say where the ringleaders were heading when they left? We didn't spot them in any other place we passed, though a few of the others are in a pub round the corner.'

'No. I called a couple of other pub managers nearby, we have an unofficial agreement about tracking troublemakers, but no one else has reported any problems. I didn't recognise any of them.'

One of the bar staff, a young man, chipped in. 'A couple of them were talking about casual work on the ferries. I didn't hear any details though. Don't know if that helps.'

Lydia handed her card to the manager. 'If anything else does occur to you, please get in touch.'

'Could they be from one of our ferry ports?' Jimmy said on their way to the door. 'That might mean Poole or Weymouth. Weymouth's only ten miles away.'

'The Weymouth link is a possibility. Andrea Ford is based there. I wonder if information about our planned meet up slipped out somehow? One thing's for sure. After what we've just heard, it's clear those thugs were looking for trouble and that worries me. And why the hell wasn't she here, with or without her informer?'

* * *

Detective Inspector Kevin McGreedie's attitude towards his second in command, DS Lydia Pillay, was a shade ambivalent and he felt guilty about it. She was a first-class detective who worked extremely hard and she had a sharp brain. During the six months that she'd worked for him, she'd never given him any cause to doubt her loyalty and commitment but the uneasiness was always there. It wasn't the fact that she was from an Asian background, nor that she was an obviously committed feminist. Neither of these caused him the slightest problem. No, it was the fact that Lydia had been Sophie Allen's protégée before the young detective unexpectedly transferred to the Regional Financial Crime Unit in Bath for two years. Now she was back in Dorset, at Bournemouth CID, in a move that had obviously been engineered by her previous boss. Or had it? Kevin was also aware that Lydia's sudden departure from Sophie's Violent Crime Unit at Dorset's police headquarters may have been brought about by some unexpected rift between the two women. He'd never managed to find out what it had been, though. One of his own junior detectives, Jimmy Melsom, had left the unit soon after Lydia and claimed to be unaware of any disagreement. But Jimmy wasn't the most razor-sharp analyst of human interaction, particularly when it came to women.

So where did Lydia's real loyalties lie? It wasn't a problem of any consequence to the work of the department, so why did he feel so guilty? Sophie was one of his closest friends as well as a county police colleague, but he was aware that she had unofficial contacts, and a lot of influence, in many police forces across the country, particularly since her very recent promotion to detective superintendent. He was beginning to wonder if the "old boy" network that had once been so influential in policing was being replaced by an "old girl" structure, closed to the male members of the profession. It was a little unsettling for traditional male officers like him, promoted through the ranks and lacking a university degree. Yet he knew from his younger days just how much crap women officers had been forced to endure in decades past. Part of him felt it was about time they gained the upper hand.

Kevin had decided to pay a brief visit to his Bournemouth CID office on Saturday afternoon because he knew Lydia was due to meet an informer in a backstreet bar over in Dorchester, arranged by a local detective, and he had uneasy feelings about the planned encounter. Lydia's current investigation was the result of a Home Office request that county forces try to get to the bottom of the methods used by criminals to smuggle "illegal materials" into prisons on their patch, identify the people involved and organise some arrests. Apparently, the justice department had just digested the fact that the situation was getting out of hand, something the prison service, and most police officers, had known for several years and had predicted as soon as the government began to cut back on prison budgets. Did anyone in their right mind think that an increasing prison population could be adequately supervised by fewer prison staff without problems following closely behind? Some politicians did, obviously, and now someone on high had got the message. A unified effort was called for, and a local police officer nominated to coordinate the investigation into the criminal gangs that supplied the illicit goods from outside the prison walls. With two prisons in the county, Dorset should be one of the leaders. It was the government's usual answer to any problem — neatly shift the responsibility elsewhere. And Lydia had been keen to get involved. She had approached Andrea Ford, the detective with the most contacts in the area around Portland prison. Andrea had never inspired Kevin with confidence. He'd often felt uneasy about her off-piste role in West Dorset, added to which he'd never entirely trusted her judgement. Getting close to criminals was like being a trapeze artist, and needed a highly developed sense of balance. Andrea Ford had a very outgoing personality and a willingness to hurl herself into raucous social situations, but in Kevin's opinion she lacked insight, added to which there was something unsettling about her attitude to criminals, though he couldn't quite put his finger on what it was.

The door opened. An angry looking Lydia Pillay stalked in, accompanied by Jimmy Melsom.

She threw her bag on her desk. 'What a fiasco. Ford didn't turn up, the informer may or may not have been there, and I got threatened by a gang of racist thugs who were in the pub. The whole thing fell apart. Bastards.' She switched the kettle on and spooned some instant coffee into an empty mug. 'What are you doing here, boss? You shouldn't be in today. You need your time off.'

That was the thing about women officers. They always found the time to comment on personal difficulties, whatever the situation. Kevin had kept Lydia up to date on the latest course of chemotherapy that his wife, Laura, was undergoing, and she never failed to remind him when he needed to get home or collect Laura's prescriptions. Lydia had even gone shopping for groceries for him. She really was unnervingly organised. But was it any surprise, considering who her boss had been?

He shrugged. 'I was out anyway to collect a few things from the shops, so it isn't a problem. No need to make a fuss about it.' He regretted the last remark as soon as he'd spoken. The words sounded ungrateful.

'No, but you need to switch off sometimes, boss. Laura needs you at the moment. Not that I don't appreciate your interest, but I'm a big girl now. I know how to look after myself. And Jimmy was around. I'd kept him informed of where I was.'

Kevin became even more irritated. 'I'd have done the same for anyone under my command. It's not because you're a woman, you know. You've got to see beyond the easy reason.'

'Do you know more about Ford than you've let on, boss? Is that what's worrying you?'

'No.' He shrugged again and turned away. 'Let's discuss this on Monday morning when we've all had a chance to think things through.'

Lydia watched him leave, then turned to Jimmy Melsom. 'Is it my imagination or did he look more worried than usual?'

Jimmy looked blank. 'You know me. I'm useless at this personal stuff. I can't read people's moods any better than the man in the moon. The boss is the boss. He's a good bloke, so I just get on with my job and leave that kind of stuff to you. Listen, I'm starving. Fancy a pie and a pint? We're off duty now.'

Lydia hesitated for a moment. 'Okay. I'm glad we came back in though. I wondered if the boss would be here, worrying. He takes his responsibilities too seriously sometimes. I didn't want him hanging around waiting for us, not with his wife as ill as she is. He's got enough on his plate.'

* * *

After a hurried lunch, Lydia finally managed to contact Andrea Ford in the middle of the afternoon.

'Sorry I couldn't make it. There was an emergency down here in Weymouth,' the detective explained. 'We only had a two-hour window to raid a drug gang. I tried to phone you but I couldn't get through. That's why I called Jimmy.' Her voice sounded distant and Lydia strained to make out what was being said. 'The signal's weak. There must be a line problem at the moment.'

Andrea's voice had all but disappeared, so Lydia gave up. Instead, she called the Dorset police communications unit to discuss the problem but was met with a puzzled response. 'We're not aware of any issue,' the technician said. 'I'll investigate and get back to you.'

Lydia sank back in her chair, deep in thought. Finally, she picked up the latest Ministry of Justice report on the prison problem and began to read it. Its contents were deeply troubling. It was clear that the smuggling of goods into prisons had got out of hand, and she could see why. The miniaturisation of mobile phones was making it almost impossible for the prison authorities to prevent them reaching inmates. The latest range would fit inside a lipstick case, designed to slide into a woman's clutch bag for an evening out, but also easily smuggled into a prison during visiting time. Particularly worrying were those made entirely of plastic, undetectable by the ageing scanning equipment installed in most prisons. They clearly made a mockery of attempts to keep high category prisoners in a communications limbo. Technology was evolving faster than the methods governments used to control its use, and would go on doing so.

Lydia read on. Smart thinking was required here, not an obvious feature of some of the justice department civil servants that she'd met at security conferences, clearly overworked and undervalued by their political masters. Every single aspect of public service was being systematically stripped to the essentials and run by stressed-out staff. It's a wonder social structures manage to keep ticking over at all, she thought wryly.

She looked at the clock. She should have been home hours ago. She slid the report and a few other documents into her bag, grabbed her jacket from the hook and was about to leave the office when her phone rang. It was the communications technician. There had been no issues with county communications over the last few days, and certainly not at midday. One of his colleagues had been on the line to Weymouth police station several times during the late morning and had reported no problems with voice clarity or broken connections.

'That isn't to say it didn't happen,' he went on, 'the gremlins can strike at any time. The log shows the call coming into your office at noon, the one your colleague took. We couldn't see any other attempts at calls around that time.'

'Thanks.' Lydia replaced the phone. Was something strange going on here?

Chapter 2: Death

Saturday Afternoon

Laura Quigley slipped into her daytime coat and draped a scarf around her neck, calling up the stairs, 'I'm just off to the shops, Tony. I'll be about an hour. Are you alright?'

She listened to the muttered, grumpy reply. She couldn't make out every word, but its meaning never varied. It was always the same when he was ill in bed like this, uttered in a self-pitying moan: *you go out and enjoy the fresh air and meet people and leave me alone here, ill in bed, festering.* Quite honestly, she was utterly fed up with him and his constant complaining. Other people with coughs and colds didn't make as much fuss as him. She knew he had chronic liver problems but who was to blame for that?

She pulled on her gloves, opened the door and stepped out into the fresh air. She tugged the door shut and, as was her habit, tested that the lock was fully engaged. She spotted one of the neighbours across the road, wiping down her front windows, and walked across for a chat. The usual stuff — the weather (chilly for the time of year), prices (getting dearer all the time), men (always moaning about something, and totally useless in the kitchen) and the state of Tony's health (worsening slowly and steadily). By the time the two women had exhausted these topics, the sky had darkened noticeably, and Laura was concerned that it would soon start raining. She gave her apologies and hastened towards the shops. She occasionally wondered whether to look for a part-time job, just to get out of the house more often and avoid the sour atmosphere created by Tony's constant complaints. She'd given up work when his various ailments had first developed, soon after he'd taken early retirement. They'd planned to fill their later years with travel and luxurious living, but his liver disorder had put paid to such fancy schemes. The reality was entirely different to the expectations she'd had just a few short years ago. Tony had turned into a lazy, grumpy, monosyllabic, brooding presence in the house and she'd grown to hate him. She must have been blind to have missed the signs all those years ago when they'd first met. Well, that wasn't entirely true. She knew she'd deliberately overlooked them because of the lavish gifts he'd showered on her and the luxury Spanish holidays they'd shared. Miserable git. Why didn't he just hurry up and die? Shocked at herself for thinking such a thing, Laura shook her head and hurried towards the local supermarket as the first drops of rain began to fall.

On her return she called her usual greeting. 'I'm back. Alright?' She walked through to the kitchen and dropped the bag of groceries on the table before returning to the hall to hang up her coat and hat. Still no sound. She called up the stairs again. 'I said, I'm back, Tony. Are you okay?'

Silence. This was unusual, but maybe he was asleep, which he often was mid-afternoon during one of his spells of sickness. She returned to the kitchen, tidied the groceries away and put the kettle on. She glanced at the newspaper. Squabbling politicians, knife crime, poverty and overpaid football stars. She sighed, extracted two mugs from the cupboard and made the tea. A couple of half-hearted stirs with an old teaspoon, a slightly soft biscuit from a dented tin on the shelf and she was ready for the trek up the stairs to her irritable husband.

She pushed the bedroom door open. He was lying on his front, his face buried in the pillow. Somehow it looked unnatural. She hurried across and grasped his hand, hanging lifelessly over the edge of the bed. It was icy cold. The mug of tea fell from her other hand, spilling its contents over the old mottled-green carpet. She lunged forward, feeling desperately for a pulse or any sign of life. There was none.

* * *

Sergeant Rose Simons, West Dorset's most experienced uniformed sergeant, sat in Laura Quigley's lounge drinking tea, her eyes flickering around the sitting room before they settled on the tearful home owner.

'This must have come as a terrible shock to you, Mrs Quigley. He was obviously unwell, but no one's ever prepared for a sudden end like that. You must be devastated. Is there anyone I can contact? Family members?' She watched Laura's face.

Laura shook her head. 'We never had kids. Tony never wanted any. I've got a sister, but she lives in Birmingham. Tony fell out with his brother and sister years ago, and they've never kept in contact.'

'We'll ask one of your neighbours to pop in. It'll be better to have someone around for a while. Maybe Mrs Grayling?'

'I'll be okay, honestly. He wasn't much company at the best of times. In some ways it's come as a relief as well as a bit of a shock. He was getting impossible to live with, especially on bad days like today. Ever since he retired two years ago, he was making my life a misery.'

Rose observed the woman closely. Would she be capable of hastening the end of the man she'd lived with for several decades? It was hardly likely, but something about the death wasn't quite right. It wasn't just the corpse's face and Laura's concern about the patio door, something else didn't make sense. It had been the neighbour opposite, the one called in by the distraught Laura Quigley, who'd told Rose of her concern. Through the frosted glass of their front door she claimed to have seen movement on the Quigley's stairs, at a time when Laura should still have been at the shops. Had it been the now-dead Tony Quigley, moving around for some reason? But his wife had said he hardly ever rose from his bed on one of his bad days. The man's slippers were still neatly arranged beside the bed, toes pointing outwards, just as she'd left them when she'd tidied the room after lunch. She was adamant that he would never have left them like that if he'd been up. They'd have been kicked off carelessly.

Could someone have called? If so, how would he or she have gained entry with both doors safely locked and the windows secured? Could the neighbour have imagined the movement? Rose was unsure. Frances Grayling appeared to be a sharp-witted and observant person, but the afternoon had been a gloomy one, particularly once the rain had started to fall. She had also insisted that the blurred figure she'd glimpsed rapidly descending the stairs in the Quigley's house had been darkly clad, yet the dead man's pyjamas had been pale blue. And she'd also been adamant about the speed of descent. Neither Quigley himself, nor his wife, could have moved so quickly. Either she'd imagined the incident or . . .

Rose looked up as her assistant, PC George Warrander, entered the room.

'The medics have finished, so they're ready to move your husband out, Mrs Quigley. Is that alright?'

Laura nodded slowly. 'Yes. Go ahead. Whatever has to be done, just get on with it. Look, I should have left him years ago. I kept telling myself that, but I was just too weak-minded to actually do it. Well, now it's happened I can't pretend to feel things that I don't.'

'What was your husband's line of work before he retired, Laura?' Rose asked.

'He was a prison officer, down at Portland.' She turned away to gather the mugs together.

'Do you keep a spare key to these French windows hidden somewhere out the back?' Rose asked.

'Yes. But it's in a little key safe, with a combination.'

'What's the combination, Laura?'

'It's Tony's birthday. Sixteen eleven. Sixteenth of November. Tony used it for all his combinations.'

* * *

'What do you think, boss?' asked George Warrander as they made their way back to the car.

'My nose is twitching a bit and you know what that means,' she said.

'Maybe you're going down with a cold?'

Rose looked exasperated. 'I'm the one who cracks the jokes around here, Georgie boy. Don't try to muscle in or I'll transfer you to the night shift on New Year's Eve. No, there's something not right about that death. I think I'll give Barry Marsh a call and talk it over. I know our local CID will need to get involved but I'm still allergic to Stu Blackman. With family liaison looking after the merry widow, we've got some time to dig around a bit. Did you have a chance to check out her supermarket receipt? Do the times tally?'

'Exactly with what she and the neighbour said.'

Rose often displayed a hard-bitten, couldn't-care-less attitude but George had quickly learned that this was all for show, part of her coping mechanism. Her offbeat humour was merely a shell, and the quirky behaviour was only partly successful in camouflaging the very efficient and organised approach to work that lay underneath, along with a surprisingly caring attitude. Not that Rose didn't have a temper. He'd been on the receiving end several times and didn't enjoy the experience one bit.

'Was there something else that made you suspicious, boss? That movement spotted by the neighbour could just have been a trick of the light.'

Rose pursed her lips. 'His face and eyes were a bit pink. Maybe it was down to his illness or the medication he was on, but it sounded a little warning bell.'

George looked puzzled. 'So?'

'It can be a sign of smothering, a pillow or cushion pushed hard into the face. The paramedic spotted it too.'

'Ah. And that combination on the key safe was too easy to guess. For someone who knew him, anyway.'

'Exactly.'

George unlocked the car and waited patiently as Rose walked around the vehicle scanning it carefully, even though it was raining. He'd given up trying to point out the odds against a mad assassin fixing a bomb to the underside of her car, and now merely sat in silence.

'One day, Georgie boy. One day. And then you'll be glad that I bother to check it out.'

George wondered if it would ever be worth rigging up a spoof bomb, complete with flashing lights, just to see the effect when she spotted it. No, that would be too cruel. It was her idiosyncratic quirks that made her into the person she was, and he didn't want to destroy their special relationship. He was very lucky to be her work partner, and he knew it.

He slid into the car and waited while she walked across to the last member of the paramedic team, busy packing his kit into the ambulance. She was back within a couple of minutes, looking cheerful.

'See? I told you it was going to be a good day,' she said as she settled into the passenger seat. 'Gotta date with him. He's off duty tonight, so we're going out for a curry.'

'Good for you, boss. But take my advice and steer clear of the Vindaloo.'

'Okay, okay, Mother Hen. No need to nag.'

George thought it wise not to remind her of their last Indian meal. Her stomach still sounded like a set of leaky bagpipes hours after the meal was over. Instead, he tried the diplomatic angle. 'Seems a nice bloke. Good looking too.'

'Hands off, Georgie boy. He's all mine. Maybe I could dip him in curry sauce and lick it all off.'

George looked at her with horror. 'Chocolate, boss. It's chocolate. Maybe honey. But definitely not curry sauce. Trust me on that.'

'No imagination, that's the trouble with you younger generation. But maybe you're right. Let's get going.' She waited until they turned onto the main road leading into the town centre, then added, 'Maybe stop off at that chocolate shop on the High Street?'

* * *

George Warrander was scheduled for an extra shift that night, working Dorchester's town centre. Maybe it didn't quite present the challenges facing the police in some of Britain's more notorious inner-city beats, but the pub and restaurant area of the town was still fairly lively. He was kept busy by the boisterous groups of youngsters roaming the nightspots, noisily moving from one favoured location to another. George was a natural at this kind of work. It was only a few years since he'd been a student in Bournemouth and he'd loved the nightlife. Maybe Dorchester's social scene was lower key, but he knew what attracted the youngsters and, more importantly, he knew the kind of behaviour that might spark off trouble. Better to head it off before friction started, rather than waiting for a fight to begin.

He spotted the off-duty Rose Simons a couple of times during the evening, although he doubted that she'd noticed him. She'd looked entirely focussed on her date, and quite right too. The first occasion was when he saw her enter a pub in the early part of the night, although he'd had to look twice to assure himself that it really was her. He'd never seen her so dressed up before, even at the police Christmas party. She was wearing a tight-fitting red dress and heels. He only noticed the dress because she'd unbuttoned her coat as she approached the doors. Good for her! It was all too easy to make lazy assumptions about how a middle-aged person ought to behave, particularly when she was your boss. Later, he'd spotted her through the window of the curry restaurant, laughing at something either she or her date had said. George kept a closer than usual eye on the immediate locality. He didn't want his boss's evening out spoiled by any thoughtless morons out on a rampage. She deserved time for a spot of romance in her life, and George would do his best to ensure she got the chance.

He turned and watched a group of about a dozen men walk past, heading for one of the town's less salubrious pubs further down the street. They'd need monitoring. They weren't the usual mix of Saturday night revellers — half-drunk youngsters tottering about in seriously inappropriate clothing. No, these men were heavily tattooed, shaven headed and intimidating, looking as if they were spoiling for a fight. George radioed back to the station. He didn't like the look of that lot one bit.

Chapter 3: Mugshots

Monday Morning

Lydia arrived at work early on Monday morning and spent the first hour looking through mugshots on the database. Surely someone as intimidating as the ringleader of the Saturday pub gang would have some kind of criminal record? She was still intrigued by the group's presence in the bar — had it been purely coincidence, or had it been the result of something a bit more worrying? Had news of the planned meet up somehow slipped out to people who had something to lose?

None of the faces she flicked through bore a resemblance to the angry man who'd confronted her. She checked the time, not wanting to be late for the morning briefing, and as she looked back at the screen she recognised the next face displayed. It wasn't the person she'd been looking for, no. Instead she found herself viewing the record of the taller, thinner man from Saturday, the one who'd laid a hand on her antagonist's shoulder, as if to calm him.

Lydia examined the details closely. Luke Boulden was a thirty-six-year-old from Weymouth who'd been convicted of several offences since his teenage years, including minor assaults and affray. None of these were serious crimes, but that could be the sign of someone who knew how to remain in the background, out of the eye of the police. Lydia tried to think back to the interaction on Saturday. She'd assumed that Mr Angry was the ringleader of the group, but this man Boulden must have had some influence, from the way he'd followed Mr Angry across the room and attempted to calm him.

It would be worth finding out more about Luke Boulden — where he lived, his livelihood, his personal circumstances. Maybe something would come out of it. Lydia printed the sparse conviction record, gathered her notes together and made her way to the briefing room, ready for the Monday morning meeting.

* * *

'Just keep it low-key, will you, Lydia? I know you're angry, but don't let it show and, for God's sake, don't upset Bruce Pitman across there. It's taken me ages to build up a good working relationship with him and I don't want it put at risk unnecessarily. Okay?' Kevin seemed more relaxed today.

'Sure thing, boss. I'll keep all the balls in the air and a smile on my face. Jimmy is coming with me to Weymouth to have a look around for this man Boulden. We'll keep you posted. See you later.'

Lydia grabbed her coat and bag and made for the door. She checked the time. They should be able to make it across to Weymouth inside an hour, enough time to see the elusive Andrea Ford before lunch. Kevin had agreed to smooth the way by contacting his counterpart, Bruce Pitman, in charge of Weymouth CID. Although Lydia's mood had mellowed over the weekend, she was still puzzled by Ford's non-appearance on Saturday and wanted to get to the bottom of the problem, if there was one at all. During the drive she thought back to that morning's meeting, particularly her boss's supportive attitude. Clearly, he'd also been upset by the no-show, particularly since it had potentially put Lydia in danger. She had sensed his unease particularly when she'd shown him the criminal record for Luke Boulden.

They made good time and she dropped Jimmy at the quayside on her way to the police station. She entered the building twenty minutes earlier than she'd arranged and made her way to the reception desk, where she asked for Ford. She noticed the slight flicker of anxiety that crossed the receptionist's face.

'You're early.' The receptionist picked up her phone.

'Not a problem, is it? I'll go straight up. I have clearance, of course.' Lydia waved her Dorset police pass, walked to the security door and swiped it. She walked quickly up the stairs and turned into the corridor, where she spotted a frowning DI Pitman emerging from the general CID office.

'Morning, sir,' she said cheerfully. 'Kevin sends his best wishes.'

'Um, yes. Good. Look, I'm aware there was a bit of a mix up on Saturday. Too much going on as usual. Understand? She's in there.' He pointed to the office he'd just left. She thought he looked uneasy.

Lydia gave him a bright smile. 'Thanks, sir. I'm sure there was a good reason.'

She moved towards the CID office before he said anything more. She needed to see Andrea Ford before telling the unit commander about the item she'd spotted before leaving the Bournemouth office that morning. Better to keep it from him until later.

There were five desks inside the office, but only three were occupied. Two detectives were working in the area near the window and glanced up briefly as she passed them. Andrea Ford was alone at the far end. Interesting,

Lydia thought. Does that mean the others don't know anything about why I'm here? She could sense that Andrea was watching her as she approached, even though she appeared to be reading some documents. She decided to be formal.

'Good morning, DC Ford.' She pulled a spare chair across and sat down opposite the older woman. Ford had made no attempt to welcome her, despite Lydia's more senior rank. Well, well. She'd obviously chosen the right approach.

Andrea looked up. She put a hand to her blonde hair and attempted to smooth it back, even though it was already in a tight pony-tail. 'Look, Lydia, it was a mix up pure and simple. No one was to blame.'

Lydia raised an eyebrow and cleared her throat softly, a trick she'd learned from Sophie Allen.

There was a pause. 'Ma'am,' Andrea finally added.

Lydia smiled. 'That's better. I'm aware of the reasons why you weren't there, and your boss reminded me as I came in. But what about your informant? Did he or she turn up at some point?'

Andrea shrugged. 'I don't know. He hasn't been in contact since.'

Lydia frowned. 'I need to get this right. Do you mean he hasn't tried to contact you, you haven't managed to contact him, or both?'

'Both.'

'But you have tried? To find out, I mean? Who is he, Andrea? Can you tell me?'

'No. That was part of the agreement we made. I'd keep his identity to myself.'

'How does that square with Saturday? You'd arranged for me to meet him. Didn't that present a problem?'

'I'd promised him that it would go no further than you. And you wouldn't ask anything about him. You agreed, remember?'

Lydia frowned again. 'Of course I remember. So he's not responding to your calls?'

'No. I only have a mobile number for him. I don't know where he lives.'

'You must know something more about him. You said he had inside knowledge of the local prison system.'

'I told you. I made a promise to keep what I knew secret.'

Lydia thought for a few moments. How good an actress was this woman? She seemed to be unaware of the other weekend news. Time to tell her? 'Are you aware, Andrea, that a recently retired prison officer was found dead at his home in Dorchester on Saturday afternoon? His name was Tony Quigley. Was it him I was due to meet?'

'Jesus.' Andrea looked shocked. It was impossible for Lydia to see if she'd turned pale, such was the thickness of her make-up. But her hands, gripped tightly together on the desktop, started to shake.

'So, it was him.' Lydia said.

Andrea nodded.

'It looked at first as though he died from natural causes, but the local plods were a bit suspicious. We know the official reason for his early retirement was ill health, but that was only partly true. There were rumours that he was bent. Did you know?'

'No.' It sounded somewhat hesitant.

'Officially, they won't know any more about the circumstances until after the post mortem. If it shows anything unusual then the big guns will be wheeled in. You know who'll be in charge, don't you? Anything else you want to tell me before it's too late?'

Andrea shook her head, though she still looked miserable. Lydia left the office and knocked on the DI's door. Pitman needed to be kept up to date on the news. Kevin McGreedie had insisted on it.

* * *

'Wow, Jimmy, that's brilliant.'

Lydia met Jimmy in the prearranged cafe, where he told her he'd managed to discover some useful information about Luke Boulden, the thin man from Saturday's pub encounter, including his work address.

'Do we pay him a visit?' he asked.

'Let's keep it low-key at the moment. We'll have a quiet look around just to see the lie of the land.'

They drove the short distance to the quayside area, parked the car in a secluded spot and went for a walk. Lydia was wearing a long coat, a woolly hat, boots and gloves. She hoped that this was sufficient for her not to be recognised if they did happen to come face to face with Boulden. She'd insisted that Jimmy also wore a hat and kept his collar up, despite his grumblings. Anyway, it would help to keep the chilly wind at bay. She looked around. In summer, this place would be heaving with tourists, all visiting the quaint shops, cafes, pubs and chandleries. But today, on a cold Monday in late January, it was almost deserted. The few people who were out braving the chill hurried along the pavements and walkways, trying to get out of the increasingly biting wind. Even the dogs, trotting along beside their owners, seemed somewhat unenthused with being outside.

The duo reached the commercial port area and wandered through the open gates as if they were a couple of dozy tourists. The place was almost deserted, unsurprising considering the loss of its cross-channel ferry service to local Dorset rival Poole. They stopped every twenty yards or so and looked out across the bay, pointing at landmarks as if they were tourists spotting points of interest, all the while noting any workers in the vicinity, although such people were few and far between. Some repair work was going on to the quayside further along the jetty, so the two detectives wandered in that direction, still acting like dim-witted sightseers. Although the workmen were clad in high-visibility jackets and hats, the foreman stood out because of his height. Lydia nudged Jimmy.

'Is that him? He's got the height and could be quite thin under all those clothes.'

'It looks like our bloke. You stay here. I'll get closer,' he said.

Jimmy wandered towards the group, pulling his woolly hat down and wrapping his scarf around his chin and neck. The tall man glanced at him and he turned back to Lydia, standing with his back to the group. They strolled off.

'It's him. I'm sure of it.'

'I wonder if some of the others in that group were also in the pub on Saturday. It's impossible to tell when they're wrapped up against the wind like that. They must be bloody freezing. I know I am!' She stamped her feet. 'Let's get back.'

Chapter 4: Promotion

Monday Afternoon

'Hi, Benny.' Sophie Allen pushed open the senior pathologist's office door and backed in, trying to balance two brimming champagne flutes. A folder of documents was tucked under her right arm. 'I've probably overfilled them but I haven't spilled any yet.'

'This is so typical of you,' he said. 'Any normal person would have made two journeys or called for help. Or maybe even waited to pour the champagne until you were in here and had my desktop available?'

She scowled. 'Wouldn't have had the same dramatic effect.' She carefully put the glasses down and pushed one across the desk surface. 'Anyway, here you are, as promised.'

'Am I meant to make a solemn speech?'

'Only if you must. Just knock it back, as far as I'm concerned.'

They chinked the flutes together and each took a sip.

'Seriously, congratulations,' Benny said. 'I'm still a bit concerned though. You always said you'd never go above

DCI. I'm still uneasy at the thought of you flying a desk rather than trampling about in the outside world. Is your sanity going to be at risk here?'

'It's not a problem, Benny. The vacancy was there, ever since Matt Silver got his promotion. They wanted me in the job, so we negotiated a special deal. I'm still heading up the unit, but as a detective superintendent rather than a DCI. I get more money and a bigger office, but I'm also more involved in the senior decision making. They get to keep me in Dorset. It's been on the cards for some time, ever since the Met decided to start phasing out the DCI role. Other forces were bound to follow suit. It's meant to streamline things, lead to faster decision making and save money.' Sophie rolled her eyes at him and took another sip of champagne.

'How's it gone down at home?'

She grimaced. 'It's a bloody nightmare. Martin keeps saluting me and calling me *ma'am*. And as for Jade, well, she uses the word *super* as often as she can. Meals are *super*, TV programmes are *super*, parties are *super,* even school dinners are *super*. It's driving me mad. I tell you, if it goes on much longer I'll walk out on the two of them. What did I ever do to deserve a husband and daughter like them?'

Bennie grinned. 'That's one of my best friends you're talking about there. He might expect me to start looking after him, doing his laundry and stuff. Even kipping down on my sofa. I know he's a close friend, but I don't want my own relationships ruined. No, just stick with 'em, Sophie. They'll run out of enthusiasm soon enough.'

'Hang on, I said I'd walk out on them. It'd be me trying to kip on your sofa and my laundry you'd be doing.'

There was a moment's silence. 'Uggh. You mean your undies and stuff? What, me? I might be gay, but there are limits.'

'Enough said. Down to business? What have you got for me?'

He swallowed another mouthful. 'He was suffocated. Clear as day. Do you want a look?'

They went through to the theatre where Bennie pointed to the corpse spread out on the bench. 'Cyanosis of the face was obvious when he first came in, though it's gone now. But there's the usual slight bruising around the mouth and nose, and oedema of the lungs. Lots of other clues in the lungs as well. No doubt about it. I hope forensics are examining the pillow. They should find his saliva all over it.'

Sophie frowned. 'Anything else?'

'Light bruising around the neck from someone's fingers. He was pushed down into that pillow, hard.'

'Any traces of a fingerprint pattern?'

He shook his head. 'Gloves. Whoever did it wasn't stupid.'

'That means they were prepared, which goes against it being a domestic,' she said. 'Maybe someone was outside watching and went in right after his wife left. Unless she's involved in some other way.'

Benny raised an eyebrow. 'Am I meant to hear these rambling thoughts of yours?'

'Just keep them to yourself. Anything else of interest?' she asked.

'His heart was in poor condition, his lungs were a bit dodgy and he had cirrhosis of the liver. I'd guess he'd been a heavy smoker and drinker. What was his line of work?'

Sophie pursed her lips. 'A prison officer, though he retired early a couple of years ago.'

'Lots of stress, then. No wonder he smoked and drank.'

Sophie glanced at her watch. 'I'd better be off. I want to pay a quick visit to the Quigley house. It's on the way to the office and I might catch Dave Nash still there.'

Benny laughed. 'Women! You're all alike. Any excuse to drool over a bloke with film star looks. Good job he's not my type.'

She punched him gently in the stomach.

* * *

The Quigley house was on a modern estate, built in the eighties. The gardens were all well-established, with mature shrubs and a few decorative trees scattered among the lawns and flower beds. Not that many had foliage left on them at this time of year, just a few Leylandii and a decorative holly in a garden a few doors away from the Quigley house. Sophie noticed the absence of a lawn or flower beds at the Quigley home. The front garden had been paved over completely, with nothing to soften the starkness of the geometrically arranged paving bricks. She parked her car in the road, showed her warrant card to the uniformed constable on duty at the front gate and ducked under the crime-scene warning tape.

'As she entered the house, Dave Nash, Dorset's senior forensic officer and George Clooney lookalike, appeared in the hallway, looking around him as if he was about to leave.

'All finished, Dave?' she asked.

'He looked at her in surprise. 'I didn't expect you along, Sophie. It was Stu Blackman from CID who lodged the request for forensics. What brings you here?'

'I've just come from seeing Benny Goodall at the hospital and thought I'd call in before I go back to base. Anything interesting cropped up?'

The forensic chief pursed his lips, causing Sophie to wonder what it would be like to snog him. Most of the female contingent of Dorset police were probably having similar thoughts. She forced herself to concentrate on what he was saying. 'There's no sign of a forced entry, if that's what you mean,' he said. 'If someone was here, they came in via the patio door at the back, which would have been easy if they knew or guessed the combination to the key safe. Or someone let them in. No fingerprints anywhere, though. We found a few dirt stains on the rug just inside, but that's not really a surprise. That's what the rug was there for, so it may not be relevant.'

'But? Come on, Dave. I can see by your face that you're holding something back.'

'A streak of dried mud on the top of the fence at the bottom of the garden. It's unlikely to have come from here, because the lawn extends right to the fence. Come and have a look.'

He dropped the bags he was carrying and led the way through a neat sitting room to a patio door that looked out across the small rear garden. The late Tony Quigley had obviously not been a keen gardener. The rear area was almost entirely set to grass, although a few decorative pots stood on the patio, still containing some dead or bedraggled looking plants. Dave pointed to the timber fence that marked the property's boundary.

'Close to the left-hand corner. That's where we spotted the mud streak. It looks to be soil from the vegetable bed on the other side. It's level with their main entry from the road. If someone trotted down their driveway and vaulted the fence, that's exactly where you'd expect a mark to be.'

He unlocked the door and led Sophie across the scrawny grass to a point where she could peer over the lightweight barrier. It looked to be about five feet in height.

'Ideal for an intruder, that garden, isn't it? With all those shrubs, they'd be unlikely to be spotted if they were quick,' Sophie mused.

'That's what we thought. It was a bit of a drab afternoon on Saturday, so that would help even more. This is all conjecture, mind. Until we get the lab tests done on the soil, we can't be sure.'

Sophie took one final look at the scene then followed Dave back towards the house. 'I'll get a door to door started. Maybe we'll be in luck and someone will have spotted something suspicious,' she said. 'Did you get any footprints from the soil on the other side?'

'No. The owner's a keen gardener. Can you believe that he dug over that patch yesterday morning, ready to plant spuds? He said it looked a bit flattened but didn't consider delaying, so you're out of luck there.' He looked at his watch. 'I need to be off, Sophie. We've got another team up at Guys Marsh prison checking some stuff that's been smuggled in and looking at a breach in the perimeter fence.'

Sophie frowned. 'The dead guy here was a retired prison officer, but at Portland.'

'Coincidence, surely. By the way, there's some interesting stuff in a wardrobe in the second bedroom. I'll leave it to you to form a judgement.' He picked up his bags and hurried out to his car, followed by the other two forensic officers, who'd finished packing away.

Sophie followed them out and spoke to the constable on duty. 'Listen, I'll be here for about half an hour, so go and get yourself a cup of tea in that cafe along the road. Just make sure you're back here in about twenty minutes.'

He smiled at her gratefully. 'Thanks, ma'am.'

Sophie watched him drive his squad car away. She remembered the unmitigated boredom of standing guard at a crime scene from her days as a young uniformed constable in London. She would take the opportunity, now she was alone, to have a good look around, starting in the front hallway. The walls were painted a pale lemon colour, with white skirting and doors. Two brightly coloured prints hung on the walls. She took a closer look. They had a Spanish feel to them, particularly the one of a white villa basking in sunshine. Interesting.

The other rooms on the ground floor yielded little of interest. The woman of the house clearly liked light romance fiction, judging from the small number of books on the shelf of the lounge and the magazines in the rack beside the large television. Actually, large was a completely inadequate description for the monster that dominated that part of the room. A few football magazines lay on a shelf beside it, but no other reading matter that would give an insight into the dead husband. The room lacked character, as did the garden, visible through the patio door.

Sophie walked through to a neat kitchen/diner. It had all the expected mod-cons and looked relatively new. As in the lounge, the decor and fittings looked recent. She knew that the couple had lived in the house for almost two decades, so had all of this obviously recent refit been paid for out of Quigley's retirement lump sum? Sophie finished in the kitchen and returned to a small drawer unit in the sitting room, flicking through the contents that she'd spotted earlier. She quickly found some invoices and receipts that suggested a complete refit of the house a year or two before Tony had retired. Moreover, there were a stack of receipts for trips to Spain, some dating back almost a decade. Surely the amounts shown here were beyond the salary of an ordinary prison officer? Sophie laid the bundle aside and, having finished looking through the ground floor rooms, climbed the stairs and started on the bedrooms. She found little of interest in the main bedroom, but in the fitted wardrobe of the second bedroom were those "interesting items" Dave Nash had mentioned. A real mink coat worth, she guessed, almost a thousand pounds. Then a small jewel box that was half hidden on the shelf below the coat. It contained a selection of gold jewellery, probably worth another few thousand. This was puzzling. Although she hadn't met Laura Quigley, the report from the local CID had suggested that she was a rather timid, nondescript woman. It didn't add up.

When Sophie was in the bathroom, working her way through the contents of the medicine cupboard, she heard a noise from the ground floor. Was that the sound of something being moved in the room below? She listened carefully. There it was again. It sounded as if someone had pulled a chair aside to give easier access to the shelves behind, something she herself had done no more than ten minutes earlier. Who could it be? She tiptoed back to the front bedroom and peered out. The uniformed officer had not yet returned, his squad car was nowhere to be seen, as she'd expected. He still had half of his allocated twenty minutes to go. Someone must have come in while she was working her way through the contents of the cupboard in the back bedroom. But she'd locked the door behind her, hadn't she? The person below had now moved to the kitchen at the back of the house. Sophie could hear the sound of cupboard doors opening and closing. What could they be looking for? Could it be Laura Quigley, back home for some reason? But the duty constable had told her that the widow was staying with her sister in the Midlands for a couple more days at least.

Sophie pondered. Should she call for backup? But how would she explain the missing duty officer at the front gate? Her decision to give him half an hour off was strictly against the rules. There was probably a sensible explanation for the presence of someone below. Maybe it was one of the forensic team returning to collect a forgotten item. But she couldn't recall seeing anything out of place during her own search a few minutes earlier.

She picked up a heavy ornament from a window shelf on the landing, then made her way to the top of the stairs and started to creep slowly down. She arrived at the turning point, near the bottom of the stairs and heard a creak nearby. Someone was approaching, creeping along the hallway from the kitchen. Sophie raised the bronze figurine above her head. As long as the intruder wasn't armed, she stood a good chance of coming out on top in any struggle. She slid around the corner and gasped.

Chapter 5: Tears of Laughter

Monday Afternoon

The two women sat at the kitchen table, tears of laughter running down their cheeks.

'I think I'd have stood a good chance with anyone else,' Sophie said. 'Even with the knife you were carrying. But you're some kind of black belt, aren't you? I'd have come off worse for sure. Christ, what a scare you gave me.'

Lydia was indignant. 'Think I wasn't scared too? It's been a recurring nightmare of mine, being in a house alone with a deranged killer. I watched too many horror movies when I was a teenager. I was convinced the creaking on the stairs meant only one thing. Someone with a huge knife was coming for me.'

'We're both bloody mad, Lydia. But it's lovely to see you, even in these crazy circumstances. I need a cup of tea. Do you think the widow Quigley would object?'

'Not if she doesn't know, ma'am. I'll do it and tidy everything away afterwards.' Lydia got up, filled the kettle and pulled a couple of mugs from their hooks.

'Where did you say Jimmy was?' Sophie asked.

'He dropped me off and went to the local nick. I thought one of us should find out what we could from the squad car crew who were first on the scene a couple of days ago. He's coming back a bit later to collect me.' She popped a tea bag into each mug.

'So why are you here exactly? I was too hysterical a few minutes ago to take in your explanation.'

Lydia poured the tea, then turned to face her erstwhile boss. 'I'm not surprised. I wasn't exactly coherent. It's this initiative to reduce smuggled stuff going into prisons.' She described the weekend's events and the reason for her visit to Dorchester.

'So,' said Sophie, 'our Mr Quigley, the victim here, was some kind of police informer, according to your contact? What was her name again?'

'You mean Andrea Ford? She's one of the local DCs in Weymouth. Haven't you ever come across her? Middle-aged, a bit sassy, bottle blonde?'

'I think she might have worked on one of my early cases in Dorset. She wasn't blonde then, but she was a bit full of herself if I remember rightly.' She looked at Lydia. 'Have you got some doubts about her?'

'Let's say I'm a bit uneasy. And I'm pretty certain Kevin feels the same, though he wouldn't say so. You pick up on these things, don't you? Sort of spotting the things that have been left unsaid.'

Sophie smiled wryly. 'Oh, yes. It's one of the things that make a good detective into an outstanding one. I always thought you had it, Lydia, and I'm so glad you haven't lost it.' She paused. 'There's something that doesn't quite make sense, you know. In what you've told me.'

Lydia looked blank. 'Sorry?'

'Well, if Quigley was the informer and was due to meet you both, what was he doing in bed? I know he was unwell but, from the wife's and the neighbour's accounts, he seemed to be making "a something" out of "a nothing."

So, was it an excuse to get out of the meet-up? Even then, surely he'd have tried to get a message to Andrea Ford? And if he didn't, shouldn't she have been a bit more concerned about his absence than she appeared to be?'

Lydia frowned. 'What are you suggesting, ma'am?'

'I don't really know. It just seems so peculiar. I'll need to mull it over for a while. I probably need to see the delectable DC Ford myself sometime soon, now she's admitted to knowing Quigley. I may just throw that into the conversation and see what ripples it creates. That's if you don't mind me trampling in your muddy puddle.'

Lydia shook her head. 'No, of course not. You're the boss. Always were, always will be. And it means I can get on with my real task, sorting out this prison problem. The thing that worries me, though, is that I seem to have crash-landed into the middle of your murder investigation. Is it going to be a problem?'

Sophie looked at her and smiled. 'Hardly. We may have to share information, but I don't see how it affects your current role. Anyway, I handpicked you all those years ago when I was setting up the unit. We've always been a great team.' She paused. 'Lydia, isn't it about time we put the past behind us?'

Lydia eyed her warily, and then returned the smile. 'Of course. Water under the bridge and all that. I wonder how Kevin's going to take it though. My guess is that it's the one thing he's uneasy about, the fact that you and I used to work together so closely. It'll be worse now with your promotion. Congratulations, by the way. I always knew you'd be a chief constable one day. You've only got a couple more promotions to go.'

'Pah,' Sophie snorted. 'You can wipe that thought from your mind. My original plan stays in place. Five more years, then it's back to university for me. I'll complete my doctorate, then take up a post in criminal psychology at Oxford. Maybe six years, I don't want to overlap with

Jade. It would be a bit much for her to have her mum at the same university, so I'll wait till she's finished.'

'That's great news. I didn't know. What'll she be doing?'

'Medicine at Keble, though it's not a foregone conclusion — she's still got to get the exam results they want.' Sophie took a sip of tea. 'Are you happy, Lydia? In your new role, I mean?'

'Oh, yes. It's a dream come true being back to Dorset. You were right. It was good experience for me in the fraud unit in Bath, but ordinary CID work is really my thing, and Kevin's great. I worry a bit about him though. His wife's really not well.'

'Laura's cancer is terminal, and she's only been given until the summer. It's so sad. She's a lovely person. I worry that Kevin will go to pieces, so you need to keep me posted. We can all chip in if the worst happens.' She looked at her watch. 'I'd better be off. I was finishing when I heard you prowling about. Maybe we ought to have an official joint meeting. Can you mention it to Kevin, and sort something out for a couple of days' time? There's no point in us going over the same ground twice, so we ought to plan ahead. Okay?' She finished her tea, stood up and made for the door, before turning. 'It's lovely to have you back on board, Lydia. I've missed you.'

* * *

'So, do we have a case, ma'am?' Barry Marsh, Sophie's second in the Violent Crime Unit, pulled his chair closer to the table. 'Rose Simons thought so when she called me on Saturday, but I did tell her that the final decision would come after the autopsy. What did Dr Goodall have to say?'

The core team of three detectives were sitting at the round table in their main office, sipping mugs of tea. It was Sophie's rule — coffee in the morning but tea in the afternoon.

'No doubt about it,' she answered. 'Apparently Benny made his mind up within a few seconds of seeing the corpse. Our Mr Quigley had a lot of health issues, but they didn't kill him. He was smothered. Probably a pillow or something. I've asked the forensic squad to prioritise a check on the soft furnishings in the bedroom. But there may be a lot more to this than meets the eye.' Sophie told them about her unexpected meeting with Lydia Pillay at the Quigley house, and what it might mean for their murder investigation. She looked across the table at the Violent Crime Unit's junior detective. 'Rae, you get an incident board set up, then find out what you can about Tony Quigley and his wife. All we know so far is that he was a prison officer at Portland until he took early retirement two years ago. Maybe someone bore a grudge against him from back then. But he and his wife seem to have been living a lifestyle beyond what I would have expected. Barry, can you contact the prison governor at Portland and fix up an appointment for us tomorrow? Don't give too much away but let him know we want to find out all we can about Quigley. Let's get busy.'

Rae Gregson returned to her desk. She'd become used to this kind of research in the time she'd been with the unit. It had become one of her key specialities — seeking out background information on suspects, victims, family members and contacts. And with such an unusual name as Quigley, it shouldn't be a difficult task. As the afternoon wore on, the bank of information grew. Tony Quigley had been born in the mid-fifties in Kent to a local Gravesend father and a Polish mother. His marriage to Laura in 1983 was his second, but her first. Neither of his marriages seemed to have produced any children. He'd joined the prison service in his thirties, a year before marrying Laura and they'd moved to Dorset in the late 1990s, presumably because of his posting to Portland prison. Tony had obviously been a keen darts player, his name appeared regularly on team sheets for the Highlander pub in

Weymouth, although that appeared to have stopped shortly after his retirement from the prison service two years previously, in 2014. Surely stopping work meant that more time was available for hobbies? Most people were looking for extra activities to fill the void, not cutting back. Maybe it was the start of Tony's health issue showing itself, when his liver disorder began to make itself felt. Rae would need to check with his doctor.

Quigley had always owned a car, right from his early years in Dorset, when he'd had a small hatchback. But later this had changed to a series of upmarket Mercedes saloons. Rae frowned. Not your average vehicle for a bottom-rung prison guard. Maybe he'd done a lot of overtime and anti-social shifts, or he'd inherited some money.

Rae then turned to his passport usage. This generated some really interesting information — twice-yearly trips to Malaga in Spain. These weren't always at the same time of year, so it didn't look as though he and Laura owned a time-share apartment. Worth further investigation? She noted it down, and moved on.

Chapter 6: At a Low Ebb

Monday Night

Sergeant Rose Simons slammed the rear door of the scum-wagon, the secure van used by the local uniformed police to transport drunks, drugged-up yobs, pimps and thieves to the local cells. She looked at her watch: only another three hours until the end of their shift, and then it was home for the night, and a soft bed. She yawned and tapped the driver's door.

'Okay, sunshine. Take it away.'

She watched the van drive off in the direction of Dorchester's police station, and turned wearily to her sidekick, George Warrander. 'Come on, young George. Time to get back to work. There's still an hour or so before the pubs shut, so let's go walkabout. I caught sight of you on Saturday evening, by the way. Were you trying to hide? You seemed to dodge out of the way pretty quick.'

George laughed nervously. 'Not really, but I did see you in that curry place.'

'Were you doing what I think you were? Patrolling about outside to keep the area quiet for me?'

He was trying to look as if the thought hadn't crossed his mind, but Rose knew him too well. 'Sort of, in an indirect way. It was the usual Saturday night and I was just keeping an eye on things. There was a group of about eight men wandering around the area. I thought they were looking for trouble, but nothing much came of it. Odd, because they looked like real tough nuts, out for a rumble. Maybe they spotted that we were monitoring them, so they didn't push their luck. They weren't our local yobs, but I sort of recognised one or two of their faces. I wonder if some of them were from Weymouth?'

'So, were they up to something?'

'It was odd. They'd go into one of the bars, talk to a couple of the locals, then head off somewhere else and do the same thing. They ended up in the Highlander Bar and a bit of an argument started but we were nearby and calmed things down. They did as they were told, and there were no more complaints. But I really didn't like the look of them. There was something a bit strange going on, but I couldn't put my finger on it. How did your date go, by the way?'

His boss grinned broadly and tapped her nose. 'That's between me, him and the bedpost. Definitely not for public consumption, though I have to say, Georgie, your chocolate trick worked a treat. I'm gonna put you in for promotion as soon as I can. You deserve some kind of a reward. Now, let's get moving.'

They meandered slowly through the town centre, following a route that took them past most of the pubs, bars and clubs, not that Dorchester had many of the latter.

'So, this group of men that caught your attention on Saturday night. Should we be worried about them? Or are you just being a teensy bit paranoid?'

George didn't answer immediately. 'It's hard to say. There was something different about them, they weren't just your usual run-of-the-mill yobs and they didn't get drunk. Now I think about it, it was almost as if what they did was planned. We watched them go into three bars, and the pattern was the same in each, as far as I could see.'

'Have you had a look at any mug shots since?'

He shook his head. 'Am I allowed to? They didn't commit a crime.'

'You have reason to suspect that they were up to no good. I'm happy with that, so when we get back to the station, indulge that curiosity of yours and look at a few faces. Weymouth, you say? There's a good few rogues down there.'

* * *

At the same time, Andrea Ford was sitting by herself in a secluded alcove in a Weymouth wine bar, sipping at her drink. The large glass of sauvignon blanc wasn't unusual, but the fact that she'd opted for a table in the shadows was most uncharacteristic. Normally she'd have been perched on a bar stool, on prominent display, chatting to staff and fellow customers alike, but not tonight. She'd been feeling at a low ebb all day, just as if some life force had been sucked out of her by a hungry insect that feeds on emotion rather than blood. Maybe that wasn't far from the truth. Fucking Lydia Pillay. Miss Perfect, Miss Nosey, Miss Bloody Ethnic Minority. Plus a newly appointed detective sergeant with a reputation for efficiency and a point to prove. No, she, Andrea, should have seen the trouble coming. Too many balls kept in the air for too long. Was her whole life about to go tits up? Well, at least she had tits. Not like that skinny Asian bitch, with her boy's body.

'Hi, Andrea, I nearly missed you, sitting in the shadows. You look as though you need cheering up. Can I get you another? Something stronger maybe?' The speaker was a local accountant, a pale, slightly damp-faced middle-aged man with a developing paunch.

Andrea forced a smile and opted for a brandy on the rocks. She really didn't feel like conversation at the moment, not with Simon Osman anyway, but it wouldn't be wise to refuse his offer. She needed all the allies she could muster and couldn't afford to offend anyone who might help her right now. Not that Simon was likely to be of any direct use, but he might know someone who could get her out of her predicament.

Simon reappeared a minute or two later and slid a glass across the table towards her.

'This looks like a double,' she said. 'Are you planning to get me pissed?'

'It had crossed my mind,' he replied, smiling. 'No, I thought you needed something to bring a bit of colour to your cheeks. You look a bit peaky. Had a bad day?'

She gave him a thin smile. 'You could say that. Stress at work. I won't bore you with the details.'

'You need to relax a bit and enjoy life. Do you want to come back to my place for a bit of, um, fun?' He winked at her. 'I don't mean right now. We can take our time over these drinks.'

That was the thing about Simon. So predictable. Always hopeful, believing every time that he was in with a chance, despite the regular rebuffs. She eyed him knowingly and leant forward so that he had a better view of her cleavage. 'Why not? I'm not likely to get a better offer, am I? Not in this fucking waste of a town.'

She noticed the surprised look on his face. He hadn't bargained for that, had he? That'll teach him! She finished her drink and he ordered another round.

They left the bar three-quarters of an hour later, her arm linked through his. She was already planning how she might best use a little emotional blackmail on him during the coming days and forge some new alliances. Though she'd have to steel herself to get through a night with the flabby, pink and slightly damp financial consultant first. She tried to mask a shudder.

Chapter 7: Furious Activity

Tuesday

Frustrated, Sophie slammed the receiver down. Oh, these constant budget cuts! She could rarely get in touch with the person she wanted at the time she wanted. This time it was Andrea Ford, clearly someone she needed to speak to. Apparently, she was out of contact. She wasn't in the office, she wasn't out on a routine operation, but nor was she answering her phone. Yet Andrea's fellow CID officers didn't seem unduly worried. It seemed that she'd been given a slightly maverick role in order to monitor local criminal activity, an initiative that apparently had paid off. Drug-dealing, extortion and pimping seemed to have been kept under control in the area, largely due to the information she supplied.

Her overall boss, DCI Bruce Pitman, didn't seem concerned that she was out of contact. 'That's the way she operates,' he explained. 'I'll get her to contact you when she shows up, probably later today.'

Sophie felt uneasy. Such a scheme was good on paper and, when it worked, it supplied useful intelligence. But it left the officer concerned highly vulnerable unless a well-organised support system was in place. That didn't seem to be the case here. Everything seemed to be a bit lackadaisical. It hadn't been the case with Lydia a few days earlier — she had Jimmy Melsom on standby and her unit boss unofficially dropped in to monitor events. Maybe a trip down to Weymouth was needed? She could check on procedures, particularly in light of her new role.

She made her way along the corridor to her boss's office. Detective Chief Superintendent Matt Silver was at his desk reading a set of Home Office documents when she entered with a mug of coffee for him.

He looked up. 'Perfect timing. My eyes were beginning to glaze over. What can I do for you?'

Sophie explained her concerns. 'Can I pay a visit to check it all out? Bruce Pitman doesn't seem overly worried, but I'm very uneasy, particularly given the events of the weekend.'

'Of course. I know we haven't hammered out a complete role description for you yet, but this fits what we had in mind. Keep me informed, will you? I don't like the sound of it either.'

Sophie finished her own coffee, and left the building. It was only a twenty-minute drive to Weymouth, so she could be there and back by early afternoon.

* * *

'Detective Superintendent Sophie Allen.'

My, that sounded impressive. Sophie smiled inwardly. It was if the receptionist had been given an electric shock. She sat up straighter and swallowed hard.

'Right, ma'am. Who have you come to see? I can let them know you're here.'

'CID. Bruce Pitman if he's here. If he's not, anyone else will do. I also need to see Andrea Ford.'

Sophie noticed the nervous flicker cross the receptionist's face.

'She's not in yet, ma'am. We've been trying to contact her. I'll call through to DI Pitman.'

'Okay,' Sophie replied. 'I'll head on up.'

She decided not to hurry up the stairs, imagining the panic that would be rippling through the CID office as news of her arrival spread. The receptionist's phone would be red-hot, as she scrambled to give the local unit a few precious seconds of warning. They'd all appear to be hard at work when Sophie walked through the doors in less than a minute's time.

And so it was. Sophie couldn't help but smile, particularly at one young man who'd come out of the toilets just ahead of her. He entered the CID office and stood scratching his head in bemusement at the furious activity that greeted him. People were studying documents intently or energetically pressing keys on computer keyboards. At a desk near the doorway, Bruce Pitman seemed to be deep in conversation with his second in command and hadn't spotted that the document he was holding was upside down. None of the room's occupants were looking at her directly, but she could feel them all nervously watching her out of the corners of their eyes. Time to take the bull by the horns.

'Morning, everyone. Morning, Bruce.'

Bruce Pitman looked across, as if he'd only just spotted her. 'Morning, ma'am,' he replied. 'This is a pleasant surprise. To what do we owe the honour?'

'Shall we go into your office? There are a few things we need to discuss.'

His expression and his exaggerated hand gesture, implying that she was just some fussy woman in need of humouring, angered Sophie. He indicated the open inner office door and led her through. No point in pulling any punches. 'The murder of Tony Quigley up the road in Dorchester on Saturday. The link between him and Andrea Ford. The fact that she seems to have gone walkabout. Doesn't any of that worry you?'

Bruce Pitman was a big man, well over six feet tall and broad-chested. He stood too close to Sophie, looking down at her.

'Andrea's often late in on Monday and Tuesday mornings. It's not something that overly concerns me. I told you that on the phone.' He paused. 'Ma'am.'

'Don't try to intimidate me, Bruce. It won't work and it's likely to have the opposite effect to the one you want.'

He moved back and leaned against the desk but said nothing.

'You also said that she wasn't responding to phone calls, either to her home number or her mobile. How common is that?'

'We haven't had reason to call her before.' Now his tone was sulky.

'Where does she live? In Weymouth?'

Pitman nodded.

'I want to check on her right now. Give me someone who knows where she lives. It'll only take a few minutes, and it will set my mind at rest. Who can you spare?'

'Tommy Carter, maybe. He only lives a couple of blocks away from her flat.'

'Well, get him sorted, Bruce. And stop being so resentful. If something has happened to her, I've probably saved your bacon by forcing the issue. Get Carter organised, will you? Because I want to go right now.'

* * *

Tommy Carter was the bemused looking young man who'd walked into the CID office ahead of Sophie. He still looked preoccupied on their way down the stairs and out of the building. Sophie wondered if he ever showed anything other than puzzled bewilderment. At least he was dressed fairly smartly. He chatted amiably until he finally twigged that she was a superintendent, and then he fell into an embarrassed silence.

They reached Andrea's flat within a few minutes. Carter glanced around as they climbed out of their vehicle.

'Can't see her car anywhere,' he said. 'It's a cream BMW convertible. Can't miss it.'

'Has she had it long?' Sophie asked.

He shrugged. 'Maybe a couple of years? I think it was new about the same time as I joined CID here. We kidded her about it. You know, fast woman in a fast car.'

Sophie sighed. 'No, I don't know. Why should a woman in a flashy sports car attract any more comments than a man in one? For God's sake, we're living in the twenty-first century. Anyway, what was her reaction to this *teasing*, as you call it?'

Carter thought for a moment. 'She seemed okay about it. She didn't snap at us or anything. Well, not often.'

'She's the only woman in the unit. Maybe she just felt the best option was to grin and bear it. But just let me warn you, Detective Constable. You make any such patronising comments to a female officer under my command and I'll have your guts for garters. Understood?'

Carter looked crestfallen. 'Sorry, ma'am.'

There was no answer when they pressed the button on the entry intercom for the apartment, so Sophie tried a neighbouring flat, and talked her way in. Andrea's flat was on the first floor, at the end of a short corridor. She rang the bell but there was still no response. She tried the door handle and found that the door opened at her touch. The lock showed no signs of damage. Why had the place been left unsecured? The reason became clear as soon as they entered. The contents of a small cupboard unit in the corner had been tipped out onto the floor.

'Police,' Sophie called loudly. 'If there's anyone here, come out now.'

She reached into her bag and pulled out a Taser, Carter following suit. 'We'll do a quick search in case she's here, but don't touch anything.'

The other rooms had also been hastily ransacked, with drawers upended and cupboards emptied, their contents strewn across the floor. There was no sign of Andrea.

Sophie called the office they'd left just ten minutes earlier. She then made a phone call to Dave Nash asking for a forensic team to be sent down without delay.

What had happened here? More importantly, where was Andrea Ford?

Chapter 8: The Affair

Tuesday Afternoon

The forensic unit arrived quickly, having finished their work at Guys Marsh prison that morning.

'You certainly know how to keep us busy, Sophie,' was Dave Nash's terse comment. 'We could have done with a rest, but there's obviously no chance of that with you around.'

Sophie poked out her tongue at him, stood to one side and watched the team get to work. It was obvious that whoever had ransacked the flat had been thorough, even if it looked a mess. Every drawer and cupboard had been cleared, and most of the contents lay strewn haphazardly across carpets, rugs and work-surfaces. It looked very much as if there had been a purpose behind the break-in, a search for something. Maybe the culprits had been looking for incriminating evidence, something that could be used against them. The jumbled spread of items seemed to lead to that conclusion, suggesting a hurried scrabble through drawers and cupboards. Andrea's jewellery, some of it obviously valuable, had been left untouched.

Bruce Pitman arrived shortly afterwards. He'd been through Andrea's work schedule for the last week, looking for possible leads as to her whereabouts. Nothing had showed up.

'I'm gutted,' he said. 'I can't believe this is happening.'

Sophie looked at him, saw the haunted look in his eyes. 'Was there something going on between the two of you? Was that why she was able to take such liberties? Own up, Bruce, because I need to know. This is no game, not any more. My guess is that she's lying face down in the dirt somewhere, with a hole in the back of her head. So stop pissing me about and tell me.'

He shook his head slowly. 'We had a short fling last year. It was over months ago, but she was still using it to manipulate me. She threatened to tell Chrissie if I didn't cut her some slack.'

'That, of course, makes you a suspect, so you're off this case immediately. I'll get a formal statement from you later, but you need to be out of here. You're suspended as of now, so go home and don't try to get back into your offices. If you make any attempt to influence any of your team, I'll have your guts. Give me your keys.'

Without a word, Pitman handed them over and left. Sophie phoned Matt Silver to let him know what had happened.

'Have we got someone who can take over from Pitman temporarily?' she asked. 'I want someone I can trust. No, wait. I'll get his DS to take over but bring Barry Marsh down to keep an eye on things. He might get some useful nuggets about Andrea. I'll float between here and Dorchester, because there's an obvious link to Tony Quigley.'

'Sounds good to me,' Matt said. 'Expect me in about twenty minutes. I need to find out what's been going on down there. Kevin's been on the phone with some of his concerns about Andrea Ford. Can you make sure no one has a chance to remove any incriminating data from their network? It's unlikely, but I'm worried in case there's an insider. I'll get a techie person down as soon as I can.'

Sophie drove back to the local police station and hurried to the CID office, to be met with three anxious faces. It had finally sunk in that something serious had happened.

'Listen, everyone. I want you all to log off your computers right now. Leave all official items on your desks, collect anything personal you need and leave the room. I suggest you wait in the canteen. Once a support team arrives from headquarters, you'll be allowed back in and work will continue as normal. DI Pitman is off the case now, but he'll be back once we've cleared this up. As of an hour ago, DC Andrea Ford is a missing person. Once we get up and running, tracing her whereabouts becomes our overriding priority, so think back over the last few days. Anything at all that might give us a clue as to her whereabouts will be vital. Go and get a cup of tea. It's going to be a long day.'

* * *

First on the scene was Dorset police's senior IT Technician, Ameera Khan. She froze all accounts and allocated temporary ones that allowed the local CID staff to get back to work. The enforced lock-out had lasted less than an hour but it meant that none of them had a chance to delete or alter any data held on the system. This was an unlikely possibility, but one that had to be faced. Ameera then mirrored all the network data onto a hard-drive unit. Particularly important were all recent documents, emails, calendars and logs relating to CID work. Checking would start immediately on her return to her facilities at county headquarters.

'Can you check something for me as soon as possible?' Sophie asked. 'I need to know if any data was altered or deleted in the two hours before I arrived. Only files accessible to CID. Can you do that?'

'Of course, ma'am. I can do it right now,' Ameera said. 'The server's log file will show what you need. It records all activity.'

She tapped a few keys and watched the screen fill with information.

'Nothing was deleted. A few documents were open and being worked on. I can have a closer look at them later, but it doesn't look as though anything suspicious happened.'

'Do you mind if I send one of my team to give you a hand looking through Andrea's stuff? Rae knows the kinds of things to look for. She's still at HQ. I can tell her to meet you when you arrive back.'

'Sounds good to me.' Ameera gathered all her equipment together and left.

Matt Silver, Sophie's boss, arrived shortly afterwards, closely followed by Barry Marsh. The three of them decided on priorities in the search for Andrea Ford. Sophie had the ominous feeling that the task would be a difficult one. The missing officer was in all likelihood already abroad, having seen the writing on the wall, or was dead. Sophie's instincts opted for the latter, but she didn't share her pessimism with the local officers. She drew the three remaining ones together for a briefing.

'We want to know everything about Andrea,' she told them. 'Her private life, her family, her friends. How often she sees them. Secondly, her current work here in CID. What investigations is she involved with? Who does she meet? How often? Has she made enemies? Lastly, there's her private social life. My understanding is that she's a bit of a party animal. So, where did she go? Did she have some regular haunts? Who did she meet there? She still has her mobile phone with her, and I want an urgent check on her account. At least one of you must know her personal mobile number?' One of them raised a hand. 'Contact her service provider and get a record of all calls and texts, incoming and outgoing, for the past week. Barry's going to be building up a timeline of her activities since Friday. Saturday seems to be key, because that's when her behaviour became erratic. If you already remember anything that could be remotely useful, let him know now. I want all this done by the end of the afternoon, then we head out into the town and visit every likely bar, pub, restaurant, cafe and club to try and trace her movements. If you discover even a hint of her whereabouts during the weekend, let Barry know immediately. Her life may depend on us building up a picture and acting on it quickly.'

'What's happened to DI Pitman?' Doug Jessop, the local DS, asked.

'He's at home. You may know that there was brief relationship between them, although Bruce says that it's been over for a while. Procedure dictates that he stays away until we get this mess sorted. We'll be seeing him again a bit later. That information remains in this room. Don't any of you dare share it, even with your nearest and dearest. Everything is a bit tangled because of the parallel investigation into prison smuggling that Lydia Pillay is running. I'll be in overall charge for the foreseeable future, reporting to DCS Silver. You, Doug, take a lead role, teamed up with Barry Marsh here, who's from my unit. You know the local situation. He knows how I operate and what I want. Let's get busy.'

The first significant fact to emerge was that Saturday's supposed raid on the drug gang was more low-key than Andrea had suggested to Lydia. In fact, the word "raid" was a bit of a misnomer. It had been the co-ordinated arrest of three teenage dimwits who'd been trying to sell soft drugs to youngsters outside the local football training ground, in full view of the volunteer helpers. One of these was a recently retired fire officer who took a dim view of the activity. Moreover, Andrea's presence hadn't actually been required, and the police officers involved had been surprised when she turned up. It seemed likely that Andrea had been looking for a way to avoid the planned meet-up with Lydia, and had jumped at the first opportunity that presented itself. She had returned to the station at two, then disappeared, not to be seen there again until Monday, and then only until early afternoon. She'd clearly been shaken by Lydia's revelation about Tony Quigley's death. Her colleagues remember her being uncharacteristically quiet, and she'd left after lunch before they even realised she was gone. Apparently, the only person to have had a lengthy chat with her was the unit's boss, DI Bruce Pitman.

Sophie looked across at Matt Silver. 'Time for a visit, don't you think, sir?'

* * *

It was late afternoon by the time the two senior detectives drew up outside Bruce Pitman's house. He had a wife and two teenage children, though they were all out when Sophie and her boss were shown in. Matt Silver had asked Sophie, as the SIO for the case, to take the lead in the questioning. He would observe and make contributions only if necessary.

They sat down around a low coffee table in the sitting room. 'Where do you want me to start?' Pitman asked.

'Our priority is to find Andrea, so you need to focus on anything that might help,' Matt replied. 'The other stuff can wait until later. This isn't a formal interview, not yet. You must have been turning things over in your head, looking for bits of information that might lead us to where she might be. Have you come up with anything?'

Pitman shrugged. 'Nothing substantial. She was a regular in the bars and restaurants around the town. She was a member of a local gym but was thinking of ending her subscription because she rarely had the inclination to go for a workout, or so she said. The trouble was, Andrea kept herself to herself. The rest of us didn't get to know her all that well.'

Sophie was exasperated. 'Bruce, you had an affair with her, for God's sake. Yet you talk as though she was just another detective in your squad. Who are you trying to kid? If we've got to push you for information, then we bloody well will. Tell us how your affair started.'

Pitman was pale and looked ten years older than when Sophie had first called in on him early that morning. 'It was after our Christmas party last year. Chrissie decided not to come. We'd been going through a bit of a rough patch, partly because she was stressed out at work. She's a nurse at the local hospital, in A and E, and her job's become a nightmare. I wasn't much better. Anyway, she was on a late shift that week, so I went alone and offered Andrea a lift. We all know she likes a bit to drink, so we always make sure she doesn't drive. But she didn't want to be collected. She didn't tell me why at the time, and I didn't realise that she'd booked an overnight room in the hotel where we had the function. Well, I didn't until she started coming on to me, near the end of the evening. She was making things pretty obvious, and that's when she told me she had a room upstairs.'

'And you, poor innocent soul that you are, didn't think of trying it on with her, of course. You were entirely the wronged party, seduced against your will by this cunning temptress? Don't make me laugh, Bruce.'

Pitman looked at her bleakly. 'Okay, have it your way. Whoever was at fault, that's how it began. And once it started, I couldn't give it up. It went on for about six months, until she got fed up with me. I got dumped in favour of a hedge fund manager she met in a local wine bar. That's it.'

'This is all so much crap. You had a six-month fling with one of your unit's junior detectives. You did it, by your own admission, while your wife was stressed out and under pressure. You could have ended it after the first night, if it was what you claim, a simple case of two over-inebriated partygoers who couldn't keep their hands off each other. But I know what you're like, Bruce. I know perfectly well that you use your intimidating size and your alpha-male status to get what you want. No, I think there was more to it than you've said. But we don't have time for it now. We have to find Andrea. So where was this wine bar? And who was this hedge fund manager?'

He shook his head. 'I honestly don't know. She seemed to be familiar with every upmarket bar and restaurant in the area. She took me to a fair number of them, but I couldn't tell you which ones she liked best. Anyway, there are only five wine bars in the town, so it's got to be one of those, surely.'

They heard the front door slam and footsteps in the hall. A teenage girl put her head around the door.

'Hi, Dad. I saw the car in the drive and thought you must be home.' She smiled nervously at the two detectives, and then disappeared. The stairs creaked, followed by the sound of an upstairs door closing.

'Holly?' Matt Silver asked.

Pitman nodded. 'She's fifteen. Paul is a year younger. He'll be at basketball practice.'

Sophie sat thinking for a while. 'This threat from Andrea, that she'd spill the beans to your wife, did she really mean it?'

'I didn't want to chance finding out. It was too risky.'

'So you calmly accepted her request. What was it you said? To cut her some slack? It just doesn't square with your character, Bruce. I can't believe that a man like you would meekly go along with anyone's demands, let alone a younger woman. What else was going on? Were there other threats?' She watched his face, waiting for a response. None came. 'There were, weren't there? Against your family?'

Pitman looked at the floor.

'Who was pulling her strings? Didn't you ever try to find out?'

'I just wanted a quiet life,' he replied. 'For me and my family. That's all I wanted.'

He was beginning to look like a broken man. Time for the key question.

'Yesterday. Your CID team said that Andrea seemed withdrawn and anxious after she'd seen Lydia Pillay. She was clearly shaken by Tony Quigley's death and wouldn't confide in anyone else. You were the only person she spoke to at length before she vanished, so what was said?'

Pitman shook his head like a wounded bear. 'I never knew about this guy, Quigley, not until yesterday. When Pillay told me about his death, I didn't really understand what she was going on about, particularly since I hadn't been told about this planned meet-up on Saturday, the one that didn't happen. When I finally got to see Andrea, she was nearly in tears. I'd never seen her like that before. She's been round the block a few times and is pretty hard-bitten. She seemed able to take all the knocks life could throw at her. But this had got to her.' He paused as if to choose his next words carefully. 'She was really scared, that's the conclusion I've come to. But she wouldn't tell me what she was afraid of, not directly. She just said that she'd been bloody stupid. I asked her what was wrong, I really did, but she wouldn't say. She said she'd figure a way out of it all. I told her that if there was anything I could do to help, all she had to do was ask. She just gave me a withering look and left. That was it.'

'And you've still no idea what was bothering her?'

'No. Something linked to this Quigley guy, obviously. But beyond that . . .' He held his hands up.

Nothing else seemed to be forthcoming, so Sophie and Matt stood up to leave. At that point the front door opened again, and they heard footsteps coming towards the lounge door. It opened and a dark-haired woman in a nurse's uniform walked in.

She stopped short. 'Oh.'

'We're just leaving,' Matt said. 'Matt Silver and Sophie Allen, from police headquarters. We'd like to stay and chat, Mrs Pitman, but we have a missing officer on our hands and time is ticking by.'

They left Pitman to explain to his wife why he was at home, and why two senior officers from headquarters had come calling.

* * *

Sophie and Matt arrived back in the incident room at Weymouth police station to be met by Barry Marsh. 'We may have found her car,' he said. 'It's just been radioed in, so it's not yet confirmed. It was in a disused quarry out near Kimmeridge, and pretty well incinerated, but the team that spotted it are fairly sure it's the right model and colour. It's still warm and smoking slightly, so they're guessing it was dumped sometime earlier today. We'll have to wait for confirmation from forensics though.'

'What do you think?' Matt asked Sophie.

She grimaced. 'It can't be good, can it? Ransacking her flat and torching her car? It's a gang at work, wiping any tracks that might lead their way. She knew something and they're making sure it doesn't get out.'

'But Quigley's house wasn't ransacked and his car wasn't torched,' Matt said.

'Maybe they didn't see him as the main problem. Maybe Andrea was always the more serious threat and they were watching her to see how she reacted after Quigley's death. They held off until they could see what she was going to do. I don't know, Matt. This is all supposition, but I'm pessimistic about our chances of finding her alive. Somehow, she's managed to irritate a group of nasties. I think it might be somehow linked to Lydia's investigation, but beyond that, I'm in the dark. But whatever my suspicions about Andrea's fate might be, we've got to concentrate on finding her while there's a chance she's still alive somewhere. I've been wrong before.' She looked across at her number two who was standing gazing into space, frowning. 'Out with it, Barry. You've thought of something.'

'They might have made a slip up, ma'am. If that is Andrea's car, and if it went out to Kimmeridge by the obvious route, they might have been caught on CCTV. There's a petrol station on the corner, as you turn off the main road. One of its cameras angles out across the road and catches everything that's turning off down the hill. I don't just mean a glimpse, it's really clear. I'll get onto them right away. We might just be in luck.'

Chapter 9: No Skinny Dipping

Tuesday, Late Afternoon

The old quarry near Kimmeridge was a gloomy, dank place. It had once been used to extract chalk, but this activity had ceased decades, maybe even centuries, earlier. It was now overgrown with brambles and other coarse shrubs, interspersed with discarded bits of metal, torn plastic fertiliser bags and a few items of dumped furniture. It was small and hardly had room for the police car that blocked its entrance, not with the smouldering shell of the burned-out convertible occupying the centre of the small enclosure. At least, most of it was burned out. But not quite all. The wreck was covered with a fine powder, and an empty fire extinguisher was lying on the ground nearby.

'I think you did a good job there, George,' Rose Simons said. 'Maybe there's something left that the forensic girls and boys can play with. Come and have some champagne.'

George Warrander looked at her, his face streaked with sweat and particles of soot, puzzled. 'What? Oh, I get it.' He wiped his mouth with his sleeve, took the offered bottle of mineral water and drank greedily. He then sat down on a rock near the one his boss was perched on. 'That was hot work.'

She nodded sagely. 'I know. It was quite tiring watching you, but I thought I'd better not interfere. Boys and bonfires go together so well. That's what my mum and dad used to say. But you'll need a shower, Georgie, and the sooner the better. Once the techs arrive we'll hot-foot it to the beach and you can indulge in a bit of skinny dipping if you like.'

He glared at her. 'It's January, boss.'

She feigned surprise. 'So it is. It'll just have to be a hot shower back at the station, won't it? So when am I likely to see that glorious young body of yours? Anytime soon?'

'Are you allowed to say things like that? I mean, if our roles were swapped I'd be disciplined for saying such things to a young woman officer. The press would have a field day. How come you're able to get away with it?'

Rose tapped her nose. 'Friends in high places. And talking about our elders and betters, that looks like the local field marshal coming along the road now.'

She struggled to her feet as a convoy of cars approached at high speed, with Sophie Allen's silver saloon in the lead. Soon, the small quarry was a hive of activity as forensic staff began the process of examining the wreck and searching the area. As soon as their presence was no longer required, Rose and George set off back to their base for a shower and some long overdue food.

* * *

Lydia Pillay was beginning to make progress in her attempts to identify the group of men who'd confronted her in the bar on Saturday. A somewhat grainy set of CCTV images, extracted from the Dorchester pub's CCTV recording, had helped, along with some careful use of social media postings. One of her hunches had been right.

They were all part of a loose-knit agglomeration of far-right extremist groups, set up to counter what they saw as the "pollution of our country" by non-European — that is, non-white — ethnic groups. Their social media posts were vile in the extreme but so far there was no evidence of any link to her investigation into prison smuggling. She was beginning to wonder if any such link existed. Was she letting her emotions get the better of her? It was all very well spending time probing a racist gang of thugs, but not at the expense of her allocated task. The problem was that something kept niggling away at her, she couldn't help suspecting that a link did exist. Why had the gang been there, in that bar, at that time, just when she was due to meet the information source? It was the comment that the bar manager had made, that the ringleader seemed to be on the lookout for her, that kept bringing her back to this thought. Anyway, she had no other lead to follow at the moment.

She looked up as her boss came into the room.

'That Luke Boulden you've been looking into? His younger cousin was in gaol for GBH about ten years ago. Guys Marsh, up near Shaftesbury. Apparently Boulden was a regular visitor.'

'Do you know the cousin's name, boss?' Lydia asked.

'Shane Thomas. There was always speculation that Boulden was involved in the altercation that led to Thomas's trial, but there was no proof. It might be worth looking into. By the way, why did we have Boulden's photo on record? What had he been lifted for?'

'Selling stolen goods. It was about seven years ago. He got a suspended sentence and seems to have kept his nose clean since then. Apparently, he's ex-army.'

Maybe things weren't going quite as badly as she'd feared, now they had another name to work with. There was a chance it would generate something of interest. She realised the cause of her worry. Her only opening so far in the prison smuggling investigation had been Andrea Ford and her supposedly anonymous source. But now, with the source dead and Andrea missing, how was she to make any progress?

Kevin must have seen the anxiety on her face. 'Listen, Lydia, I know this job is a pig. These kinds of government initiatives always are. I asked you to take it on because you're the best I have at this kind of thing. But don't think you have to carry it all yourself. Look me out for a chat if it's necessary. It's always good to get another perspective. How's Jimmy, by the way?'

'Fine. He's a solid, reliable guy. He saved my bacon on Saturday, and I'm really grateful for that . . .'

Kevin nodded gently. 'But?'

Lydia shrugged. 'There aren't any buts. I know I can depend on him. I've always known that. We worked together a few years ago, back when I was a DC in the VCU and he was in Swanage. We complement each other, boss.'

'You mean you're the brains and he's the brawn. I'm fine with that, as long as it works, and I've no reason to think it isn't. Just don't beat yourself up if progress seems slow. You'll get there, I know you will.'

Kevin turned away and made for his office and, after a few moments' thought, Lydia walked across to Jimmy Melsom to give him the latest snippet of information. Then she made herself a coffee and settled down at her computer terminal. So many investigations seemed to go this way these days. Rather than spending time out in the big wide world asking questions, there seemed to be endless hours in front of a computer screen typing search queries. It might be preferable when the weather was foul, but less appealing on a bright, fresh day like today. Jimmy was doing the background search on suspects using the routine criminal databases. Her task would be to attack from more unusual angles, looking for snippets that might open up an unexpected line of enquiry. If she was lucky.

* * *

Back in the old quarry at Kimmeridge, the initial news from the forensic unit was not encouraging.

'Professionals,' Dave Nash pronounced.

Sophie frowned at him. 'Come on, Dave. Apparently young George Warrander bust a gut trying to get the fire out before the car burned up completely. Are you saying that he wasted his time?'

Dave grimaced. 'Not entirely. He's a bright lad, you know. He went for the most sensible part of the car, the passenger side glove box. There are a few bits and pieces that are charred but we may get something from them. But how relevant is it likely to be? Surely they'd have emptied it of anything incriminating? What are we looking for anyway?'

She shrugged. 'I don't know. What I'd really like to know is whether Andrea was in it when it was brought here, but we're more likely to find that out from the CCTV that Barry's chasing up. Did they use petrol to start the fire?'

'Yeah. The pattern of the fire suggests someone opened the rear door on the driver's side and flung petrol around from a container.'

'And the container itself?'

'Not in the car, which is a bit strange. Usually it'll be in a plastic bottle, and that gets burned out in the blaze. No evidence left behind apart from a few residues of charred plastic. Doesn't look like that here, though.'

Sophie looked pensive. 'Well, at least we didn't find her body in the car. That would have been the pits. I was imagining nightmare scenarios on the way here.'

Suddenly they heard a shout from one of the search officers poking through the tangled undergrowth at the rear of the quarry. Most of the rubbish strewn around had obviously accumulated over a period of years. But at the rear of one of the bushes was a relatively clean-looking metal vacuum flask, slightly dented as if it had been hurled over the top of the bramble thicket. The forensic chief fought his way through the bushes, picked the flask up carefully in his gloved hand, loosened the top and sniffed cautiously.

'That's it,' he said. 'Petrol. What bloody idiot would torch a car and then chuck it down at the scene rather than taking it away?'

'You answered your own question,' Sophie said. 'An idiot. Which gives me hope. What other mistakes might they make?'

Barry Marsh's car appeared around the corner and drew in at the side of the lane. 'We're in luck,' he said, hurrying over. 'That CCTV records twenty-four seven, and it's angled across the road, just like I said. I've copied the recordings to a flash drive. But the car wasn't dumped this morning, it was earlier this afternoon.'

'That figures,' Sophie said. 'It ties in with what Rose Simons thinks. Hers was the first squad car here. George Warrander had a go at the blaze with a fire extinguisher and may have prevented a total burn out. I hope his efforts were worth it. He was covered in smuts and his eyebrows looked a bit scorched. He's a good lad.'

Chapter 10: The Watchers

Tuesday Evening

'It may take longer than we thought, ma'am. Just warning you. Even then, we may turn up nothing. Do you want me to continue?' Rae was back in the Weymouth CID office having spent several hours with Ameera Khan at county HQ, sifting through the data taken from the station's local server.

'Have you found anything that suggests it's worth continuing?' Sophie asked.

'I think so. Andrea Ford wasn't the best at keeping records of what she was up to. Whoever described her work as off-piste was a bit wide of the mark. She was so far off that at times she was practically invisible. She wrote less than any other member of that CID team.'

'So, there's not much on the system from her, not for the last few weeks?'

'On some investigations she kept things to the very minimum she could get away with. It was just a feeling, but it seemed to me that she might have been holding back on stuff in some of her case reports.'

Sophie looked puzzled. 'What do you mean?'

'There was nothing on how she got hold of information, or anything that would allow someone else to follow it up. Nothing on her contacts. I know most of us don't like the report writing and sometimes try to cut corners, but she had it down to a fine art. But as I said, it was only for some of her investigations. Most of them are fine. In fact, it wasn't cutting corners at all, because it must have taken time to work out what to include and what to leave out, all without raising suspicion. She did it really well. Hats off to her.'

'Something's troubling you, Rae. Come on, out with it.'

'I can't put my finger on it, not yet. But if you give me another day or two I'll get to the bottom of it, one way or the other.'

Sophie needlessly tucked a few loose wisps of hair behind her ears, a sign that she was troubled. 'No one here seems to know what she was up to last week. She seems to have always been a bit of a loner which, I suppose, ties in with her role. So do we assume that some part of it was somehow linked to Lydia's inquiry into prison smuggling? And was this Tony Quigley character involved more deeply than we thought?'

Weymouth DS, Doug Jessop, hurried into the room, out of breath.

'Ma'am, we think she was in one of the local wine bars last night. The barman recognised the photo and said she was usually there two or three times a week. He said she left quite late, with a local guy.'

'Do we know who he is?' Sophie asked.

'Simon Osman, a financial consultant.'

'What's he like?'

'Never had a problem with him as far as I know. He's always seemed above board. Sociable sort of guy.'

'Okay, Rae,' Sophie said. 'Keep working at that data tomorrow, but keep me posted as to how worthwhile it is.

As soon as you feel that you're not getting anything useful out of it, hot-foot it back here, because I can use you. We could use you this evening anyway. No one down this end of the county knows you, and that's a bonus.'

* * *

After dark, two cars pulled up outside a secluded detached house in a tree-lined residential street in Weymouth. Sophie followed Barry out of the lead vehicle, glancing around. There seemed to be no pedestrians about, even though it was still early in the evening. A fox scurried across the road only twenty yards away, stopping midway to sniff the chilly air. It turned its head to look at the detectives, trotted across to the other side of the road and disappeared into an overgrown front garden. They were joined by Doug Jessop from the second vehicle, and then Rae drove up. She parked further back along the street, and remained in her car, as did the local DC in the second one. Sophie didn't want to cause alarm among the neighbours. Three detectives would be more than enough.

'This is it,' Jessop said. He unlatched a small wrought-iron gate and strode the short distance to the porch, which glowed orange in the light of a lamp above the door.

Sophie and Barry stood back and waited while Jessop rang the doorbell. A few seconds later the door opened, and a middle-aged man with a round face and tousled hair peered out at them. He didn't speak.

'DS Jessop, CID. Are you Simon Osman? We're here regarding a missing person, and we believe you may be able to help us. Can we come in and have a few words?'

The man opened the door wider. 'How can I help?' he finally said. 'Is it someone I know?'

The detectives went inside and waited while he closed the door.

'Is there somewhere we can sit down, Mr Osman?' Sophie asked. 'It's been a long day.'

They followed him into a spacious sitting room facing out to the road. Sophie and Doug Jessop sat down, while Barry remained standing close to the door.

Sophie waited until Osman was seated. 'One of our officers, Andrea Ford, has gone missing. We're obviously concerned and are trying to trace her whereabouts.'

There was a brief pause. 'Why are you asking me?' Osman said.

Sophie looked at Jessop.

'Because she left the New World wine bar with you last night,' Jessop said. 'Around ten? Is that right?'

Osman frowned. 'We only went as far as North Street together.'

'What did you do then?'

'I walked back here. It's only five minutes or so, and I don't drink and drive. Getting some fresh air at night clears my head.'

Sophie noticed the moisture on his face. Was he nervous, or did he always perspire like this?

'Go through the events in more detail, please,' Jessop said, 'and give us some times.'

Osman shrugged. 'I arrived at about nine. Andrea was already there but I didn't spot her at first. She's normally perched on a bar stool, chatting to whoever happens to be around, but last night she was sitting at a corner table by herself.'

Sophie watched him, trying to weigh him up. He sounded very guarded. Did that just reflect a cautious nature, or did he know more than he was letting on? 'How well do you know Andrea, Mr Osman?' she asked.

'We're acquaintances rather than friends,' he said. 'I've known her a few years because we both like that wine bar. We bump into each other there occasionally, and have a chat. That's what happened last night. It wasn't planned or anything.'

'So, you just happened to leave together, is that what you're saying?'

Again there was that slight pause before he replied. 'Well, we did have a short conversation and I bought her a drink. I hope she's okay. She's a nice person, always happy to have a gossip whenever we run into each other.'

'What was she wearing?'

Osman frowned. 'A deep red pair of trousers, sort of maroon I suppose, and a cream blouse. She put on a black leather jacket when we left.'

'Boots or shoes?'

'Short boots, black ones.'

'What did you chat about? During this "short conversation?"'

'Nothing much. Just catching up on how we both were. General chit-chat.'

Sophie had noticed the absence of a ring when he'd first opened the door to them. 'She's an attractive, single woman, Mr Osman. Outgoing personality, too. Are you telling me that you haven't tried to get to know her better?'

'She's not really my type, to be honest. We don't have a lot in common. She's into parties and that type of socialising. I like the theatre and the arts. But she was a nice person to chat to. Does that help?'

Sophie looked impassively back at him. 'I hope you're not lying to us, Mr Osman. This is a missing police officer we're talking about, and you might well be the last person to have seen her before she disappeared. You need to think about that. Trust me, we don't take prisoners when it's one of our own. If you know anything that might have a bearing on her disappearance, however unimportant it might seem, you should tell us. If you're holding back on anything, we'll find out. And I'll have you. So, anything to add?'

He shook his head.

'Well, if you do think of anything, please get in touch immediately. We need to be off.' She stood up and led the way to the door. 'I'll leave Sergeant Jessop here so you can make an official statement. It needs to be detailed. We'll be going through it tomorrow, fact by fact and line by line. Don't leave anything out that might prove to be important. Okay?'

She dropped her contact card onto the table in front of him. 'Tell the DS if you remember anything else. Please stay around and be in touch if you need to.' She turned to Jessop. 'Go through every detail with him. Barry and I need to check something out, but it shouldn't take too long.'

The door closed behind them, and they went out to the road. Sophie glanced along the street.

'That car's still there,' she said. 'Forty yards away, under those trees. Someone in the front.' She took out her mobile phone and called Rae, still sitting in her car fifty yards away on the other side of the road.

'Rae, turn around and head off back the way you came, but then go around the block. Pull in at the other end of the road so that you get a good view. There's a car parked halfway along the street with someone in it. They might be watching us. I'm going to walk along there and try to have a word. If the car heads off, follow it, but keep well back. Let us know where you are. Don't do anything rash, okay?'

Rae turned and drove off, heading away from the suspicious vehicle. Less than two minutes later, Sophie spotted a set of vehicle lights appear at the far end of the avenue, only to be quickly extinguished. She crossed the road and walked briskly towards the suspicious vehicle, a heavy torch in her hand. It started up when she was ten yards away. She switched the torch on and shone it towards the driver, but the car accelerated quickly past her. It was a powerful BMW saloon, dark in colour, and she only saw one occupant, the driver, a middle-aged man. Sophie wasn't sure that Rae, in her small hatchback, would be able to keep up with it if the driver decided to put his foot down. She hurried back to her own car, climbed in beside Barry, who was already in the driving seat, and they set off. As they drove away, she caught sight of Jessop and Osman just coming out of the house.

'No need to push it, Barry,' she said. 'I don't want him catching sight of us, and we have Rae in front. Let's see how she does.'

Rae's voice came over the radio. 'I don't think he's spotted me, ma'am. He's sticking to the speed limit, heading west towards the town centre. I've let a couple of other vehicles get between us, so I think I'm safe.'

There were a couple of minutes' silence, then, 'He's approaching the main bridge over the river. Still going west.'

'Okay, Rae. Stay back and out of trouble. We have the registration number, so this is just a bonus. We don't know who he is, but he was definitely keeping a watch on Osman's place. I want him to think he's got away with it.'

'Understood. He's crossed the river but has turned off the main road. He's heading uphill. The signs say Westham and Lanehouse. Does that help? It's getting a bit trickier because the other cars didn't turn off. It's just him and me now.'

'Okay,' Sophie replied. 'We're catching up with you. I think I can see your lights in the distance. Barry says there's a junction ahead of you. Slow down and try not to reach it until he's already moved off.'

'He's just turned right. The sign says Lanehouse and Charlestown. We're approaching a fish and chip shop. He's taken a left. It's tricky because he's not indicating at all, not once, and he's going faster. Wow. He's gone. The driver put his foot down, ma'am, and he was off like a rocket. I'm not trying to keep up. I can just see his lights in the distance. He might be turning right. I'll trundle along and have a look. I think I can see you in my mirror.'

Barry stayed fifty yards behind Rae and followed as she turned right into a side road. Where was she? Sophie craned her neck, trying to spot the small hatchback. It was parked at the side of the road, its lights off. They drew in behind it. Rae's voice came across the radio again.

'I think he's up in that cul-de-sac. Shall I take a walk, just to check?'

'Wait for Barry. You can go together. It'll be better camouflage. He's just coming now.'

While Sophie watched, Barry reached the small car. Rae was already on the street, waiting. She slipped her arm through her boss's, moved in close and the two of them meandered slowly along the road, appearing to converse quietly. They were back within a few minutes.

'The car's in a parking area. I think it serves two or three rows of houses with a path to each. No one around. They must have got out pretty quick.'

'We'll sit tight for a while in case someone reappears.'

The wait proved to be a waste of time. The night grew darker as clouds moved in from the west and obscured the moon. After half an hour, Sophie decided to abort the watch and return to the police station. But the question remained. Who had been watching Osman's house, and why?

Chapter 11: Convent Girl

Wednesday Morning

Martin Allen opened one eye and tried to focus on the bedside clock. Six thirty. Another fifteen minutes before he had to get up. Then he realised that there was no warm body beside him. Sophie must already be up and around, despite her late return the previous night. He slid out of bed, put on his dressing gown and made his way downstairs to the kitchen. His wife was making sandwiches, and a flask was sitting on the kitchen table beside an empty backpack. She was wearing her favourite "action" clothes, as she called them — tan cord trousers, brown ankle boots and a thin wool jumper in a mottled pattern. Her brown leather jacket was on the back of a nearby chair. She looked up.

'Sorry if I woke you. I was trying to creep around quietly, but I managed to knock the wastepaper bin over.'

'It doesn't matter,' he said. 'You know I like to have a couple of minutes with you before you head off on a case. Didn't you sleep well?'

'I was fine until six, and then those noisy birds woke me. I decided to get off early to beat the traffic. Sorry I was in so late last night, you know what it's like.'

He put his arms around her. 'Of course. Don't worry about it. What's happened?'

'One of our Weymouth detectives has gone missing. She's closely linked to that death on Saturday.' She shook her head. 'Things don't look good.'

'There's not much I can say, is there? Just look after yourself, Sophie. Please.'

She returned the hug, then broke away and began to pack the food and drink into the bag. 'Emergency rations, a life saver.' She glanced at the clock. 'I need to be off, honey-bun. Not sure when I'll be back, but I'll message you. Maybe a casserole again? See what Jade says.'

'Leave it with the Senior Chef and his trusty assistant,' he replied. 'We'll do our best to keep you fed and watered.' He massaged her buttocks. 'Now get yourself off, you've gotta show them who's in charge.'

'Sure thing, boss,' she replied, smiling. 'Anything you say.'

He slapped her playfully and she gave him a quick kiss on the lips before grabbing her bag and making for the door. Sod. It was raining. Even so, she had the feeling that it might be a productive day. Since the weekend, Martin and Jade had stopped teasing her about being *super,* so things were undoubtedly looking up on the home front. At work, of course, things would only get worse.

* * *

The mysterious BMW belonged to Liam Fenners, resident of a corner house that backed onto the parking area where the car had been left the night before. According to the DVLC, he'd bought it second-hand two years previously, and the license, insurance and MOT certificate were all up to date.

‘Find out what you can about him, Tommy. It might give us another lead. We got nowhere last night, so we dearly need another angle if we hope to find Andrea before it’s too late.’ The Weymouth detective Sophie was addressing, had seemed slightly dozy the previous day, and no wonder. Like the rest of the local team, he’d worked long hours since Andrea’s disappearance had been confirmed. The squad were shaping up well.

Appearing in the doorway, Barry Marsh shook his head in response to her look of enquiry. ‘None of the search teams came up with anything,’ he said. ‘They were out until midnight, knocking on doors and looking around likely spots in the town. Not a sign of her anywhere. Nothing from any of the neighbours in her block either, which is a bit strange. Two of them say they often spot her on her way in and out, but neither has seen her since Monday evening. As far as I can see, there’s three possible explanations. She’s done a runner, maybe abroad. She’s been abducted and is a prisoner somewhere. Or she’s dead. Take your pick. I haven’t mentioned that last one to any of the locals, by the way, but they all know it’s a possibility. What do we do now?’

Sophie thought for a few moments. ‘Once Tommy’s got the background on this Fenners guy, we’ll go back to his place and have a look around. Then we’ll pay him a visit, either at home or where he works. I’ll need to call Rae first to see how she and Ameera are getting on with analysing all the computer stuff. It would be a good idea if you and I could find the time to go back to Andrea’s flat. Maybe before seeing Fenners? Forensics will have just about finished, so it’s time we got a feel for the place. Maybe there’s something there that might give us a clue as to where she is.’

It didn’t take long for Tommy Carter to find some basic information on Fenners. He worked as a general labourer at the local docks and lived with his wife and two teenage children, a fifteen-year-old daughter, Kerry, and

Danny, who was thirteen. Having listened to Carter's report, Sophie and Barry left the station.

The rooms of the flat were tidier than on Sophie's previous visit. All Andrea's belongings had been tidied away, although probably not in the right places. They walked quickly from room to room, looking around as they went, absorbing the atmosphere of Andrea's home and getting a feel for the kind of person she was when off duty. They followed this with a detailed search, in the unlikely hope that they might spot something that would yield a vital clue to Andrea's whereabouts. Sophie examined the framed photographs, turning them over to check for writing on the rear, but to no avail. They mainly featured Andrea in a variety of sunny, holiday settings.

Again, the paintings caught Sophie's attention. 'Do these look Mediterranean to you, Barry?'

He looked over her shoulder. 'It's possible. They could be Spanish. Or maybe Italian?'

The prints showed coastal views, blue sea and sky, often forming a backdrop to crumbly, sun-bleached villas.

Sophie looked through the contents of a book cupboard. There were few books in it, but it did have an old scrapbook in the corner, so she took it across to the window to get a better look. She turned the pages slowly.

'She was a convent girl. It's a scrapbook of a school trip to Spain that she went on. Look. She won a prize for it.'

Barry came across and peered at the handwritten diary entries, sketches, maps, extracts from pamphlets and a few faded photos. The prize certificate was stuck to the inside cover page. "Andrea Ford, Form 5C. First Prize." The citation read: "Well done, Andrea. This is such a lovely piece of work. The trip obviously meant a great deal to you and shows that you can do excellent work when you try."

'Well, maybe that tells us something, don't you think?' Sophie said. 'Does it imply that she was usually a bit half-hearted about her school work?'

Barry shrugged again. 'That applies to half the population, doesn't it? It summed up my school years, anyway.'

'But you work like stink now. I can't say the same for Andrea, going by what we've found out about her. She was a good bit older than you but still a DC. Why didn't she ever get promotion? Didn't she want it, or didn't she ever show the aptitude? Listen, Barry, when we get back can you follow up on that? You won't find the full reason in her personnel record, but a couple of off-the-record chats with her ex-bosses might give us the answer.'

Andrea's main bedroom was furnished in a sumptuous deep red, giving it a feel that was both welcoming and slightly exotic. Sophie recognised the style — that of a woman looking to impress her boyfriend. Or boyfriends. She looked through the wardrobe, and then tackled the drawers. Most of the clothes were as Sophie expected, but with a few more upmarket dresses and some very pretty lingerie.

Barry was searching the kitchen, examining the contents of each cupboard. He came across two matching cups with Spanish images stamped on the front. From the cutlery drawer, he pulled out a sugar spoon with a Costa Del Sol handle.

'Ma'am! More Spanish stuff,' he called out.

Sophie stood for a moment, and then returned to the wardrobe, pulling out a flamenco style dress that she'd glanced at earlier. The label showed it to be made in Spain. She then opened one of the bedside drawers. A couple of well-thumbed travel booklets for the south of Spain lay inside. It looked very much as though Andrea had paid several visits to Spain in recent years. Probably not relevant to her disappearance, but useful background.

The second bedroom was evidently used as guest accommodation, and was decorated in a more neutral style. The cupboards were largely empty. A small bureau stood in one corner, and in the drawer Sophie found Andrea's passport and various other travel related documents. She flipped through this paperwork but there was little of obvious interest.

She took another walk around the flat. There was no evidence of children ever having stayed there. No toys, no reading material for youngsters, no DVDs of children's films. They already knew that Andrea had no children of her own, but it also looked as though she rarely, if ever, had young relatives to stay. Not unless they brought their own toys and reading matter. She looked at her watch. Time they were on their way.

They left the flat and retraced their route of the previous night, when they were on the trail of the black saloon. They found it still sitting in the same parking area. Sophie decided to have a few words with the house occupants if they were in, and left Barry in the car.

The small house was an end of terrace with a front and side gate both set in overgrown hedges and both decidedly rickety. The garden was untidy and infested with weeds. Sophie made her way to the front door.

Chapter 12: Prison Visits

Wednesday

Lydia Pillay and Jimmy Melsom were heading across the rolling countryside south of Shaftesbury to Guys Marsh prison. They'd spent the morning at Portland, speaking to senior staff about the realities prison governors confronted in the current climate, and the problems they had in attempting to counter the smuggling that was rife.

The governors' main concerns were drugs, weapons and miniature mobile phones. 'Drugs provide an escape from the harsh daily reality,' one Portland officer had told them. 'That's how the prisoners view them. But the mental health problems they create are horrendous. And if they go berserk when they've got a weapon on them, even if it's homemade, the resulting injuries can be dreadful. Our fight against the smuggling is never-ending, and we're hampered by staffing shortages and a lack of resources. The mobile phones are a real issue. Without them, the smuggling would be a lot harder to arrange. These latest miniature ones are a pig to deal with.'

'How's the stuff coming in?' Lydia had asked.

‘Well, the old-fashioned methods were to get the stuff direct from visitors, or it was chucked over the perimeter. But these days drones are the problem. It’s unbelievable what they can do. They’re fitted with cameras and the operator can see exactly where they’re going. They can direct the things to within a yard or so of a target.’ The officer paused. ‘Course, all these problems started with the budget cuts and the drop in staff numbers.’

‘I can imagine.’

The drive north east to Guys Marsh passed largely in silence. The prison staff’s description of the difficulties they faced had been sobering, and their dedication impressive. They often worked in extremely challenging circumstances, and there was no doubt that the prison was under intense strain. Would Guys Marsh be any different?

The answer was no. A different prison, but facing the same problems: overcrowding, under-resourcing and overworked staff. Psychotic drugs, mainly so-called legal highs, were freely available, smuggled in by all kinds of circuitous routes. Debt among prisoners. The bullying and assaults resulted in many prisoners living in constant fear.

If the smuggling chains could somehow be broken, the atmosphere within Dorset’s prisons would improve. But who was behind it? Whoever it was, it must be a highly lucrative operation. The people at the top of the smuggling gangs would be raking in the cash. Surely this would show up in someone’s financial records, wouldn’t it, once they had a few names to work with?

Jimmy spent most of the drive back to Bournemouth staring gloomily out of the window. Finally he said, ‘They’re such depressing places, aren’t they, boss? Remind me never to end up in one.’

Lydia laughed. ‘Why, were you considering it? Bloody hell, Jimmy, I just can’t imagine you in a place like that. It would just about finish you off.’

‘By the way, did you get anything out of the deputy governor at Portland about the dead guy, Quigley?’

'Yes, though he was a bit reluctant to say much. Understandable, I suppose. But there was a cloud of suspicion hanging over Quigley. The thing is, we've been given an idea of how this stuff gets smuggled in, but there's always been an additional problem of bent staff turning a blind eye in return for cash. No one wants to talk about it to outsiders like us, but even though the numbers will likely be small, it has an effect. I reckon Quigley was on the make. We have strong suspicions but no proof. You know what we need to do now, don't you? My favourite phrase?'

Jimmy looked blank for a while, then brightened. 'Follow the money?'

'Dead right. You know, the boss was right about my two years with the fraud unit. It's proved invaluable.'

'Oh. That boss. Didn't you say you'd bumped into her a couple of days ago?'

They approached a roundabout and Lydia changed down a gear. 'That's right. It was weird the way it happened. Anyway, she's offered us full support because our two cases overlap. So we're kind of back working for her again. Just like old times, Jimmy, when we were both rookie detectives with a lot to learn.'

Jimmy said nothing. He had mixed feelings about Sophie Allen, caused partly by his belief that he hadn't shaped up to her exacting standards. The problem was, she liked people who were real quick thinkers, like Lydia and that Rae Gregson. And Jimmy knew that he wasn't in their league, not in terms of coming up with ideas. He was a plodder, a grafter, someone who needed to be told what to do. Once he had a clear set of instructions to follow, he'd work like stink and get the results. Oh well. Not to worry. He was happy enough working in the Bournemouth CID unit and he admired his senior officer, Kevin McGreedie. Good bloke, even if he did support Arsenal.

* * *

Lydia was busy working on her weekly report on the prison smuggling problem. This was required by the chief constable's office. Not that the chief herself had demanded it, it was a Home Office diktat, driven by the peculiarly British practice of never trusting public employees to just get on with their jobs.

Her boss, Kevin McGreedie, walked into the room. 'Worthwhile visits?'

'Well, yes, although it didn't tell us anything we didn't already know. But it was good to see the issues in real life. It's utterly different reading about these things and then seeing the effects being played out in front of you. You see the stresses and strains. We wondered how the staff coped and kept their sanity, but then they probably think the same about us.' She paused. 'Did you want to see me about something in particular, boss?'

'I just want you to be extra careful, Lydia. What with Quigley's murder and Andrea Ford going missing, we need to reinforce all our precautions. Log all risks when you, Jimmy or anyone else is out on a visit. No one goes out alone, and all details are checked with me beforehand. Okay?'

Lydia frowned. 'But I always do, boss. You know that.'

'Yes, I know you do, but it's now official. Jimmy needs to know as well. Sophie Allen's been on the phone. She seems to think things could get nastier. Christ. It's like bloody warfare.'

Lydia could sense that he was still feeling down.

'Well, at least I'm starting to make headway, boss. I've got a few useful leads to follow up. Jimmy's on one now. But there's something else.'

Kevin waited, eyebrows raised. Finally, she said, 'We've been given this job because we have two prisons on our patch, in Dorset I mean. But I've been talking to my opposite numbers in Wiltshire and Hampshire. The problems are exactly the same, of course, and we're sharing useful info. But it makes me think. What if this isn't just a local problem? What if the organisers of all this smuggling are spread across a whole region? Maybe the gang doing our prisons is also operating in Winchester and Devizes, and others besides. The amounts of money involved must be enormous. Someone is making a lot of dosh out of this. It's almost a military operation. Okay, there may be some small-scale operators getting stuff in to family members and pals that are locked up, but a lot of it looks third party. That ties in with what's happened to Quigley and Andrea. Maybe they thought they were dealing with small fry, but they weren't. They trod on some fairly significant toes, serious heavyweights who didn't like the thought of their operations being upset. The whole process, boss, none of it is amateurish. It's slick and smooth running. It might even be a group that's operating on a national scale.'

'Heaven forbid,' Kevin said.

'Nevertheless, we have to consider it. Here we all are, blundering around in our local areas just like the Home Office asked, but all we might be doing is scratching the surface. If so, it'll be like a hydra. We cut off a head in one locality and it'll just grow another somewhere else.'

'So, what do you suggest we do?'

'Well, I'm too junior to have any clout with the Home Office. But someone on high might have more influence. Sophie Allen's running this murder and missing person enquiry so she's too busy, but what about her boss, the DCS? Would he be able to stir up some interest?'

'Leave it with me. I'll keep you posted.' Kevin stopped at the door, turned and said quietly, 'Lydia, you never fail to impress me. Great thinking.'

Chapter 13: Danny Fenners

Wednesday

What do you do when your dad's a crook, your mum's always drunk and your older sister makes a bit of extra cash at school by allowing boys to feel her breasts at a pound a go?

Thirteen-year-old Danny Fenners had spent countless hours pondering such questions, often lying awake late into the night. He just wished his family was normal, like the ones he saw on TV. In those normal families the parents were mostly happy and only had a few rows, meals were prepared in a proper kitchen and were eaten at normal times around a table, people talked to each other about things, instead of shouting and screaming abuse, doors were opened and closed quietly instead of being hurled open and slammed shut in a rage. If only he had a family where he wouldn't feel the need to hide away from his parents and the constant threat of violence simmering just under the surface.

Danny kept a secret diary, hidden in an old biscuit tin stashed behind a pile of jumpers on the top shelf of the wardrobe in his bedroom. Not that he really needed to keep it so well hidden. His parents showed little interest in him or his possessions, and much of the time he was left to fend for himself. It wasn't a proper diary, he knew that. He didn't write stuff in it every day, just when an idea struck him, or when he needed to let off steam. It was mostly his hopes and dreams, interspersed with entries that recorded the harsh realities of his home life. He also wrote down some of the things his granddad told him.

His grandad was the person he loved most in the world. Old Charlie Bailey was a man of integrity. He'd even explained to Danny what the word integrity meant, and why he was proud to describe himself in those terms. Danny wasn't entirely sure he fully understood, but he did know that his grandad led a well-ordered existence in his little retirement bungalow, a five-minute walk away from the perpetual chaos of Danny's home. How had this man of integrity managed to father a sluttish woman like his mum? Danny often wondered about this. But he knew the expression "black sheep," and had seen how the rest of the Bailey family kept her very much at a distance. His aunts and uncles seemed fairly normal, and Danny was perceptive enough to realise that they all kept their eye on him, even if from afar. His Uncle Jim, some kind of engineer, talked to him about the importance of education, and his Aunt Joyce always asked about his health. She told him about hygiene and why he should keep himself clean. He knew why she said it — the Fenners' house always looked as if a herd of warthogs had just been on the rampage through it. Danny was proud of that comparison. He'd invented it himself for an essay entitled *My Home* that he'd had to write at school the previous year. His English teacher had complimented him on his writing style and his imagination. The trouble was, none of it had been made up.

Danny also knew that his uncle and aunt had given up all hope for Kerry, his older sister. The last straw was when she'd smuggled a bottle of vodka into her cousin's birthday tea, got drunk and told the adults to "go and wank yourselves off, you fuckers." She'd been fourteen at the time. Danny could understand their attitude. Kerry could be really rude without even trying. He used to suggest to her that she should work a bit harder at school, but she just looked at him scornfully and replied with one of their mother's favourite expressions: 'fuck off, you twat.'

Still, Danny knew that hidden away deep inside, there was still a big sliver of decency in her. She was unhappy, that's all, and the hard face she presented to the world was a cover. But every day that cover was fixed more firmly, and soon the real Kerry would vanish forever, submerged in a dark bog of cynicism, coarseness and animosity. At least she still washed every day, unlike his mum. And Kerry still looked after him. She made sure he had clean clothes each week and that he had money for dinners. If their mum couldn't be bothered, Kerry would sneak it out of her purse when she wasn't looking. Mum was usually too drunk to notice anyway.

Danny's thoughts strayed to his father, and he shuddered. His grandad always said that the moment she met Liam Fenners, his youngest child had been lost. Mind you, he said to Danny, she'd always been weak-minded, even as a girl.

'See your uncle Paul and Aunt Penny? They both got on well at school, and they're in good jobs now. They've got nice homes. But your mum? She was always getting herself into trouble, no matter what we did. It's the luck of the draw, I suppose. Must be something in the genes. What other reason could there be? Now you, Danny, you take after my brother, Dickie. He died in a car crash before you were born. He was always good with words, like you. Dickie went to university and studied literature, and then he got a job as a journalist on a top paper. You could do that, or something like it. You may have Asperger's, but that shouldn't hold you back. You're a clever lad. If you've got brains, then the world's your oyster.'

Danny always puzzled over this expression. How could the world be an oyster? He ought to look it up sometime, maybe when he was next in the school library. Mrs Rendall, the librarian, often talked to him about the meanings of words and phrases when he was in during rainy lunchtimes. He'd sometimes watch a group of older pupils who spent one lunchtime each week doing a crossword from that day's paper. They were clever. One of the girls in the group was in Kerry's class. She always said hello to him. 'Alright, Danny?' she'd say, and he would smile back, and wish his sister was more like her. He bet that girl never staggered home at night, drunk and spewing up her tea.

As for his father, Liam, he preferred not to think of him at all. His dad worked at the docks, dealing with freight, until Weymouth docks lost its main ferry contract, some years ago now. From that point on, his work hours were cut, and he began to get involved in various shady enterprises. Danny didn't know exactly what he did now, or who he worked for, but he occasionally spotted him and his mates leaving one of Weymouth's pubs in the middle of the afternoon. They looked vicious and swore a lot. And when they were drunk, they shouted insults at anyone who looked foreign, even women and children. The victims of the abuse would walk away in a hurry. Sometimes they were in tears.

When his dad was at home, Danny kept well out of his way. His father made fun of Danny's fondness for books, so he stayed in his bedroom if he wanted to read. He stayed there a lot, mainly because he hated watching TV when his father was in the room. He would hurl abuse at the people on the screen, stuff like, "What a wanker! . . . Look at the fucking tits on her! . . . I'd fuck her over a tree trunk any day of the week . . . He's a fucking poof. Cut his cock off and stick it in his fat gob! . . . See that fucking darkie? He oughta be back in the fucking jungle."

When it started, Danny would slip out of the lounge and retreat to his room to lose himself in a book. Even worse was when his dad's friends came round, particularly that Irish one, that Leary. He wasn't very tall, but he frightened Danny. He'd stare at you with those piggy eyes and he always looked as though he wanted to punch someone. He had a dog that growled all the time. It growled at Danny, and he was scared it would sink its teeth into him. Even Kerry avoided Tonto Leary and his dog.

Danny couldn't wait to get through school so he could leave home, and never come back.

He was learning to play the alto saxophone and had one on loan from the county music support team until he could get enough money to buy his own. He was due to play in a forthcoming young musicians' concert and had spent the first half of this morning rehearsing in a hall in the town. It meant that he'd missed a double French lesson, which was another reason to be cheerful. Rather than carrying his instrument case all the way back to school, he decided to drop it off at home on the way there.

Thus, halfway through the morning he sauntered up the path to his house, not thinking of anything in particular, when he cannoned into a blonde woman who was walking in the opposite direction. She looked pretty smart in brownish trousers and boots, and she had a leather jacket on.

They both spoke at the same time.

'Sorry.'

'Sorry.'

They smiled at each other.

'Is your name Fenners?' she asked.

'Yeah,' he replied. He didn't say anything else. His dad would knock him round the head if he knew he'd told her.

'It's just that I didn't get an answer when I rang the doorbell. Isn't there anybody in?'

He shook his head.

I'm with the police,' she said.

'Are you here about Kerry?' he asked, worried. His sister had woken him late the previous night. She had several nasty-looking gashes on her arms, sustained, she claimed, when she accidentally fell through a shop window in the town centre. She'd obviously been drinking heavily again and needed his help to clean and dress the wounds. He always felt a bit of a warm glow when Kerry asked him to help her rather than their mum. Clearly she didn't want Mum to find out about her accident.

The woman was looking at him. 'No. Who's Kerry?' she asked.

'My sister. She hurt herself in the town centre last night, but she's okay now. I put plaster on her cuts.'

'That sounds nasty, but I guess you've looked after her properly. No, I'm not here about her. I'm a detective on an investigation.'

'What, like on the telly?' Danny said. 'Wow!'

'Is that a saxophone you've got there?' she asked.

'I haven't nicked it,' he replied anxiously. 'It's on loan from school. I'm learning to play.'

She laughed. 'I wasn't implying that you'd stolen it. My daughter plays the saxophone too. She's in the Dorset schools' senior wind band. What about you?'

He shook his head. 'Only just started, I'm a junior. I've just been to a rehearsal. 'S why I'm here, to drop it off. Going back to school.'

'What's your name?'

'Danny.' He was wary again.

'Well, Danny, I'm just checking around the neighbourhood. You can mention to your parents that I've called, but I'll probably be back later. My name's Sophie Allen and I'm a detective superintendent. Okay?'

He nodded solemnly, and then turned to the door. He needed to get back to school before the end of morning break. It was double science next, his favourite subject.

Chapter 14: Danny's Diary

1st January. My new year's resolution is to keep a diary. Mrs Anders at school says we should, just to practise our writing. It also puts your thoughts in order she said. It's past lunchtime but Mum and Dad are still in bed. Kerry did us both bacon sandwiches for lunch, with ketchup on them. I might go out on my bike later or go and see Grandad.

4th January. Back to school. Everyone else was miserable, even Spoggy. I don't mind going back. I feel safe at school.

7th January. I went to Grandad's for tea. He did a stew with dumplings. It was great. He looked at my maths homework, but he couldn't help. He says he never learned stuff like that when he was a boy, just numbers.

9th January. Kerry's had to do the washing again because Mum's been in bed all day. She had to do it or we wouldn't have anything to wear for school next week. She says Mum's a lazy bitch. All her friends go into town on a Saturday morning, but she's stuck at home doing the washing and cleaning. She says she's going to leave home as soon as she's old enough. She wants to be a model.

11th January. I got an A for my holiday work in English. Mrs Anders said it was one of the best in the class. I wrote about a boy with Asperger's, like me. But it wasn't me. I made everything else up. She said there were a few grammar mistakes but I explained everything really well, and he came alive in my story about him. I even got a B for last week's maths homework. I told Mum about it but she just patted me and said, 'Good lad. Get me a fag will you?' Then she kept watching TV.

14th January. I hate PE. We did cross country this afternoon and it was freezing. Mum never bought me a tracksuit, so I was in my shorts and I borrowed a zipper from the spare kit locker. I got laughed at by Gary Spedding and his mates. I told Kerry when we were coming home, and she went across and punched him. He wasn't bruised or cut or anything. Kerry's great sometimes. She's just like Mum ought to be.

16th January. Dad's been out all day. Normally Mum and him go to the pub at lunchtime on a Saturday, but she just watched the telly and asked Kerry to get a pizza for dinner. Then she got angry because Kerry got one of the best ones and Mum said it cost too much. Kerry just swore at her and said she'd pay for it herself if Mum was going to be that mean.

19th January. Dad was horrible this morning. Even more than usual. He wanted Mum to wash some clothes of his but she was still in bed so he told Kerry to do it. She was just on her way out to school so she said no. Dad hit her so she kicked him. Then he punched her, and she cried. I tried to help her up so he hit me and called me a freak. Then he went out. I hate him.

20th January. We had a rehearsal for the concert this morning. I took my sax home before going back to school and there was this woman there who was knocking on our door. She said she was a detective and showed me her ID card. I was a bit nervous. I thought she was there about Kerry breaking a shop window last night but she said she wasn't. She said it was ok for me to tell Dad, but I've decided not to. He might get even angrier than he was yesterday. Why can't I have normal parents like other people? Ones that are kind to you.

Chapter 15: Liam Fenners

Wednesday

'What was that all about, ma'am?' Barry asked as Sophie climbed back into the car.

'It was the son, Danny. He seems a nice lad, though he's obviously worried about his sister. Do you know, I wonder if he's autistic in some way? There was something a bit odd about the way he talked, but sort of innocent too. The house looked at bit shambolic, judging from the quick view I got through the front window. And did you see those hedges? They're so overgrown they're taking over the garden.'

'Where to now?'

Sophie looked at the time. 'Let's go down to the docks to see the father. Time's moving on and we're no closer to finding out where Andrea is, despite the number of people we've got out looking for her. It's grasping-at-straws time, I think.'

They pulled up outside the harbour office with its view across the water to the Isle of Portland. Not that you could see much of it this morning, with the thin drizzle falling from leaden skies. The wind was picking up again and Sophie wrapped her scarf more tightly around her neck and zipped up her jacket.

They hurried towards the reception desk where Sophie flashed her warrant card.

'We need to speak to Liam Fenners,' she said, 'and quickly. Where can we find him?'

The receptionist eyed her warily. She checked her screen. 'He's out on the far jetty with a repair squad. I can get him in for you, rather than having you wander around outside.'

'That's fine. Is there a room we can use?'

Again, the wary look. Understandable really.

'I'll just let my manager know.' She reached for her phone. After a minute or so, a thin man in a suit emerged from a side door and hurried across to meet them.

'I hope it's nothing serious,' he said. 'Can I help in any way?'

'If you could just find us a room suitable for an interview, please.'

'You can have my office.' He pointed to the door he'd just come through, and they went in to wait. The office was small, with three chairs placed around a desk.

At first sight, Liam Fenners was pretty nondescript. He was in his late thirties, hair already greying, with washed out blue eyes. His face was pale and blotchy. He was undoubtedly the driver of the car parked along from Simon Osman's house the previous evening. He paused some distance from Sophie, looking wary. Barry slid behind him, blocking any possible attempt to leave in a hurry.

Fenners looked Sophie up and down. 'What's up?'

'Detective Superintendent Sophie Allen, Dorset police,' she said, regarding him steadily. 'You were keeping a watch on Simon Osman's place last night. When I approached your car, you drove off in a hurry. To me, that's suspicious. Why were you there?'

'I stopped to check my phone. I just got a message. I've never heard of that guy, whatshisname.'

'That's clearly not true. You were there when we arrived, and were still there fifteen minutes later when we left. Don't lie to me, Mr Fenners, it just wastes police time. And lying means only one thing. You've got something to hide.'

Fenners shrugged. 'I've told you why I was there.'

'We have a missing police officer. Osman may have been the last person to see her before she disappeared. It's in your interest to tell us why you were watching his house. Anything to say now?'

A momentary flicker crossed Fenners' face. What was it? Uncertainty? The scowl quickly re-established itself. 'No. You've got nothing on me. And that's it. I'm saying nothing else.'

'In that case, we're going to have to take you in for further questioning. We'll continue this interview more formally, at the station. That'll give you time to reflect on your best course of action. As I just said, we're talking about a police officer here, Mr Fenners. No one's playing games, not any more. If whoever's pulling your strings has told you there's nothing to worry about, then you're being tricked, set up as the fall guy. We've got everyone from the chief constable down on this one, even the Home Office. When I get pulled in on a case, it's because it's serious. If you're hiding anything, I'll find out and your life will change for the worse. A whole lot worse.' She looked at Barry. 'Let's get a squad car here. We can't waste time.'

* * *

Sophie sat with Matt Silver, informing him of their progress — or lack of it. 'He's not talking, Matt. He sits there and just stares at us. I don't know whether he's been told to do that, or whether it's his own choice. So we're back to square one, getting nowhere fast.'

'Have you got any leads?'

‘She was sometimes seen at the local marina, even though she didn’t own a boat. Clearly she knew someone who does. Maybe we need to find out if Bruce Pitman has one. I think I’ll go round to see him again, and soon. There’s a lot of other stuff I need to ask him, and I haven’t got my head round it all yet.’

‘Will you have to let Fenners go?’

‘It looks like it. For now, anyway. All we’ve got is his suspicious behaviour last night. We’ve nothing else on him at the moment. It works in our favour in a way, because we’ll watch him like a hawk. He’s not exactly one of Weymouth’s brightest, so my guess is he’ll contact someone before the week’s out. We just need to be sure that we’re there when he makes the attempt.’

Chapter 16: Anglers

Thursday

Mickey Spiller clambered over the last few boulders and stepped onto the rocky shelf. He turned to check where his young nephew Jamie was. The lad was only a few steps behind, surprisingly quiet in his soft-soled trainers. Jamie stepped forward, surveying the scene that spread out before him. The grey water stretched as far as the eye could see, occasionally flashing gold when the rising sun struck the tips of the small waves.

'Wow!' he said. 'This is fantastic, Uncle Mickey. It makes it worth getting up early.'

Mickey grinned. 'Even better if we catch some fish. A few other people fish from this spot, but not this early in the day. This part of Portland is one of the best in the area for fishing 'cause of the deep water, but it's a bit of a scramble to get down here. We've probably got about two hours until high tide, so we'll be back home late morning, with some fish for dinner if we're in luck.'

'What sort of fish?' Jamie asked, starting to assemble his rod.

'If we're really lucky we might get a cod or two or some flatfish, but even mullet will do. Or pollock. It's too early in the year for bass or mackerel. Let's just see what happens. To be honest, anything will suit me. There's less fish around than when I was a lad. That's why you need a good spot like this, with deep water. And the right tide. I've got enough bait to last us a good few hours, so let's get set up. We'll do your rod first.'

After assembling their tackle and attaching an eelworm to the hooks, the anglers cast their lines out into the cold water and settled back to watch. It was very calming to be out here, staring out across the gently moving sea. It felt as if they were perched on the very edge of the landmass. Herring gulls were busy on the surface, along with some black-headed gulls.

'If we're lucky, we might see some dolphins,' Mickey said. 'There's a pod lives in Weymouth Bay, and they move up and down the coast as they fancy. I've sometimes seen them from here.' He took a pair of binoculars out of his rucksack and laid them carefully on a rock. 'I'll leave these out ready. If you leave them packed away and then spot something interesting, by the time you've got the binoculars out and adjusted, it's too late, the dolphins have gone. You've got to be prepared, like if you're taking photos. You've got to have the camera ready. Wildlife doesn't wait around posing for you.' He looked at his nephew. 'Are you warm enough, Jamie? Keep your gloves on. It's always your fingers that get cold first.'

His nephew's eyes were shining with excitement. That's the problem with big city living, Mickey thought. You never get to do simple things like this. He settled back in his small canvas chair. This was the life, even on a chilly January morning. He'd ensured that his young nephew was well wrapped up against the cold. He was down from Birmingham for a week's convalescence after surgery, and it wouldn't do for him to get chilled.

His rod twitched, and he started reeling in. A grey mullet soon lay in the plastic bag beside them and it wasn't long before Jamie was pulling in another, larger than the first.

'Well done, Jamie. We've made a good start. Definitely fish and chips for tea tonight. Your Aunt Nikki cooks great chips, you'll see.'

The two anglers had caught several more fish by mid-morning, including a cod landed by young Jamie, but once the tide had turned, all fish activity seemed to cease.

'We'll give it another half hour, then we'll pack up,' Mickey said. 'The fish'll move out to deeper water with the tide.'

Jamie was getting a little bored by now. 'Can I use your binoculars, Uncle Mickey?'

He scanned the horizon, then looked along the shoreline.

'There's something in a pool along there,' he said, pointing at a spot a hundred yards or so to the west. 'It's big.'

Mickey took the binoculars from his nephew and focussed on the spot he'd indicated. What was that, lying pale and glistening in the rock pool? He adjusted the focus and gave a jolt. He began to feel rather sick.

* * *

Sophie Allen brought her car to a stop at the end of the clifftop track and climbed out. She tied a scarf around her neck, pulled on a pair of gloves and, with Barry Marsh beside her, hurried across to the vehicles clustered in the small turning area at the end of the track.

Two uniformed officers were standing at the top of the rocky slope, and they straightened up as the detectives approached.

'Bit chilly up here,' Sophie said.

'Not so much down below, ma'am,' said a young WPC. 'They're down on a shelf that faces south east. It's out of the wind. We've got the body under a rough awning to protect it.'

'You know what I'm going to ask you, don't you? Is it her? Andrea Ford?'

'I'm pretty certain it is. But she's been in the water so . . . Down there, ma'am.' The constable pointed to a little-used path leading over the crest in front of her. 'It's a man and his young nephew who spotted the body. The lad's about twelve. They were here fishing. They're sheltering behind those rocks down there. We asked if they wanted to wait in a car but the man said he'd rather be in the fresh air. They're okay. They had a flask of hot chocolate with them, and they're both well wrapped up, so I expect they've kept warm enough. The boy's on a convalescent break, he had surgery last week to remove a cyst. I'll come down with you. I only came up here because I heard you were on your way.'

On reaching the rock shelf, Sophie had a quick word with the two anglers sheltering in the lee of the cliff with another officer, who was nibbling one of their biscuits. She and Barry then hurried across to the rock pool area, where a white nylon awning swayed in the breeze. Another two uniformed constables were standing guard. Sophie and Barry bent forward and went inside. The body lay face down in the pool, her blonde hair a tangled soggy mess. The clothes were just as Osman had described them: a black leather jacket, claret skinny-fit trousers, one leg now stained and torn, and black ankle boots. There were no obvious signs of severe physical injuries, so it didn't look as though she'd fallen or been pushed from the clifftop. Her face had undergone the usual water-induced changes, but as far as they could see, this was Andrea.

'She may not have been in the water for more than a few hours, ma'am,' Barry said. 'I've been based on the coast for years, so I've seen a fair number of drowning victims. I never met Andrea, so I can't really say for sure, but the skin deterioration is not that great. An expert will tell you more, but my guess is that she wasn't in the sea more than half a day. Could be a lot less. So how did she get there?'

'Chucked off a boat, maybe? And left to struggle in freezing January seawater. I wonder if the currents brought her in, and she's been among these rocks for a day or more.' Sophie straightened up. 'It's what we always thought, Barry. She's probably been dead since soon after she vanished. Poor woman. We'll need to wait for Benny to get to work for more information. If she was lucky, they drugged her first, so she wasn't aware of what was happening.'

'You don't think it could have been suicide?'

'Not Andrea Ford, no,' Sophie said firmly. 'Believe me, she had a pretty strong sense of self-preservation. And why was her car torched? We'll consider suicide as an option because we have to, we wouldn't be doing our job properly otherwise, but the chances are low, simply because of what happened to Quigley at the weekend. He's her information source. He's found murdered, and two days later she goes missing, and ends up dead here. No, I think we need to do another big push in the town, looking for witnesses to what happened on Monday night when she left that wine bar. Someone must have seen her walk to the car park, surely?'

She looked around at the grey sea, now flecked with white in the strengthening breeze. Two cormorants scudded low across the wave tops and disappeared from view around the next headland.

'What a place to die, out here in the freezing water. Whatever she was up to, she didn't deserve this. I'll have them, Barry. Everyone involved. I'll have the lot of them.'

* * *

'What are your thoughts, Benny?' Sophie asked. She and Barry had been watching from a distance while the senior pathologist examined Andrea Ford's body. He got to his feet and indicated to his junior that the corpse was ready to be moved.

'She drowned, as far as I can tell. I'll be examining her lungs back in the theatre, which will tell me more of course, but that's what it looks like. Though you'll be interested to know that she has a few bruises around her face and arms. They're from a couple of hours before death, judging from the stage they've reached.'

'Can you make a guess as to how long she's been in the water?'

Benny frowned. 'It's a bit tricky because if she's been in this pool a while, she'll have been exposed to water and air in turn as the tide's been in and out. But it's pretty clear that it's been a day at least, possibly longer. I should be in a position to get you a more accurate idea after the PM. It is her, then?'

'Oh, yes. That's our Andrea lying there. What you've said ties in with her being killed on Monday night. Maybe knocked about a bit, brought out in a boat and chucked overboard.'

'You need to have a closer look at this.' Very gently, Benny lifted Andrea's right hand. Sophie and Barry bent forward to look.

'There's something wrong with her little finger,' Barry said. 'It looks misshapen.'

'Exactly. It's been broken. I don't mean snapped. It looks as though it's been crushed by a rock or hammer. It's a mess, but of course any blood has been washed away by the water.'

Sophie began to feel nauseous. 'Is there any way it could have been caused accidentally?'

'That was my first thought — until I saw this.' Benny reached across the body and raised the other hand. The little finger was damaged in exactly the same way.

'So someone crushed those fingers prior to her death? Can you tell if that's the sequence?' Sophie said.

'I can't be totally sure until I do the full PM, but that's the way it looks.'

'That poor, bloody woman,' Sophie said. 'What a way for her life to end. This should never have happened. Somehow she was allowed to get herself into this position. She probably never fully realised just how vulnerable she was.'

Benny saw the resolve in her eyes. 'You're taking this personally, aren't you?'

'Not in the way you mean. I didn't know her. But she was a cop, Benny. She was one of us. We have a rule when this happens. No mercy. Total effort, with no let-up until we find the killers. The whole system swings into action, from the chief constable to the copper on the beat. I may be the SIO but I'll get all the backing and resources I need. And everyone above me, from the Home Secretary down, will be watching.'

'I don't envy you.'

She answered quietly. 'No, that part's fine. They'll all be very supportive. The people you've got to feel sorry for are the ones who should have been looking out for her and keeping her safe. If they'd been doing their jobs properly she'd have never got herself into such a dangerous situation. I haven't told you this, by the way. Forget it instantly. It's for police ears only.'

The three of them left the tent. Benny made his way towards the cliff path after the rest of his team. Sophie and Barry walked towards the two people waiting in the lee of the rocks.

'Time to have our chat with the anglers,' Sophie said. 'They'll remember today for a long time to come.'

'I think we all will,' Barry said. 'Unfortunately.'

Chapter 17: Data Analysis

Thursday Afternoon

'Am I glad to see you, Rae. Our team just isn't the same without your input.'

Sophie, Barry, Rae and Matt Silver were sitting around a table in a small conference room, the door firmly shut. Rae glowed — grateful for her boss's kind words, but also because she'd been worried about her future. She'd been concerned about what might happen at the VCU following Sophie's promotion, but there was little change as yet.

She lifted a folder out of her bag and spread the contents across the desk. 'It took us two days, but we've done as much as we could. Ameera helped me isolate the base data, and then I just got on with it. I've spotted some discrepancies. None of them are particularly meaningful in isolation but, taken together, a different pattern shows up. It'll take me about half an hour to explain. Is that okay, ma'am?'

'Of course.'

'We made a chart showing every time Andrea accessed any data, every log she completed, every document she wrote. At first glance, nothing seems to connect, does it? It's just columns of isolated figures. But then we thought we'd correlate the different sets of data, and a few surprising things came out.'

Rae pointed to a set of graphs. 'Every Wednesday afternoon her mileage claim was pretty well the same, and it continued like this for months. The other days showed the usual variations. Her mobile phone usage was pretty random, as you might expect, but not on a Wednesday. Then, there were very few calls, with one particular mobile number cropping up frequently. And look at this. Very little document activity or database access on a Wednesday afternoon.'

She turned another page. 'What we have here is an analysis of her contribution to investigations involving the whole team. Pretty standard in the main, but check this item. When it came to CID work on gambling, nightclubs and the like — the type of stuff that used to be called vice — her contribution was minimal. She was clearly involved, because the log records her as being part of the teams, but her input was zero.'

'Was she trying to spike those investigations?' Matt Silver asked.

Rae frowned. 'It's hard to say, sir, from the data. She might have had negative feelings about the work, so she didn't feel like making a contribution.'

She turned another page. 'This shows a rough breakdown of her use of the PNC for general background information. At first glance it looks pretty standard, but if you look closer it shows a high level of access to records of suspects involved in racist activity and ultra-nationalism — far right groups and the like. And that doesn't match up to what she was officially working on.'

'But we know she was working on her own a lot. Not quite undercover, but given a free rein,' Sophie said. 'Wouldn't that explain it?'

'But in that case, ma'am, wouldn't someone know? If it was official, I mean. Who was she reporting to? And anyway, to me it didn't look systematic. It looked more like general browsing, just out of interest, not like when we use the PNC during an investigation. Her other uses of the PNC were much more targeted.'

'When was this browsing?' Barry asked. 'Was there a pattern to it?'

Rae smiled at him. 'That's just it. When it happened, it was always on a Wednesday morning.'

Rae stopped speaking. The stunned silence seemed to last for a long time.

'And there was me complaining that we didn't have any meaningful leads,' Sophie said. 'Does this point to what I think it does? That Andrea wasn't just a bit lazy and disorganised, but might have been up to no good? Matt, am I wrong here?'

Silver shook his head. 'That's the obvious interpretation. There could be others but, in the end, data like this doesn't lie.'

'What was the mobile number she was calling on a Wednesday?' Barry asked. 'We ought to follow it up right now.'

'Be cautious, Barry. Find out about it but don't make a call until we're ready. This stuff is just for the four of us. We don't know how much some of the others knew about what she was up to. I just pray it was only her, but we have to tread carefully until we know for sure. We certainly need to get to the bottom of what she was up to on Wednesdays, but we should proceed very cautiously until we know what we're dealing with.'

Matt Silver stood up. 'I'm off to see the chief constable. I have no idea what she's going to make of it, but she has to be told in case we're heading into security services territory without realising it.' He paused. 'That was really solid work, Detective Constable. It needs to be kept totally under wraps. You've given us a lead into something that we didn't even know existed. Even now, we don't know exactly what it is. But it explains something, I think. Why she might have been killed when things started to go wrong.'

'We may have to bring in Lydia Pillay, Matt. I'm wondering if it was her leaning on Andrea for information about the prison smuggling that set all this off. I'll give her a bell to see if she's made any more progress on it. Maybe our two investigations are converging. And, Rae, what the DCS has said is absolutely right. When I sent you up to HQ with Ameera, I had no idea that you'd turn up anything like this. I'm speechless. Well, almost.' Sophie grinned. 'Where did you get the idea from?'

Rae smiled. 'It was Craig, my boyfriend. He was telling me about his brother, who seems to be a maths genius and works in data analytics. Apparently, he told Craig that you can come up with all kinds of correlations if you use the right queries. I just thought I'd give it a go.'

'Does Ameera know what you've done with the data?'

Rae shook her head. 'She wasn't with me when I did the analysis. But she might guess.'

'Okay,' Matt said. 'I'll have a quiet word with her after I've seen the chief. She ought to be told how sensitive this material is. Sophie, you need to work out where we go from here, and how we take the investigation in a new direction without making it too obvious to the Weymouth team. Rae, you've done a great job here. Well done.' He hurried out of the room.

Sophie winked at her young assistant. 'A bottle of bubbly for you when this is all over. So, this is what we do in the short term. Barry and I will pay another visit to Bruce Pitman. Surely he must have known about some of this? Rae, I've got some of the local uniforms out looking for the boat that might have taken Andrea to her death. Could you check up on whether they've traced it yet? When they do, you'll have to pay a visit to wherever it's kept. Maybe it'll still be there. If not, we'll need to know when it was last seen and start a search for it. Get the details of how often it was out on the water. Barry, once we've seen Pitman, we'll need to check on how Lydia's been getting on and bring her up to speed. It would be better if she came across here. Can you arrange it before we leave?'

* * *

Chrissie, Bruce Pitman's wife, was in the front garden in her wellingtons, tidying one of the flower beds. Secateurs in hand, she looked up at their approach.

'Bringers of bad news, I suppose,' she said. 'He's devastated, you know. I've never seen him so withdrawn. Her disappearance has really shaken him.'

'Her body's been found, Chrissie,' Sophie said. 'Is it alright if I call you Chrissie? In a way, I'm glad we can speak to you first. Bruce seems to find it hard to cope with me in charge. Whenever I speak to him, he comes across kind of resentful, but confused as well. He can't seem to step out of the role he's constructed for himself. Is there some way I can avoid having to pull rank on him? I don't enjoy being confrontational with fellow officers, and I know what a good guy he is underneath.'

'Is he?' Chrissie said. 'I don't know what to think any more. I could probably forgive and forget if it had been a simple brief fling with someone nice. But her? She was so . . . so *obvious.* So shallow. I mean, what was he thinking getting involved with her to that extent? I bloody hate her, to be honest. We met at various functions, and I never liked her then. I warned him what she was like. Now look at the state he's in. We're in, both of us.' She sighed. 'At least I've still got my work to occupy me. I'm on duty this weekend, which is why I've got today off. Isn't there anything you can give him to do? He's driving himself mad in there.'

Sophie shook her head. 'It's out of my hands. She was blackmailing him, according to what he told us. Now she's turned up dead. He has to stay suspended until we're sure he wasn't involved. Even then, we have to find out more about her behaviour, and that's why we're here now. I don't enjoy this, Chrissie, no matter what you or he thinks. There'll be a separate inquiry by a professional standards team, and they'll be a lot nastier than me.'

Chrissie looked bleak. 'So this will run and run?'

'Afraid so. Having a fling was one thing. Allowing her to have an influence over his operational decisions was something entirely different. That was a catastrophic mistake on his part. And we don't know the extent of it. I've got to pin him down this time, and get him to come clean on everything.'

'It may be easier than you think. He's just a lump of jelly at the moment.' Chrissie paused. 'That's all he ever was, really. Underneath. People saw the surface, the image he projected. He even came to believe it himself, and that's when things went wrong.'

Chapter 18: Still Playing Games

Thursday Afternoon

Bruce Pitman looked like a broken and haunted man. His shoulders were slumped, his face haggard, and he had dark rings under his eyes. He was standing facing the door, and eyed the two detectives warily when they entered the lounge. Chrissie was back in the garden.

'Do you want to put the kettle on, Bruce?' Sophie said. 'We can chat while you're making a pot of tea, then come back in here.'

'You've found her then,' he said. It was a statement.

How to put it? 'Yes. It's bad. Her body was found washed up on Portland Bill this morning. We think she'd been there for some time, possibly since the early hours of Tuesday morning, soon after she went missing. It looks as though she was assaulted before she went into the water. I'm really sorry, Bruce. I feel bad enough, but I can only guess how you feel. Anything else I could say would sound trite, so I won't bother. You know how I work. Now, let's get that drink made.'

The hard news, bad as it was, seemed to have a slight galvanising effect on Pitman. He straightened up, and for the first time looked directly at Sophie. 'I'll tell you everything you need to know. I'm partly to blame for this mess, and I want to clear the air. Most of all, I want the people who did this to her caught. If this is going to be the end of my career as a Dorset cop, I want it to be done right.'

'I don't think it'll come to that, Bruce. We're not automatons. Anyway, it won't be up to us, so let's just deal with the here and now.' She picked a biscuit tin off a shelf and tipped some of the contents out onto a plate. Barry took three mugs from another shelf while Pitman made a pot of tea, and carried it through to the lounge, where they settled around a low table.

Sophie started the interview, while Barry prepared to take notes. 'You said on Tuesday that Andrea blackmailed you into giving her pretty much of a free rein. That part I can believe. What I can't believe is that you just let it all happen. You must have wondered what she was up to and, knowing your inability to cope with women you perceive as powerful, you must have kept an eye on what she was doing — or not doing. So what *was* she doing, Bruce?'

'I didn't think it was anything criminal. Do you really think I would have let her get away with it if that had been the case? I may have been stupid, but I'm not bent and I don't believe she was either. It never crossed my mind. I just thought she wanted a bit more control over her work. The thing is, she kept getting good results. You just have to look at the leads she provided for us. We've got a good clear-up rate down in this corner of the county, and a good proportion of it came from her contacts. I'd have taken a tougher line if it had become obvious that she was slacking and not pulling her weight, but she was a good operative, right up until now.'

'Did you notice any patterns in the way she worked, and when? Were there regular times when you noticed that she'd made herself unavailable?'

'I didn't look at first. I was scared stiff that she was going to carry out her threat and spill the beans to Chrissie, so I left her well alone, as long as she gave me no cause for complaint. That was the deal we made.'

'So, when you met up during your affair, what did you talk about?'

'Not work, you can trust me on that. When we were, you know, lying in bed afterwards, she'd sometimes ask about my family — the kids and Chrissie. She didn't have a family, you see. I think she regretted it.'

'You said that you didn't look at first. Does that mean that you did spot some patterns emerging?'

'Just recently I couldn't depend on her being around on Wednesdays. I asked her about it and she snapped that I'd agreed to cut her some slack. That was the price I had to pay, not to ask her any awkward questions.' He hesitated. 'Look, I had to trust her. And she gave me no reason not to. As I said just now, she was still doing the job for us. The whole thing was working okay, so I didn't want to upset it. I just left her alone. With hindsight, I can see that she needed help but it wasn't obvious at the time.'

'You never wondered where she was, or what she was up to? You never tried to find out why she was out of the station so much on Wednesdays?'

Pitman shook his head. He poured the tea in silence, and pushed the mugs across the table. Was he to be trusted? Was it really the case that he hadn't bothered to find out what Andrea had been doing? Sophie was still unconvinced that a man like him would have been happy to let a woman in Andrea's position hold a trump card over him and use it in the way she did. Surely, he'd have tried to restore the natural balance of power as he saw it? Yet Chrissie had clearly said he'd always been a softie underneath. Was her opinion to be believed? Or had she been aiming to gain sympathy for her husband? Niggling at the back of Sophie's mind was the possibility that Pitman was still playing some kind of game, and was being less than honest despite his protestations. What if the reality was entirely different and he knew, even approved of whatever Andrea'd been up to? She looked across the table at him. He'd never been a person she could warm to.

She decided not to let him know of her suspicions about Andrea's activities, the tentative ideas that had formed as a result of Rae's discoveries. Why let the cat out of the bag before it was absolutely necessary? Bruce might well have guessed that Andrea's frequent Wednesday absences would be spotted at some point, so he could afford to give them that item of information.

'When did you meet when you had your liaisons with Andrea, Bruce?' she asked. 'Was it a regular day and time?'

'Not really. If it had been regular, it would have been noticed by someone on the team, so we were careful to vary it. We'd choose a possible date and time for the next date when we parted. Then we'd confirm by a brief word close to the time. Look, I made sure it didn't influence the work of the unit.'

'Emails? Text messages?'

Pitman shook his head. 'I didn't want to leave a trail.'

'Where did you go? You're a pretty well-known figure around these parts, so how did you manage it?'

'Andrea's flat. I'd park somewhere nearby, then walk there. It's fairly secluded, and her neighbours were never about during the daytime. Even in the evenings I rarely saw anyone else around.'

'Did you go out together?'

'Not really. It was too dangerous for us to be seen out in public. I think we visited one restaurant on her birthday and a bar on some other occasion.'

Sophie nodded. It didn't square with the impression she'd picked up during her previous interview, when

Pitman had spoken of several visits to bars and restaurants. He was being economical.

'Anything else you want to tell us, Bruce? Any ideas about who might have done this?'

He shook his head.

'Was it hard telling Chrissie about Andrea? How did she take it?'

'Is this relevant?' he said, showing a spark of anger.

Sophie didn't answer.

'Yes, it was bloody hard. And she's taken it bloody hard, too. I'm banished to the spare room when I need her with me more than at any other time in our marriage.' He stared across at Sophie. 'I deserve it, I suppose. Who can blame her?'

Sophie finished her drink and stood up. 'No sympathy from me, Bruce, not for you. You wouldn't expect any, and I won't disappoint you. Chrissie deserves some, but I won't offer it just now. It's the wrong time. Well, that will do for now. We need to get on with tracking down her killers.'

Sophie stalked out of the house. 'Bastard. He's still trying to play games.'

Chapter 19: Justice

Thursday Afternoon

When young Danny Fenners arrived home from school he knew as soon as he opened the front door that his father was at home. It was a kind of sixth sense that he had. The atmosphere somehow felt different when his dad's souring presence was around.

He tiptoed straight up the stairs, and made it to his room without anyone noticing. Thank goodness. He took his mobile phone out of his pocket and sent Kerry a text message. *Be careful. Dad's home.* That should do the trick. Maybe Kerry would stay away until later, hoping that Dad would go out somewhere. She'd avoided her parents completely since the fight on Tuesday morning, slipping in and out of the house like a ghost. The downside, from Danny's point of view, was that he'd only managed a few snatched words with her. He hated to see her like this, moody and sullen. If it wasn't for his regular visits to his grandad, he didn't know what he'd do. He wondered about paying him a visit now. His grandad usually came home from the Thursday afternoon club at the local social centre at five. That gave Danny about enough time to do his maths homework before sneaking out of the house.

Half an hour later, he opened his bedroom door and listened. He could hear the TV and the occasional rumble of his father's voice, probably complaining about something to his mum. Danny crept down the stairs. He was just unhooking his coat from the wall rack when his father appeared in the hallway.

'Oh, it's you. What are you sneaking about for? I didn't hear the door.'

Danny just shrugged. 'I'm going to see Grandad. It's Thursday and he usually gives us our tea.'

'Well, if you see Kerry, tell her there's stuff needs washing. Mum's feeling sick again, so she needs to do it.'

No change there then, Danny thought. He nodded and slipped out of the door as fast as he could, away from his father's intimidating presence. He prayed that he didn't turn out like that when he grew up. He'd have a quiet, tidy home with books, stuff on the walls and other interesting things. If he ever had children, he'd make sure they felt safe and happy.

He was surprised to find Kerry already at their grandad's house. She was sitting on the floor in front of the gas fire, stroking the cat. She'd hidden the bruise on her cheek with some make-up and she'd brushed her fair hair. Danny thought she looked really pretty. He gave her a hug, Grandad too. It had taken him years to get used to hugging people, but now he liked doing it with Kerry and Grandad. Like a lot of people with Asperger's, he usually avoided close physical contact.

'You're soppy, Danny,' Kerry said. 'I only stay around 'cause of you.'

She'd pulled up the sleeves on her school jumper and the plasters that Danny had put on her cuts earlier in the week were visible. They looked a bit neater though.

'Are your cuts okay?' Danny asked.

'Yeah, fine. I went to see nurse at lunchtime today, and she had a look. She said the cuts are healing well and that whoever put the plasters on did a good job. That's you, Danny.'

Danny was pleased. That's two things he'd done to help Kerry this week, even though his intervention in the row between her and Dad hadn't helped much. He smiled, and his sister smiled back. Maybe she'd stay at home after all.

'Tea's ready,' their grandad called. 'It's chicken casserole, and I want it all eaten. You two eat too much pizza and chips.'

Kerry rolled her eyes but kept smiling. Danny grinned back.

* * *

'Grandad, what does the word "justice" mean? I know what the law is. You can break the law, can't you? But you can't break justice.'

They were eating their pudding, tinned pears and ice cream, sitting around the kitchen table. Danny's grandad's house had a dining room, but it was rarely used. He preferred to use the table in the spacious kitchen, and Danny and Kerry were happier there. The dining room was too formal.

'Well, that's a hard one, young Danny. You come up with some tricky questions, don't you?' Grandad set down his spoon. 'The law is a sort of set of rules passed by parliament that forbids people from doing things that might cause others harm. Justice is the way those rules are enforced and must be fair to everyone. Theft is against the law. Justice is the way that the courts deal with it and decide on a punishment that fits the crime. How does that sound?'

Danny nodded. 'Yeah, okay.'

Kerry giggled. 'You're funny, Danny. No one else would ask a question like that. Anyway, justice doesn't work the way it should, that's what one of my teachers said. If a rich person and a poor person stole a loaf of bread from a shop, the poor person should get a smaller punishment 'cause they might be starving and really need it. But in olden days the poor person might get his hand chopped off, but the rich person would escape because he was pally with the judge. So it never worked properly, did it?'

'It's not like that now, Kerry. Judges take someone's background into account. Or they should anyway.' He looked at his granddaughter with interest. 'Is this a bit of a turnaround for you? I've never heard you talk about something you've learned at school before.'

'I'm not stupid, Grandad. I listen some of the time, when it's not boring. I quite like history when it's about ordinary people in olden days. It's the rich men that piss me off. Always having battles and wars and stuff. Ruining things for the ordinary people. I 'spect they just wanted to get on with their lives.'

Danny and Kerry were back home by mid-evening, with Kerry in a good enough mood to sort through the laundry and load up the washing machine without too many complaints. She didn't hear the doorbell ring so Danny, who was in the hallway at the time, went to answer. Two uniformed police officers were standing on the doorstep. They asked for Kerry Fenners. Danny stood open-mouthed, not knowing what to do. Should he try to keep his father away and somehow sneak Kerry out without him knowing? He turned around. Too late. His father stood behind him, already looking angry.

* * *

George Warrander walked towards the untidy front garden of the Fenner house, looking around. Some of the properties were neat and tidy, others looked to be a shambles. The Fenners' home was messy, though it wasn't the worst. 'What are we here for, boss?'

'A teenage girl, Kerry Fenners. CCTV down in the town centre caught her being pushed through a shop window a couple of nights ago, and someone needs to check that she's okay. It's taken this long to identify her from the footage. She hasn't been into casualty, apparently. It looked as though she was drunk or high at the time.'

She rang the doorbell, answered by a boy who stood in the open doorway and gaped at them. He didn't seem to know how to respond to her question. He was small and thin with dark hair and a gap in his front teeth. A man came up behind him and pushed the lad aside. His face was very red.

'What the fuck do you want?' he demanded. 'This is harassment. I'll get someone on to you.'

Rose smiled at him sweetly. 'Mr Fenners? We're here to check on Kerry. Your daughter? She might have been in an accident in the town centre a couple of nights ago. We just want to see that she's alright.'

Looking puzzled, Fenners turned and shouted, 'Kerry? Get out here, right now. What have you been up to?'

A pale teenage girl appeared, looking bemused.

'Look, Mr Fenners. Can we come in for a few moments? Maybe speak to Kerry to find out what happened? It won't take long.'

He looked the two police officers up and down. 'Yeah, alright. But it'd better not take long.' He turned to his daughter before stalking back into the living room. 'I want to see you afterwards.'

'Is there somewhere we can go, Kerry? Rather than standing here in the hall?'

The girl shrugged. 'The kitchen? That's where I was.'

They followed Kerry through to a small kitchen. She'd obviously been sorting through the laundry and loading the washing machine. She perched on a stool, so Rose did the same. George stood back by the door, pushing it almost closed. The boy who'd answered the doorbell stood just outside, looking as if he didn't quite know what to do.

'How old are you, Kerry?' Rose asked.

'Sixteen. It was my birthday last week.'

'That's fine. We're her to check that you're okay. You were caught on CCTV on Tuesday night, and we're concerned that you might have been seriously hurt.'

'Oh, that. Yeah, well, me and my mates was fooling around down in the town. I fell into a window and it broke.'

'It looked as though you were pushed, Kerry.'

The teenager shook her head. 'Nah. It was an accident. We were a bit pissed.'

'There was some blood at the scene. Did you get cut?'

Kerry pulled a face. 'A bit, but it's okay.' She touched her forearm.

'Can I see?' Rose leaned across and gently pulled the girl's sleeve up. The dressings looked neat and clean.

'The school nurse did them today,' Kerry said. 'But they were okay before then. Danny put antiseptic and plasters on when I came home after. He's a good kid.'

'Where did you get the alcohol from, Kerry? You know it's against the law to be out drinking at your age.'

The girl remained tight-lipped.

'Did you get that bruise on the side of your face at the same time?'

Kerry looked away. 'Yeah, prob'ly.'

Rose held out a card. 'This is me, and it's got my contacts on it. Will you promise to phone me if you need to? For any reason? I'm here to help. And, Kerry, try not to get drunk again. It's not clever and you could get really hurt next time.'

'You're a sergeant,' Kerry said, looking at the card.

'That's me. I'm the boss. Everyone does what I say. Well, they ought to.' Rose winked at Kerry, who gave her a weak smile in return.

The two police officers left the house, while the boy watched, his eyes wide.

'Do you know a detective superintendent?' he asked just before closing the door on them. 'She was here yesterday morning. She talked to me out at the front gate.'

* * *

They sat in the car. 'Is something going on, boss? It's just what that lad said. Has the super really been here?'

Rose grimaced. 'The ways of the high and mighty are beyond normal human comprehension. But I'll check it with her. If she's been here talking to that lad, she'll want to know about our visit.'

'There's something else, boss. The father. Well, he was in that group of nasty-looking blokes on Saturday night, up on our patch in Dorchester. The ones I thought were up to something in the local pubs. I'm not saying he was the ringleader just that he was there.'

'Maybe you need to spend some serious time on photofits. We'll see what her ladyship says. And we need to make sure this is followed up. That bruise on the girl's face looks as if she's been clouted. It might have been Dad. He looks nasty enough.'

Chapter 20: Operation Shadow

Thursday Evening

'So let me sum up. And chip in if you think I've got it wrong.' Jim Metcalfe, Dorset's assistant chief constable, sat back in his chair and looked at the three senior detectives ranged in front of him. Matt Silver, Sophie Allen and Kevin McGreedie occupied the other three sides of a table in a small meeting room at police headquarters.

'We have two sets of serious crimes that, at first, didn't seem connected, plus a couple of suspicions. The first crime was the prison smuggling, and your unit has been investigating it, Kevin, with Lydia Pillay taking the lead. The second was the murder of Tony Quigley, investigated by Sophie's team, quickly followed by the disappearance and death of Andrea Ford, one of our own people. Then there's the possibility that a shadowy group of racist thugs are somehow involved, first trying to intimidate Lydia in Dorchester at a supposedly undercover meet, then seen there later on the same day, although we don't know what they were up to. Now we think at least some of them are Weymouth based. Lastly, there's this suggestion from Lydia that the prison smuggling may be more organised than the powers that be have previously thought, although this is little more than a hunch at this stage. But all three of you think there's a good chance that the same people are involved? This gang that seems to have operated below our radar until now. Have I got it right?'

'That's about it,' Matt replied. 'But it's very worrying, Jim. If it's true, we can't go after Andrea's killers, all guns blazing, if it means we might frighten off the prison smuggling people or cause them to close down before we've got a good lead on them.'

'Why does Lydia think the smuggling is more organised than anyone previously thought?'

'The procedures are similar in every case she's reviewed,' Kevin explained. 'She's looked at what happens in most of the prisons across the south west, and she says that it's all extremely systematic. It's like a complex supplies operation. She wants permission to get an army logistics expert in once she's got all the details together, and to work with Hampshire and Wiltshire. She's been speculating that the whole thing might be masterminded by some ex-army logistics corps people that are using their knowledge to make themselves rich this way.'

Metcalfe frowned. 'That's worrying. But it might explain why they acted so ruthlessly with Quigley and Andrea. Squaddies gone bad can be brutal.'

The door opened and the chief constable poked her head in. 'I'm off, Jim. Everything okay?'

Metcalfe grimaced. 'I'll need a meeting with you as soon as we can manage it, ma'am. You need to know about this.'

She looked at the small group, and then at Metcalfe. 'I can be in at seven thirty tomorrow morning if that helps?' She disappeared.

Metcalfe turned back to the others. 'At present, we'll act as the co-ordinating group, the four of us. You three run the operations and make routine decisions as usual. But nothing must happen that could shut down any other part of the chain. Let's call it Operation Shadow for now. Agreed? Your people can be told what's going on, but only on a need to know basis. We need to be careful with the crews in Weymouth and Dorchester. We don't know how far the influence of this unknown group has spread. Keep in touch and we'll meet again in a day or two, once I've discussed it with the boss. I'll be in touch.'

Chapter 21: Horror

Friday

On Friday morning, Sophie met with Barry and Rae and told them of the meeting with the ACC and the plan to merge their investigation with Lydia's.

'I'm worried that we've had to take our foot off the accelerator a bit on the Tony Quigley angle because of what's happened to Andrea. How has that side of things progressed? Have we made any headway?'

'We haven't taken our foot off at all, ma'am,' Barry said. 'It's just because you've been so focussed on Andrea. But the squads are still out on the streets in Dorchester, and the local CID have been hard at it. We've got a much clearer picture of him now, and how he operated before he stopped work. He was on the make, no doubt about it, and it wasn't just cash he was getting. He made two or three visits a year to a luxury villa in Spain, but no money ever left his bank accounts. He drove top-notch cars, but we can't find any trace of him paying for them. It looks as if they were all gifts for services rendered while he was a prison officer. They stopped when he retired.'

'Can we get a name for whoever he was working for? Is that possible?'

Barry made a face. 'They were too clever. Nothing yet, but we live in hope.'

'Spain, Barry, Spain. There was a lot of Spanish stuff in Andrea's flat. Is there any chance it might have been the same people? The same villa even? I don't suppose their visits ever overlapped, but there might be something in common. Rae, could you match up the details of their visits — flights, destination airports and the like? Perhaps another quiet chat with Laura Quigley is in order. She's had an easy ride from us so far. Maybe it's time to turn the screw a bit and find out what she knew about those Spanish holidays. For goodness sake, didn't she ever check where the money was coming from?'

'Apparently not. But I was just thinking, ma'am,' Rae said. 'They might have met someone while they were in Spain. Whoever was paying him to turn a blind eye to the smuggling might not have wanted to meet him back here, but in Spain they'd have had time to discuss their plans to their hearts' content. The merry widow might remember a face or two.'

'It's worth a try. Leave that one to me. I can't let you two do all the work while I swan around doing sod all. By the way, Lydia may be arriving later this morning. She's bringing all of her investigation stuff across with her. It's possible that Jimmy might be with her, if he can be spared. It'll be just like old times, won't it, Barry?'

She looked at her watch. 'Time to be off to the hospital for Andrea's post mortem. Coming, Barry?'

* * *

Usually when Sophie appeared for a post mortem examination she and Benny Goodall would indulge in a bit of light-hearted banter, just to relieve the tension, but this morning Sophie was too tired to even think of a suitable comment to make. She and Benny had been friends since they'd shared a house at university, so he was able to discern her moods better than most. He noticed that Barry Marsh seemed even more muted than normal, if that was possible.

'What's turned up, Benny?' Sophie asked.

He gently lifted the corpse's left hand. 'The damage to these fingers was done just prior to her death. She had her hands forcibly held down and the fingers spread out. Do you see the slight bruising on her wrist and the back of her hand? Those are from whoever held her down. Then they struck her little finger with a heavy object, most likely a mallet or hammer. This one's worse than the one on her right hand. She was hit so hard on this side that the bone splintered. We've extracted a few fragments of wood from the underside of the wound, and Dave Nash has them for analysis. My guess is that it's boat timber of some type, but it's just conjecture at the moment.'

Sophie frowned. 'So they smashed both her pinkies and then tipped her into the water?'

Benny shrugged. 'It looks like it. It was definitely done before death occurred.'

'That's just foul. How needless, to torture her before killing her. Why would they do that?'

'Could they have been trying to get information from her?' Barry said.

'It's possible, I suppose. But would it have been necessary to go to that length? Surely if that were the case, the threat of having her finger broken would have been enough? And why both hands? She'd have been a screaming mess after the first one, and told them anything they wanted to hear. So why the second?' Sophie paused. 'No, you know what this is, Barry? We have a psychopath doing this.' She shook her head slowly. 'I thought I might never have to deal with another one after Frimwell and Duff. How wrong could I be?'

'The facial bruising was caused at about the same time. There's nothing else of major importance. Her liver was a bit ropey, so I'd guess she liked her booze, but don't we all?'

'No signs of recent sexual activity?' Barry asked.

Benny pursed his lips. 'That's a hard one. There's nothing obvious but she was in the water for a long time. What I can tell you is that there are no signs of forceful rape. No abrasions or tears.'

Sophie walked towards a small window and looked out, deep in thought. 'There must have been two or more men involved. She'd have had to have been held down while her fingers were hammered. What do you reckon, Barry? Three? One to hold her hand still, one to use the hammer and one to control the boat.'

Barry nodded. 'Sounds about right. There'll be superficial damage to the timber surface where it was carried out, ma'am, probably the gunwale. If she got splinters of wood in the wound, then it will have left traces. If it was dark at the time, would they have noticed? Can we get a search started? Maybe the harbourmaster's office has a record of boat movements for Tuesday and Wednesday. It's about time we had some luck, isn't it?'

'Don't hold your breath, Barry. They'd have slipped out to sea, hoping not to be noticed, that's my guess. But it's worth a try, and your idea of looking for the damage is sheer genius. There might still be some tissue residue from her wounds and, if so, that will nail them. You get a search organised and I'll contact Dave Nash for confirmation.'

They returned to the incident room to plan the next day's activities. Sophie would be attending her mother's wedding. She should have been relaxed and happy, looking forward to the following day's joyful occasion. Instead, she felt sick with tension.

Chapter 22: The Wedding

Saturday Afternoon

The Cliff Castle Hotel, high above the Avon Gorge in Bristol, has stunning views in all directions. From it, a visitor may look across the rocky gorge to the tree-clad southern cliffs as well as the wide, grassy Clifton Downs. Best of all, the large conservatory faces directly towards Brunel's famous suspension bridge, majestically bestriding the sheer sides of the river valley. It was in this room that the wedding ceremony for Susan Carswell and Bill Parker was to take place. Sophie was waiting in a room off to the side, along with her two daughters, while Susan's hairdresser made some final adjustments. Everything was ready. Sophie glanced again at Hannah and Jade, beautiful in their mottled-green and yellow bridesmaids' dresses. Sophie, too, wore this outfit and the same gold hairpiece. She took a quick look in the mirror. She'd do. She looked as good as she ever would, but could never compete with Hannah and Jade. Of course she couldn't. The years start to take their toll in the end, and a forty-five-year-old in a high-stress job can't expect to match the looks of two glamorous young women.

The outfits, first spotted by Hannah in a London store, were perfect. Sophie's mother, Susan, had heartily approved the dress and jacket combinations. The three Allen women looked very spring-like, just as well on this drab, grey morning. Where was the sunshine that had been forecast?

She looked up as her mother came towards her. 'Ready?' Susan asked. She looked stunning in an ivory-coloured silk skirt suit and matching hat.

Sophie gave her a gentle hug and a smile. 'I can't speak, Mum. I'm too choked up.'

'Oh, get a grip, Sophie. It's only a bloody wedding. It's not as if it's life or death, is it?'

'Okay, I feel suitably chastised. I think it's time we got moving.'

The four women left the dressing room, and were joined by Sophie's grandfather, James Howard, who was to escort the bride down the short aisle. He looked both distinguished and exhilarated, and was smiling broadly. As the group made its way into the main room, Sophie realised that James was a little wobbly on his feet, and Susan was holding him steady rather than the other way around. She smiled, calm now. The sun, finally emerging from behind the bank of grey clouds, illuminated the room.

The short ceremony began, and Susan Carswell, at the tender age of sixty-one, was married for the first time. Her middle-aged daughter, Sophie Allen, couldn't help but shed a tear for the lost years of her mother's life and the thought of her long-dead father, a man she'd never met.

Later, in the reception, after several glasses of champagne, and when they thought no one was looking, the four women came together for a hug. As they broke apart they realised that the room had fallen silent. A loud burst of applause erupted, which, of course, led to another round of champagne toasts.

It turned into a truly wonderful day, one that would live long in Sophie's memory. Later that night, as she and Martin climbed into bed, she burst into tears again.

'I'm just so happy,' she said. 'It was all so perfect, and Mum deserved it. And you kept everything ticking over. I could see you moving around, talking to everyone. I love you so much, sweetheart.'

And with that, she turned over and fell asleep at once. Martin sighed. Ah well. Probably a good thing after all that food and wine.

Chapter 23: All Solved?

Sunday Morning

The following day, Sophie appeared in the incident room, still a little disoriented from all the emotion of the day before.

'Wedding went off okay, ma'am?' Rae asked.

'Hmm, yes, great thanks. How are things here? Everything alright yesterday?'

'Oh, yes,' Rae said nonchalantly. 'We solved everything while you were away.'

Sophie opened her eyes wide.

'Only kidding, ma'am.'

Lydia assumed a shocked look. 'That was a very dangerous thing to say, Rae, particularly when you're just a mere DC and the boss is now a superintendent. Are you feeling suicidal today for some reason?'

Rae giggled. 'Maybe I should go and sit in the naughty corner.' She glanced sideways at Sophie. 'Can we see the photos sometime soon? Please?'

Sophie laughed. 'Of course, once I get myself organised. Seriously, have there been any developments?'

'I'm even more certain that it's the same bunch of guys behind everything,' Lydia said. 'George Warrander came in at the end of his shift yesterday and we sat down and had a good look at that gang of thugs. We're pretty sure that three or four of them at least were in both groups. We concentrated on the apparent ringleaders and compared what we remembered of them.'

Sophie looked puzzled. 'We can guess why they were in Dorchester that lunchtime. To intimidate you. We think they come from Weymouth, and we know that at least a couple of them work at the docks. But why were they in Dorchester that night? What were they up to?'

Lydia shrugged. 'We don't know. George couldn't work out what they were up to. I've been thinking back to my encounter with them last weekend, ma'am, particularly the ringleader. At the time, I thought that he was a bit thrown when I told him who I was, and he hesitated because he thought he was in danger of being arrested. But it might not have been down to that at all. Jimmy arrived at that very moment, and it could have been seeing him that put the guy off.'

'Which ties in with the idea that they knew full well who you were, and why you were there.'

'Exactly.'

'Have you got a name for him? The ringleader, I mean?'

Lydia shook her head. 'No. We've worked out who the other two are, the ones that pulled him away. Luke Boulden and your man, Liam Fenners. But as to Mr Confrontation . . .' She shrugged.

'So he becomes a priority. Get a photofit made up, if you haven't already done so — George can add his bit. Then we look for this guy. Agreed?' Sophie turned to Barry. 'Have you made any progress on that phone number? The one Andrea was calling on Wednesdays?'

'Yes,' he said. 'We think whoever it belongs to is based in this area. But it's an unregistered SIM, so we can't get a name. All we can tell is where it's been used, from the mast data. So we know it's mainly in Weymouth, but occasionally in other places in Dorset.'

'Such as? I can see there's more, Barry. You have that look on your face.'

'Dorchester, eight days ago, just before the confrontation with Lydia. And the same that night, just as George Warrander observed. But whoever he is, he's playing things really carefully. He's no fool.'

'But that doesn't match with Lydia's observations of his behaviour. Creating a confrontation in a pub like he did was totally stupid. What on earth was he thinking? Unless his only previous interaction with a woman detective was Andrea Ford. Maybe he knew her and found her easy to intimidate, and so he tried the same trick on you, Lydia. I really can't think of any other explanation.' She looked away, apparently lost in thought.

Lydia coughed. 'I know that look of old, ma'am. Can you share with us?'

Sophie gave a wry smile. 'Of course. The behaviour of our Mr Angry isn't what you'd expect from someone in charge. Even though Mr Angry was the main man in that group, my guess is that he's just an underling. There's someone else running all this, and he's keeping himself hidden in the shadows. Someone clever. Andrea might even have known who he was. Maybe that's why she had to be killed, because she was showing signs of wanting out. Maybe the plan was to use the confrontation with you, Lydia, to suss you out as a possible replacement. If so, the boss might have been in the pub but not in that group. Maybe he was watching and listening from the sidelines, to see how you reacted. Can we get the CCTV back from the pub and go through it? If I'm right, he'll have waited until you and Jimmy left, then followed. He might have joined up with the group, but I doubt it. If he works in the way I think, only a couple of them would know him, maybe Mr Angry and whoever his assistant is.'

‘Boulden?’ Lydia suggested.

‘Could be. If I’m right, the whole thing had a definite purpose. We keep quiet about this, by the way. Just the five of us, plus Kevin and Matt. It’s like everything else in this mess, we don’t know how far their influence has spread in the local team.’

Chapter 24: Inferno

Sunday Afternoon

Young Danny Fenners was in his room, sprawled across his bed and staring at his diary. He read over what he'd just written, checking it for errors. It wouldn't do to have punctuation and grammar mistakes in it, not if he was serious about becoming a journalist when he grew up.

* * *

I'm glad Kerry's getting better. She got me to have another look at her cuts this morning. They've nearly healed. That was because the school nurse cleaned them up and stuck new plasters on them. I think Kerry was scared by what happened when she broke that window, she hasn't been out getting drunk since then. That's really good because she might start concentrating on her school work and pass her GCSEs. She's been round at Grandad's even more than me this week. He might have talked her into working harder. She really likes history, but it's no good only working at that. If she wants to go to college she'll have to work at other subjects as well. I felt like telling her that but I didn't. She always swears at me if I try and tell her what she should do.

That woman police sergeant who came round saw the bruises on her face. That was from where Dad hit her. But Kerry didn't grass on him. She should of. He oughta be in prison for what he's done. I keep wondering about the other one, the detective. I haven't told anyone about her, not even Grandad or Kerry. If Dad knew he'd go mental.

Dad hasn't been around much since Thursday. Somethings going on. It's those bad people he meets. I think I might spy on them and see what they're up to but I'm scared. It's that Tonto Leary and his dog. It always looks at me as if it's going to rip my throat out. Tonto sniggers.

Our music concert is coming up soon. We're doing a big band medley. It's even got some fast tunes in it, Rock and Roll. It's hard to keep up and I keep making mistakes but so do all the others. Kerry and Grandad said they're coming to the concert. Mum said she might but she probly won't, she never does. I told her what Grandad said, about me going to college. She just got angry and said I have to get a job when I'm old enough to leave school. She said the same thing to Kerry. She said we needed the money. But she goes and spends it all on drink and fags. That's why Kerry sometimes nicks stuff from the shop, like pizzas and things. If it wasn't for her and Grandad we'd be starving some of the time.

Dad's just come in. I heard the door bang. I bet he's in a bad mood. He's always in a bad mood.

* * *

Danny heard the argument when he was halfway down the stairs. His father's voice, loud and angry, and Kerry's shrill, shrieking in response. He wondered what it was about this time. Although did those two ever need a reason to have a go at each other? He sat on the bottom step and listened. Dad was still going on about the police's visit on Thursday, when they came to check up on Kerry. Someone had obviously needled him about it. Maybe it was that Tonto Leary. Whoever it was, Dad was angry about it. Danny was about to move closer when he heard the inevitable thump, followed by another shriek. It sounded as though Kerry had fallen against the wall. The door was flung open and she came rushing out, her face streaked with tears. She pushed past Danny and fled upstairs to her room. Danny decided to follow.

'I'm pissing off out of here. I can't take any more of this shit,' she cried as he came into her bedroom. She was hauling clothes out of drawers and stuffing them hurriedly into a bag. 'I'm going to Grandad's. If you've got any sense, Danny, you'll do the same.'

Then she was out of the door and away. Danny was even more scared than usual. With Kerry gone, he'd be left to muddle along as best he could by himself. The thought made him feel sick. He went back to his room, crawled under his duvet and went to sleep.

When he finally woke it was dark and silent, with faint moonlight coming in through his open bedroom curtains. It was well after midnight and he was famished. He opened his bedroom door and crept along the landing, past his parents' room. He could hear them both snoring loudly. He made his way carefully down the stairs, avoiding steps seven and eleven (the creaky ones), along the narrow hallway and into the kitchen. The main lightbulb had failed several weeks earlier and neither of his parents had yet bothered to replace it. Kerry had brought down a small lamp from her bedroom and by this dim light Danny searched out two slices of bread and popped them into the toaster. He then collected a plate from the cupboard, a knife from the cutlery drawer and went to the fridge to pull out a jar of peanut butter.

He heard a gentle clunk from the front of the house and froze for a moment but there was no other sound, so he continued preparing his snack. The toast popped up, and he spread each slice with a thick layer of peanut butter. He took several large mouthfuls, swallowing hungrily. Strange. It didn't normally smell like this, did it? There was a cloying sweetness in his nose. Had it gone bad? He held the open jar up to the light but could see nothing wrong.

He heard a sudden strange sound coming from the hallway — a *whump*, followed by a thundery, roaring noise. Afraid, he wondered what to do, finally edging to the door and pulling it ajar, looking for the possible cause.

He found it. The end of the hall closest to the front door and the bottom of the stairs was a roaring inferno, with flames reaching the ceiling. Danny backed away in horror, his skin already smarting from the heat and his chest starting to tighten. Thick, black smoke was billowing towards him at ceiling level. He backed into the kitchen, pushed the door shut and, in total panic, ran to the back door, madly trying to heave it open before remembering that it would be locked. The roaring was getting louder, and smoke was seeping around the door from the hallway. He finally managed to manipulate the key in the lock and pulled at the heavy door. It opened a few inches but got stuck on the mat, which had somehow managed to curl up around his feet. He tried to slide out through the narrow opening and tripped on the doormat as he squirmed through the gap, sprawling onto the small patio outside the door. He pushed himself up onto his hands and knees and caught sight of a dark figure passing a gap in the hedge and walking briskly away. Danny crawled back into the small rear porch, fumbling for his saxophone case, which was stored in the corner. The kitchen was already ablaze, smoke starting to billow out through the open doorway above his head. His mum and dad were still in there.

Chapter 25: Bacon Sandwiches

Early Monday Morning

Sophie Allen arrived at the scene of the blaze just after four in the morning. Fire engines were still lined up along the road and an ambulance was sitting outside the Fenners' house. There was little activity by now. The fire had been put out, damping-down procedures were in progress, and many of the personnel were busy stowing their equipment back into the fire trucks. As she hurried towards the house, Sophie could see several fire-crew members still moving in and out. Rose Simons was standing at the front gate, arms folded, looking serious. George Warrander was a few yards away, talking to a cluster of onlookers. Several other groups of people were standing about chatting quietly, their faces still wearing expressions of shock and horror.

She reached the untidy hedge, some of its leaves curled and browned by the intensity of the heat from the burning building. The front of the house was a complete mess, every window blackened, timber frames charred and misshapen. Part of the roof had collapsed.

'Not a pretty sight, ma'am,' Rose said.

'The family? Did anyone get out?' Sophie asked.

'The boy. For some reason he was downstairs at the time, otherwise there'd have been no hope for him either. The girl, Kerry, wasn't in at the time. She was at her grandfather's house. They're at the hospital with the boy. He's getting a check-up, but word is that he's okay.' She paused. 'It's the parents. Both dead. They had no chance.'

'Any word yet as to how it happened?'

Rose shook her head. 'No. But there's a lot of activity around what remains of the front door. The fire chief's there with a couple of the guys. Their faces are a bit of a giveaway, if you ask me. My guess is that they've found something suspicious.'

'Okay, Rose. Thanks.'

Sophie, donned her white overall and walked towards the group standing at the entrance. She managed to catch the eye of the fire chief. She took the hard hat a nearby fire officer offered.

'Hi, Natalie,' she said. 'What are your thoughts?'

The fire chief looked at her grimly. 'Petrol. And plenty of it, poured through the letterbox. The two asleep upstairs had no chance. It would have been an inferno within a minute of ignition. We think it was a burning rag that got pushed in.'

'Rose said that the two children got out. Could you confirm that?'

Natalie Smith nodded. 'The lad was outside at the back when we arrived, with the neighbours looking after him. He was incredibly lucky. He was in the kitchen at the time, we think, and managed to escape just as it began to take hold. He inhaled some smoke, but nothing serious. We sent him for a check-up anyway, but I don't think he'll be kept in. He was in shock though. Completely catatonic. We couldn't get a word out of him.'

'He might be slightly autistic, maybe Asperger's,' Sophie said. 'This would be beyond his ability to cope. Are the parents' bodies still inside?'

'Yeah. We're just finishing checking through the place and looking for structural damage. There are still one or two hotspots that need damping down first before we can let anyone else in. We'll probably get their bodies out at first light, then I'll give the place a final check. If it's safe at that point, I'll hand it over to you. Okay?'

'Of course.' Sophie looked around her. The onlookers were beginning to drift away back to their own homes. Sophie wondered if any of them would manage to get back to sleep.

'I'll head off to the hospital and see how the boy is. You can pass on any information via Rose Simons over there.' She looked at Natalie. 'I know I've said this before, but I don't envy you this task. It must be the pits.'

Natalie looked at her grimly. 'At least the kids weren't caught up in it. That's when it really wipes me out. They so nearly could have been, Sophie. It's sheer good fortune that we don't have four bodies in there. Whoever did this, they don't deserve any leeway. It's pure bloody evil.'

* * *

Dorchester Hospital's Accident and Emergency department was serenely quiet for once, with only three people waiting in the seated reception area. Sophie showed her warrant card to the duty nurse and, a few moments later, followed a second member of staff into a small examination room that held the Fenners' youngsters and their grandfather. Young Danny looked at her, wide-eyed, as she entered. He seemed to shrink back slightly.

'It's you,' he whispered.

The elderly man and the teenage girl glanced from Danny to her, looking puzzled and suspicious.

'I'd better explain,' Sophie said. 'I met Danny a few days ago outside the house. I was hoping to see his father, but he wasn't there.' She turned to the girl. 'You must be Kerry. I think you met one of my officers, Sergeant Rose

Simons, recently? She's at the house now with the fire crew.'

'Is there any news?' asked the elderly man sitting beside the bed.

'You must be Mr Bailey. Is that right?'

He nodded slowly. 'Charlie. These two are the lights of my life.'

Sophie chose her words carefully. 'There is news, Mr Bailey, but it isn't good.' She looked at the two youngsters. 'I'm afraid your parents didn't survive the fire. It's awful news, I know, but you have to be told. It's better coming from me than hearing about it from the news or gossip. What I can tell you is that they probably didn't suffer in any way. They'd have been overcome by the smoke while they were still asleep. They may not even have woken up.'

Kerry and Danny's reaction wasn't quite what she expected. There were few outward signs of emotion, no tears. Danny reached for his grandfather. 'Does that mean we can come and live with you now, Grandad?'

The old man put his arms around his two grandchildren, tears welling up in his eyes. 'Of course. We'll manage, the three of us, won't we?'

'You'll be kept safe here for a few hours more, all three of you. One of my officers is on guard outside this ward for as long as you're here. I'll be back later on once I've decided what's best, but meanwhile you mustn't leave. I need all three of you safe. Okay?'

* * *

Sophie sent a message to her unit members telling them she wanted an early start in the morning to initiate a house-to-house inquiry in the immediate vicinity of the fire. Then she returned to the scene of the burned out house. Several of the fire tenders had already gone, leaving a scene of brooding depression. She called to Rose and George and asked if they'd picked up any useful information from the neighbours.

‘Nothing substantial,’ Rose said, ‘but a neighbour who lives a few doors away saw someone walking away from here a few minutes before the fire broke out. She was closing her bedroom curtains at the time. Apparently it was someone with a dog, but not wandering slowly like you’d expect for a late night dog walker. George has the details.’

Sophie noted the details of the neighbour, a pensioner who’d returned to her house an hour earlier. Probably better to leave interviewing her until later in the morning. It was now five, and the woman might have managed to get back to sleep. The thought of bed made Sophie yawn. If she set off for home now she could hardly expect to arrive much before six, but at least she’d have time for a shower and a change of clothes before returning to start another working day. She’d already realised with some embarrassment that the trousers she’d hurriedly hauled out of her wardrobe in semi-darkness were her decorating jeans, all spattered with dried paint. No wonder the grandfather had been eyeing her oddly — they didn’t exactly match the thin, animal-print, mohair jumper, nor her tan leather jacket.

Home at last, she put the kettle on and made a pot of tea before taking the longed-for shower. She was wondering whether Martin was awake and would appreciate a mug of tea, but when she returned to the kitchen, he was already up, laying the breakfast table.

‘I heard you come back in,’ he said. ‘There was no point in staying up there by myself, so I thought I’d do something useful. I didn’t hear you go out though. When was that?’

‘Three,’ she replied. ‘I was surprised my mobile didn’t wake you.’

‘I’ve got used to your snores over the years,’ he said, ‘they drown everything out. Even thunder doesn’t wake me now, which is a blessing. I thank the Lord every time you turn onto your back in your sleep and the tractor sounds start up. Bring on that thunderstorm, I say. We're immune in this household.'

For once, Sophie was silent. Martin looked at her closely. 'Sorry. Have I said the wrong thing? What was the call-out?'

'House fire,' she replied. 'Two dead. It was deliberate.'

Martin moved behind the kitchen chair where she'd sat down, and massaged her shoulders. 'Bacon sandwich?'

'Mmm. That would be nice,' she replied. 'Plenty of ketchup, please. I need some comfort food.'

'What is it with the police and bacon sandwiches?' Martin asked. 'I'm convinced that police work in this once great country would fall apart if the national bacon supply disappeared.'

Chapter 26: Questions

Monday morning

Sheila Drangfield was adamant. She'd seen a man walking quickly away from the Fenner house only a minute or so before the flames started flickering behind the front door. She hadn't managed to get a look at his face — he was walking away from her house — nor could she tell what colour his clothes were. The street lighting here was a little dim.

'What were you doing up, Mrs Drangfield?' Sophie asked. 'Wasn't it rather late?'

'Just one of those age things, dear,' she said. 'My son tells me I go to bed too early, so it's no wonder I often wake up in the early hours. I just make myself a cup of tea, take it back to bed and read for a while. I usually drop off again within the hour.'

'The constable you spoke to said you were pulling the curtains. Is that right?'

'Yes. I hadn't closed them properly and the moon was shining in on me, so I got up to adjust them. That's when I saw him.'

'Had you ever seen him before?' Barry asked.

'Well, that's the thing. I'm sure I've seen a man like him around here a week or two ago, with his dog. But I don't like to pry. They're not people I talk to very much, the Fenners.'

'Is there a reason for that?' Barry said. 'They're right opposite you, after all.'

Sheila frowned and tapped her fingers on the arm of her chair. 'I suppose we don't have much in common,' she said at last.

'Do some of your other neighbours feel the same?' Barry said. 'Were there difficulties with them in the neighbourhood?'

Sheila thought for a while. 'Well, I have to admit that I didn't really like them, and neither did a lot of the other people around here. We were all sorry for the young boy, Danny. He's really nice. Sometimes he does some weeding for me, and I give him a few pounds for it. But the girl, Kerry, can be really abusive. As for the parents, well. He's very rude and aggressive and she's drunk a lot of the time.' Sheila put a hand to her mouth. 'Oh. I forgot. They're not here anymore. It was just awful. No one deserves that. No one.'

'But you're sure that you've seen the man with the dog before? Round here, calling on them?' Barry said.

'Well, I think it was him. He was about the same height and build, and the dog looked the same.'

'Do you know his name, Mrs Drangfield?' Sophie asked.

Sheila shook her head. 'No. I stay clear of most of their visitors. Some aunts and uncles used to call round sometimes and they were nice people — you know, much more normal. But I haven't seen them for ages. The men who come calling on them now scare me a bit. If I'm out in the garden I move round to the back. There's too much swearing and I don't like that.'

'If you do think of anything else that might help us, please phone. I'll leave my contact card,' Sophie said.

Walking back, Barry turned to his boss. 'The youngsters might know who he is, ma'am. Should we ask them?'

'It's a tricky one. I don't want to alarm them, and I don't want to put them in any more danger, which is possible if whoever did this thought they might be able to identify him. But that's a threat whether we talk to them or not, and we need to find out what they know. Whatever happens, we can't leave them in their grandfather's house. All three of them are too vulnerable. We're going to have to put them somewhere safe for a while, certainly until this is all sorted. It's tragic. They're already in enough turmoil as it is. Have the other neighbours come up with anything useful?'

Barry shook his head. 'Not a thing. Either no one saw anything, or they're too scared to speak up. From what Mrs Drangfield said, some of them must have seen these people visiting the Fenners, but my guess is that they're worried about a possible backlash. That fire-bombing was a pretty stark warning.'

'Our problem is that while we're embroiled in Lydia's investigation, we have to play it slowly. We can't go hell for leather after these thugs until we know the extent of their involvement. We can't afford to give them any prior warning and put Lydia's investigation at risk, particularly since hers is still in the early stages.' Sophie sighed. 'It's a bloody nightmare.'

* * *

Lydia, along with Jimmy Melsom, was collating the information about prison smuggling that was beginning to come in from the police forces in other counties. As it accumulated, she grew ever more convinced that she'd been right. There were just too many similarities for it to be mere coincidence. Times, vehicle descriptions, quantities of materials seized, models of drones, batch numbers of seized miniature phones, even the lawyers used — common features were beginning to emerge. Even more interesting, she'd discovered that Luke Boulden and Liam Fenners had both been in the army, and had possibly left under a cloud. She was waiting for further details from army records. She knew already that both had served in logistics, supplying equipment to front line units. Logistics expertise was the very skill required for sourcing the kind of items prisoners wanted. Maybe it was time to interview Luke Boulden. She'd need the approval of her two bosses first, though. It was a real pig, working for two senior officers. They were both great people, but Kevin and Sophie had different approaches to their jobs. Sometimes Lydia had the feeling that she was constantly running from one to the other.

Her phone rang. She listened in astonishment to Sophie's account of the house fire that had killed the Fenners.

'Do we need to move on Boulden?' Lydia asked. 'He could be next. And he's our only other possible lead at the moment.'

'Is anyone aware of our interest in him?' Sophie said. 'Has he been interviewed or anything?'

'No. Kevin suggested a softly, softly approach.'

'In that case, leave him at present but keep him under surveillance if you can. I've a feeling Fenners may have been targeted because we'd shown too much interest in him. It wasn't just us. Rose Simons from the local uniformed squad called at the house to follow up an incident with the daughter, and I went there and spoke to the son last week. It's quite possible that one of the gang leaders got jittery and thought Fenners might be about to spill the beans. How are you getting on with your inquiry?'

Lydia told Sophie what she was thinking.

'All the more reason to take things slowly with Boulden. We can't afford to lose him as a potential witness. Christ, Lydia, everything would be so much simpler if the two things weren't so tangled up together. Listen, phone Kevin and bring him up to date with the news from last night. Barry and I will be back in later this morning, so we can have a briefing then. Get Rae to join you and Jimmy looking into the army background, it might throw up some more names. Then get her to keep an eye on Boulden. You know, Lydia, I can't help thinking that there might be someone clever at the back of all this, pulling the strings and providing the brainpower. And raking in the cash. The people we've come across so far aren't nearly in that league, not even your Mr Angry. I mean, how stupid was that, deliberately causing a confrontation with a police detective? No, there's someone else behind it all. And he's not out there getting his hands dirty. We need to find him, whoever he is.'

* * *

Danny Fenners was sitting up in bed when Sophie and Barry returned, wide-eyed and solemn as usual. His grandfather was sitting in a chair reading a newspaper and Kerry was thumbing through social media posts on her mobile phone.

'Be careful what you post, Kerry,' Sophie said, taking a seat in a plastic chair Barry had hauled off a stack in the corner.

Kerry gave her a withering look. 'I'm not stupid, you know. My friends want to know what's going on, that's all. I won't give anything important away.'

'We'll be moving you to somewhere safe, all three of you,' Sophie replied. 'Once we've organised that, you mustn't post anything that might give a clue about where you are.'

'I said, I'm not stupid,' Kerry replied angrily, but put her phone away.

'Are you both really detectives?' asked Danny. 'Like what you said on Wednesday? Who's the boss one?'

Barry grimaced and pointed to Sophie with a flourish. 'She is. She's a detective superintendent, which is pretty high up, believe me. I'm just a sergeant. I drive her around from place to place, and get her some coffee when she needs it. She makes all the hard decisions, and I just go along with them. We've got some questions for you, Danny. Both of you, in fact. We want to know about any visitors that have called at your house recently. Maybe workmates or friends of your parents? Or anyone else who you've seen in the neighbourhood?'

'Why?' Kerry demanded immediately. 'And all this secrecy and protection, why are you doing it?'

'Because the fire was started deliberately, Kerry,' Sophie answered. 'Someone wanted your parents dead, or one of them at least. Whoever did it didn't care who else was caught up in the fire. My guess is that it would have suited them if all of you had been killed, which just goes to show what kind of people they are. I have to find out who it was and get the evidence to arrest them before they try the same thing again on someone else.'

Kerry looked at her through narrowed eyes. 'Okay,' she finally said. 'But I don't know anything about it. I was round at Grandad's.'

'I know you were, Kerry. And you were lucky. If you'd still been at home, you'd probably be dead. Fires don't tell one person from another. They kill anyone who's in the building.'

'But not Danny. He got out.'

'That's why I need his help. Can you tell me everything you remember, Danny? Take me through what happened, minute by minute. Can you do that for me?'

Danny nodded. 'I think so.' He described the events of the previous afternoon and evening, from the argument between Kerry and their father to his escape through the kitchen door.

'Did you see anyone, Danny? Was anyone hanging about or walking by?'

Danny shook his head emphatically. 'No,' he said, dropping his eyes. 'No one.' He looked as if he wanted to cry.

* * *

Sophie and Barry made their way back to the car. 'He knows more than he was letting on, ma'am, don't you think?' Barry said.

'Yes. The classic signs. My guess is that he's scared. The family set up must have been odd, Barry. Those three seem so close, so natural together, even though he's their grandfather rather than a parent. So what was wrong with their relationship with their real parents? They're displaying so little grief. Their grandfather was clearly upset but he's trying hard not to show it. Those two kids, though, they're not sad at all. Maybe the fire did them a favour. Kerry had already walked out, and my guess is she intended it to be permanent. I wonder if she hated her parents? Could it have been an abusive relationship? We'll need to follow it up. Danny's autism means that he'll show less emotion than an average child of his age, but even so. Maybe he was terrified of his parents too. From the interview we had with their father, I can't say I'm surprised. He came over as an out and out thug.'

Barry frowned. 'Could we be barking up the wrong tree, ma'am? If what you're suggesting is true, it's possible that those two youngsters could have started the fire, just to give themselves an escape route from an abusive home. Is it possible?'

'We have to consider it. I don't think Danny could have done it, or even been involved in any direct way, but the girl is totally keyed up and tense. She reacted defensively to almost everything I said. And according to Rose Simons, she has a history of erratic behaviour. Maybe we should get Rose to have another chat with her. I think you're wrong, though. That fire was too well planned, too callous. It was cold-blooded murder, not the reaction of a sullen teenager. Inexperienced sixteen-year-olds don't start fires in that way.'

Chapter 27: Sausage and Chips

Late Monday Afternoon

Simon Osman locked the door of his town centre office and made for his car, ready for the short drive home. A heavily built man suddenly materialised beside him, sliding out from the shadows cast by the nearby shrubs, and making him jump.

'Christ. Why did you have to appear like that, Bill? You scared the living daylights out of me.'

'You know why. I can't afford to be seen talking to any of you, and the cops are probably still watching your house. I wondered if they were watching this place too, but it doesn't look like it. I've been checking the area out for the last ten minutes and didn't spot any obvious signs. Thank God for police funding cuts. They've made our job a lot easier. There aren't enough nosey cops left on the payroll to watch everyone they're interested in all the time.'

Osman was still jittery. 'What happened to Fenners? I heard his place was fire-bombed. Was that really necessary?'

'Ask no questions, hear no lies. Move on, Si. Let's not dwell on the past. You're the one who's always said that.'

Osman glanced around, but they seemed to be alone and unobserved. Pinpricks of perspiration glinted on his forehead, despite the cool early evening breeze. There were a lot of questions he should probably be asking, but his mind seemed stuck in a loop. His throat felt dry.

'The cops might be back, Si. If they're doing the job they're paid for, they'll come calling on you again. You're the only link they have now, and there was nothing to tie you to her death. Just don't panic. Stick to the story we rehearsed, okay? They'll have to give up in the end 'cause there's nothing to go on. I made sure of that.'

Finally, Osman summoned up the courage to ask what had been bothering him for hours. 'But why kill Fenners like that? His wife's dead as well. His kids could have been caught up in it.'

'You didn't need to know. But since you've asked, there were too many cops calling on him and I guessed he was gonna break. My sources told me they were gonna offer him a new identity somewhere up north, with protection, if he gave evidence. It was all too chancy for us, Si. But there's no need for you to worry, not if you stick to what we agreed. We can keep going just like before. The cops have got nothing on us, trust me.'

And then the dark-clad figure was gone, back into the shadows. Simon Osman shuddered. He hated fire, and burning homes filled him with horror. It took him a while to calm down enough to walk the few yards to his car and clamber unsteadily inside. Even then it was several minutes before he felt calm enough to start the engine. What had gone wrong? More importantly, was there some slight chance that he could extricate himself from this violent, tangled mess? He had no idea if there were other local cops who were in on the scheme, watching with redoubled intensity now that Andrea was dead, cops who were far cleverer than she ever was. If he tried to make contact with the police, he might be walking into the very trap that he'd just been warned about. Fuck. What a complete mess.

* * *

Late that afternoon, Danny Fenners was declared fit and ready to be discharged from hospital but he, Kerry and their grandfather didn't leave by the main entrance. While press officers from both the police and the hospital made a public statement to the waiting reporters, photographers and film crews, the trio were led out of a rear exit and into waiting, unmarked police cars. Barry and Sophie travelled with them in the lead car, and a small group chosen from Greg Buller's security unit, including several firearms officers, trailed along behind in a nondescript van.

'They're officially called the security unit,' Barry told Danny as Sophie steered the car out onto the main road, 'but we call them the Snatch Squad. They're a pretty tough bunch, believe me. Anyone who tries to mess with them will come off second best.'

Kerry did her best to appear bored and unimpressed. 'Where are you taking us?' she asked.

'You'll still be in Dorset, but well away from the Weymouth area. It's probably only for a couple of weeks, maybe less. Once we get things sorted out and we've made a few arrests, you can go back home.'

'My concert is on Saturday. I can't miss that,' Danny protested.

'Okay, leave it with us and we'll organise that for you.'

Kerry looked at Sophie shrewdly. 'It's more than just the fire, isn't it? You wouldn't be doing this just because some nutter burned our house down. Dad was up to something, wasn't he? Is it like some kind of gang war, the type they talk about on the telly? Guns 'n stuff?'

Danny turned to her. 'Shut up, Kerry. You're talking too much.'

His sister looked daggers at him but lapsed into silence, chewing her fingernails.

'I wish I could explain, Kerry, but it's too early in our investigations. You're on the right track, though. That's all I can say at the moment. That's why it's so important that you tell us anything that might help us. I want both of you to have a think about it. There'll be someone with you all the time, so if you do remember anything else, just tell them.'

They drove to a quiet cul-de-sac in Wareham, where the police service owned a secluded safe house a little apart from the other residences. Greg Buller kept his van back on the main road, so the only vehicle that pulled in at the house was the unmarked car. Rose Simons and George Warrander were already inside, having arrived much earlier to check the area. They waited while the group assembled in the sitting room.

Kerry was not pleased to see Rose, even though the police sergeant was temporarily in plain clothes.

'Not you as well,' she complained. 'What is this? I'm being victimised.'

'I'm deeply hurt,' Rose said with a smile. 'I'll have you know that I'm well known for my loving and caring attitude towards small, furry, homeless creatures. And I brought chocolate.' She took a packet of assorted chocolate biscuits out of her bag and spread them onto a plate on the nearby table.

'Don't think you can bribe me into doing what you want,' a surly Kerry replied. 'I'm not stupid.'

Coming in behind them, Sophie sighed. 'You've told us that three times now, Kerry. None of us think you're stupid. We're just trying to keep you safe and make you feel welcome. Why not relax a bit and give us a chance?'

Kerry curled her lip but said nothing.

'Rose and George will stay for a few hours, and then they'll be replaced by one of my officers who'll stay overnight. Remember, no one must know you're here. It's possible that all three of you are in danger. I told you that the fire was started deliberately. It's what we said earlier, in the car. We think your father might have been involved in something illegal and that he was thinking of coming to us to give evidence. Someone guessed and decided to stop him. Whoever it is, they're still out there, and they might think you know about them.'

'But we're just kids,' Kerry said, thrusting her hands into the pockets of her jeans. 'No one would bother with us.'

'You're sixteen now, Kerry. Your evidence would count in court. That changes things.'

Meanwhile, Barry was watching Danny. The young boy was pale and he stared at his feet, squirming. His grandfather, Charlie Bailey, saved the situation. 'Let's all have a nice cup of tea. I'm parched. And those choccy biccies look too good to ignore.' He picked one up and took a large bite. The two youngsters followed suit, while George Warrander went to make tea.

'Danny and I'll have coke,' Kerry called after him. 'Make mine a diet one.' She stared challengingly at Rose.

'We can do that,' Rose said. 'I got loads of stuff. Listen, George is a mean cook. What do you fancy for your tea? You must be starving. Would sausage and mash be okay? With onion gravy? Or would you prefer chips?'

The atmosphere gradually became more relaxed, so once they'd had a quick cup of tea, Sophie and Barry decided to leave. The two youngsters were watching TV, Rose was chatting with Charlie and George was in the kitchen, cooking sausage and chips for five. He'll make a great catch for some lucky young woman, Sophie mused. She thought back to the time, four years earlier, when she'd first interviewed George as a witness, and he'd asked her about the possibility of joining the police. It had been a propitious moment. He'd shown real talent and commitment, and had proved himself to be the perfect foil for the highly experienced but rather too cynical Rose

Simons. She'd blossomed in the role of mentor. A win-win situation.

* * *

Danny was tucking into a second helping of chips, lavishly coated in ketchup, when he started to speak.

'I might have seen someone last night, when I got out of the kitchen. There was a load of smoke and my eyes were stinging, but I thought I saw a man. He was walking away. In a hurry.'

Rose decided she'd have to go carefully. She ate another mouthful of food. 'Do you think he might have been involved, Danny?'

The boy shrugged. 'Dunno.'

'Did you recognise him? Had you seen him before?'

'Might have. It could've been him.'

Rose finished the last of her chips. 'Could it have been someone your dad knew?'

Kerry was sitting bolt upright, staring at her brother. 'Why didn't you tell us earlier? Was it that Tonto Leary?' She put her hands flat on the table and leaned forward. 'Bastard. Fucking murdering bastard. I always hated him.'

'So you both know this man?' Rose said. She noticed that Charlie was looking bemused. 'Did you know him, Mr Bailey?'

'Never heard the name. Mind you, I didn't go round their house very much. I wasn't really made to feel welcome, even though Sara was my daughter. The only time I visited was when I knew these two were going to be there on their own. Sara was always trying to get money from me, and I got fed up with it.' He turned to his grandchildren. 'Why didn't you ever mention this man to me if he worried you so much?'

'He was only there a few times and it was recent. And I didn't want to think about him. I hoped he'd just go away and never call on us again,' Kerry said. 'He used to look at me, you know, as if he couldn't wait to get his hands on me. Eugh.' She shuddered.

'His dog growled at me. All the time,' Danny added. 'Like a low rumble in its throat. Every time I moved it watched me. It had great big teeth and it dribbled. I always thought it was a wolf.'

'Anything else we should know about this man?' Rose asked.

The two children shook their heads.

'In that case, I'd better report in about him.' She went to call Sophie.

Chapter 28: A Shadowy Web

Monday Evening

Lydia scrolled through her emails. At last, the Ministry of Defence had sent the information. She opened the first of several official-looking messages from the armed forces records office. Liam Fenners had served eight years in a logistics corps unit operating out of barracks in north Wiltshire but had been discharged five years ago after he'd stolen some communications equipment. Very interesting.

The next email confirmed Lydia's theory. Luke Boulden had served in the same unit and, guess what? He'd been discharged for the same reason, at the same time.

Lydia hurried to Sophie's office, where she found her temporary boss packing some paperwork relating to Tony Quigley into a folder.

'It's coming together, Lydia,' she said. 'I thought it would. There's more work to do though. I still think there are more people involved. Let me have a look at those emails.'

She read the two printouts. 'The details are a bit thin, but it looks as though they were caught pretty easily. That means they didn't think things through when they stole the stuff, which suggests to me that they're doers rather than thinkers. Someone else is doing the planning and pulling the strings.'

'Should I go up to Buckley Barracks tomorrow morning to see if I can dig anything up? It's just north of Chippenham, so I can get there in about two hours.'

'Absolutely. You can ask about these two, but try to find out if anyone remembers others who might have been involved. And do it carefully. Will you take Jimmy with you?'

'I think so. Is that okay?'

'Of course. Being a bloke, he might be able to find someone who's willing to open up a bit over a coffee. You know, Jimmy can be a charmer when he tries, particularly if he finds someone to talk football with.' She waved her sheaf of paper in the air. 'Somehow this all links together, Lydia. There's a shadowy web of people involved, and we need to work out who's who and how they're connected. This might be the breakthrough we need. Let Kevin know what you're doing and make an early start tomorrow. And good luck. Oh, one last thing. There might be someone going by the name of Leary involved. Tonto Leary. Why Tonto, I haven't a clue. It'll be a nickname from way back when. But it's the kind of stupid nickname that squaddies give each other. Officially we don't know about him, so you'll need to be very careful about bringing it up.'

'Okay. I understand. We don't want to give anything away needlessly. Who was it who said "softly, softly, catchee monkey?"'

'Hmm. It might have been Baden-Powell, but some people say it has a Ghanaian origin. You know how people argue over the origins of clever sayings. It definitely applies in this case.'

* * *

Sophie, Barry and Rae sat around a table with two sets of documents spread out in front of them.

'There's got to be a connection between these two,' Sophie said. 'Andrea and Tony Quigley clearly knew each other, but we have no evidence for it. Surely there must be something that links them? Ideas, anyone?' She leaned back and yawned. It was getting late. 'The trouble is, I don't know what we're looking for. Did you say there was nothing in the Spanish connection, Rae?'

'No. They both had holidays there, but I've checked back through every single flight they took. They never went at the same time, though the flights went to the same airport. Malaga.'

'Could they have been using the same hotel or villa?' Barry asked.

Sophie leaned forward. 'Now that's an interesting idea. What if one of the gang leaders has a villa out there, and used it to reward our two? Laura Quigley might remember where she and Tony went, and why. The trouble is, we haven't found anything of Andrea's that tells us where she stayed. No photos, no diaries, no social media posts.'

'Do you think the Fenners ever went to Spain, ma'am?' Rae said. 'Is it worth asking those two children?'

'That's another great idea. How come it's you two that are coming up with this stuff? I must be losing my touch.' Sophie looked at her watch. 'You'd better be getting across there, Rae. You're due to relieve Rose Simons in an hour. Spend some time getting to know the kids, then ask them about holidays. Careful though. That Kerry's as sharp as a blade but she's suspicious of everything and everyone. You won't be able to get round her with food either, not tonight, because apparently George has just cooked them all sausage and chips. Who can compete with that?'

'I'll think of something.'

* * *

Rae arrived at the safe house within the hour, laden with bags of crisps, puffs, nachos and an assortment of dips.

'I come bearing food,' she announced. 'But I expect I'll have to eat it all myself. I've heard that you've all had sausage and chips.'

The teenagers looked at her warily. Charlie gave her a polite smile and raised his hand in welcome.

'I'm Rae Gregson, a detective constable. That means I'm at the bottom of the pecking order, just like George.'

'Rose said you'd be the overnight watch,' Charlie said. He looked at her warily. 'If something did happen, could you cope? I mean, you'd be by yourself.'

Rae laughed. 'I'm tougher than I look. And we have a fast response unit in the neighbourhood, patrolling around in an unmarked car. No need to worry.'

'What's the difference between a detective and an ordinary policeman?' Danny asked.

'We solve crimes,' Rae said as she sat down. 'Ordinary police try to prevent crimes from happening. But they also help out with investigations. There are more of them than us. But remember, there are lots of policewomen, Danny. They aren't all men.'

'It's just a phrase,' Kerry snapped. 'Danny didn't mean anything by it.'

'I know that. But it's important that women's contributions are recognised. Surely you understand that, Kerry? In fact, Dorset's chief constable is a woman. She's one of the most senior police officers in the country. Anyway, let's talk about other things. Have you all decided where you'll be sleeping tonight? And have you left somewhere for me? I don't really want to end up on the couch.'

Kerry looked puzzled. 'I thought you'd be up all night, keeping watch.'

'That won't be necessary. It's not as though there's a mad assassin out there, desperate to liquidate the three of you. Moving you out for a few days is just a precaution. And no one knows where you are, not even the local Weymouth police. Anyway, I've been at work all day and I'm really tired. I couldn't stay awake all night even if I wanted to. To be honest, my plan was to sleep on the couch in here. It would be better if I was downstairs. But you must promise not to blunder in and wake me too early in the morning. I can be a bit grumpy if my beauty sleep is disturbed. Now, who's for a few crisps and nachos, or is it only me?'

Rae collected some dishes from the kitchen and tipped some of the nibbles out. Despite the sausage and chips, the youngsters soon joined in.

'These always remind me of a holiday I had in Spain,' Rae said. 'I wondered if I'd meet a tall, dark, romantic Spaniard and fall in love. It didn't happen though. Have you two ever been to Spain?'

'Yeah,' Danny replied. 'We went twice. It was brill.'

'Did you stay in a nice hotel?'

Danny shook his head. 'We were in a sort of house with a low roof. But it had a swimming pool and everything.'

'It was a villa, Danny,' Kerry said. 'That's what you call that type of place.'

'They're a bit expensive, aren't they? I couldn't afford to rent one,' Rae said.

'It was someone Dad knew. We went swimming in the pool every day, didn't we, Kerry? It was amazing. I learned how to bomb into the water. Mum did her nut 'cause she kept getting soaked.'

'Whereabouts in Spain was it? Can you remember?'

Kerry replied quickly. 'It was in Malaga. And don't think I don't know why you're asking. I keep saying to you lot, I'm not stupid.'

Rae thought for a moment. 'So, you'd prefer me to be absolutely open with you, Kerry?'

'Yeah. Why can't you just trust us?'

'Is it possible that the villa was owned by someone involved in crime? Someone who owed a favour to your dad?'

'Yeah, obvious. Why else would we stay there for free?'

'Did you ever meet anyone there? Did anyone come visiting?'

'Once. But Dad used to go out some evenings to meet someone. I watched once from my bedroom window. He got picked up in a big black car in the lane outside the villa.'

'Was the person who came to call Spanish? Or was he British?'

'He was from around here, I think. He said something about Weymouth as if he knew the place.'

'It wasn't that Tonto Leary, the one Danny told Sergeant Simons about?'

'God, no. That scumface doesn't have a villa in Spain, but he's used the same one we were in. I heard him talking to Dad about it once. He's a moron.'

'Did you ever hear this visitor's name? Do you remember what he looked like?'

Kerry shook her head. 'He only came once, and I only saw him for a minute. And it was years ago. But he sounded as if he owned the place. It was something he said to me as I got out of the pool. Something like, what do you think of my pool?'

Danny looked anxiously at his sister, seemingly mystified. 'You're scaring me, saying all this,' he said.

Kerry looked at him. 'I hated Mum and Dad, Danny. You know that. But it doesn't give someone the right to burn our house down and kill them, and nearly kill you. Dad was into something he didn't want us to know about. It was obvious. It was bound to be one of them that did it. And that Tonto Leary was the worst of the lot.'

'It would help if you could remember the address of the villa,' Rae said hopefully, but Kerry shook her head.

'It was called Rosina,' Danny said.

'Danny has a really good memory for stuff like that,' Kerry said. 'He remembers all kinds of weird stuff. There were lots of other houses the same, all along that lane. It took us a long time to find it the first time we went. We should have got a taxi from the airport, but Dad said the bus would be cheaper. We had to walk miles up this steep lane, pulling our cases. Mum was crying 'cause her feet were so sore. So was Danny. Mean skinflint.'

Old Charlie had been listening in to the conversation. 'I might still have the postcard your mum sent,' he said. 'I keep them pinned to the fridge for a year, then I put them in an old biscuit tin.'

'That would be very helpful, Mr Bailey. I'll get someone to visit your house and collect it tomorrow.'

Rae was pleased. There might be enough here to go on. She wondered how her two bosses would fare tomorrow when they interviewed Tony Quigley's widow, Laura.

Chapter 29: The Villa Rosina

Tuesday Morning

Having been back in her house for twenty-four hours, Laura Quigley was forced to admit that she missed Tony's company, although not as much as she'd feared. The problem had always been his grumpiness and his dictatorial manner. He had a habit of boasting to all and sundry that he was an old-fashioned, unreconstructed male, and that he couldn't be doing with all this modern "sharing and caring stuff and nonsense." After all, what were wives for but to do the domestic chores? On being treated to his pronouncements, most people moved off as soon as they could. A few, men of course, nodded in agreement, while their wives looked on with pursed lips and narrowed eyes. Laura cringed with embarrassment. Why couldn't Tony just shut up sometimes?

Well, he was permanently shut up now and, in the main, Laura had few regrets. For the first time in decades she could please herself. She could eat what she liked, when she liked and where she liked. The house was so much tidier without Tony's bits and pieces littering the tables, shelves and floors. Dirty washing was in the laundry basket, towels on the towel rail. And the whole house smelled so much nicer. The icing on the cake had been the unexpectedly large cheque from Tony's insurance company. With her other cash, she now had the money to do whatever she felt like doing. She'd come out on top at last, and for once her life was looking just that little bit rosier.

She was sitting in her lounge enjoying a relaxing cup of coffee when the doorbell rang. She glanced out of the window and saw a man and a woman, both smartly dressed and looking like officials. Insurance? Police? Council people? She opened the door to them, led them back into the lounge and offered them coffee. Well, one of her guesses had been right. The woman had introduced herself as a detective superintendent. Was that more senior than a sergeant? Laura guessed so from her air of authority. And quite clever too. She settled back in her chair and listened to what they had to say.

'We're getting closer to the people who killed your husband, Mrs Quigley,' the woman said. 'We think there was more than one person involved in the planning, although we don't know how many came into your house that afternoon. We want to lift them all at the same time, so we've got to make sure we've identified and located all of them. There are a few questions we want to ask you about Tony's contacts. You've had a couple of holidays in Spain in recent years. Is that right?'

Laura nodded, smiling. 'Yes, down in Malaga. It's beautiful. I loved those holidays. Well, we both did.'

'Where did you stay?'

'In a villa belonging to a friend of Tony's. He said it was someone from the prison service and we got it cheap. I never got involved with the money side of things, but Tony said we'd saved ourselves a lot.'

'Can you remember the name of the place? Or the address?'

'It was called Villa Rosina, but I don't know the address. Tony dealt with all of that. We'd get a taxi from the airport or to take us out to a restaurant, although we didn't do that very often. The villa was a lovely place, a real sun trap. It had a pool and a really pretty shrubbery. I can remember saying to Tony that it was prettier than all the other villas around. Tony watered the plants every day. I think that was part of the deal.'

'Do you know who the owner was?'

Laura shook her head. 'No. Tony never mentioned it as far as I can remember, and I never asked, not after the time he shouted at me.' The detective raised her eyebrows. 'The first time we went, I told him we ought to get them a present, but he was a bit negative about it. I thought the least we could do was send a card saying how much we were enjoying staying in their villa. I wrote it and asked Tony for the name and address, but he flew off the handle and tore it up. He was like that sometimes. Moody. Well, not just sometimes, he was moody a lot of the time.'

The detective's eyes were fastened on her, probing. 'Was he always a bit moody, Laura, or was it just in recent years? Since he retired? Or a few years before that?'

Somewhat taken aback by the question, it took Laura a few minutes to work out just when her husband's grumpiness began. 'Well, he can't have been too bad when we first met because I'd have never settled for him if he'd been like it then. When we were first married and living in the Midlands he was okay too. When I think about it, it must have got worse about ten years or so ago. That was when he started really snapping at me. Mind you, he was never any help around the house, even when we were a lot younger. He expected me to do all the work, even when I had a job.'

'Let's be honest, Laura, even these days it's not that unusual, is it? Part of the blame has got to lie with us women and the way we pamper our sons. And, if you ask me, too many seem to enjoy playing the martyr, they quite like their partner being helpless.' She paused. 'Sorry. I digressed. I'll get back on track.'

Laura caught the slight smile of amusement on the sergeant's face.

'Were you aware of anything that was bothering Tony at work?' the woman said. 'Did he ever mention any concerns he had? I know the local CID has already asked you this question, but please bear with me.'

'Tony never talked about his work to me. Never. It was pointless me asking because it would only set off one of his moods. But there did seem to be something bothering him, starting from about five years after we arrived here.'

'When was that?'

'We came here about fifteen years ago.'

'Okay. That's all the questions I have at the moment, Laura. But there's something else I need to mention. You were meant to inform the local CID when you felt ready to return home. You didn't, and we only found out by accident.'

'I just felt I needed to come home,' Laura said, thinking it sounded a bit lame. 'I missed the place. My sister's was fine for a short while, but you miss your own home, don't you?'

'I can understand your feelings, Laura. But it's my job to keep you safe. Something happened at the weekend that caused us to have serious concerns. We just can't have you staying here by yourself, I'm afraid. Is there no chance of you being able to return to your sister's for a few more days?'

Laura shook her head. 'We had a bit of a falling out, actually.'

'Okay. If I remember rightly, you had an offer from a neighbour, a Mrs Gibson. Do you think that offer might still be open? There are reasons why I don't want you here until we're sure it's safe.'

Laura looked shocked. 'Well, I imagine Jane would still have me if it's that important. Is it really so bad?'

'We don't know. But I always plan for the worst. That way I keep people alive.'

Laura's hand went to her mouth. 'Oh, my goodness. I didn't realise things were that bad. Yes, Jane lives opposite. She's the woman I was chatting to the afternoon Tony died.'

The detective smiled at her. 'Barry here will go across and speak to her. Better to be safe than sorry.'

Chapter 30: At the Barracks

Tuesday Morning

Buckley Barracks is situated in the north Wiltshire countryside. The area doesn't have the rolling beauty of Salisbury Plain further south, but on this crisp, sunny winter's morning, the trees and hedgerows sparkled and it looked enchanting. Lydia and Jimmy turned off the main road toward the army base.

Lydia showed her identification to the sentry at the gate. 'We're here to see Captain Hudson,' she said. 'We have an appointment.'

They were directed to the main reception office where, after a few minutes wait, he escorted them along a corridor and into an office. They were greeted by a tall officer with a thickly freckled face and sandy hair. He stood up and walked around his desk to greet them.

'I'm Colin Hudson, in charge of security. I've a vague idea why you're here, and I've done a bit of preparation for you.'

Lydia smiled at him. 'Thanks.'

He pulled some documents out of a drawer in his desk. 'I've found the records of the men you mentioned in your request form. I'm allowed to share with you anything that I think might be relevant to your criminal investigation, but no other stuff. I only got a hazy idea from the ministry's message, so you'll need to fill me in on the details. Just to reassure you, I'm aware that all information relating to an ongoing serious crime investigation is confidential. Whatever we discuss in here won't leave this office.'

Lydia gave him a brief description of the Operation Shadow investigation, along with her theory that the smuggling operation in different areas might be organised by the same gang, some of whose members could well be former logistics corps soldiers. 'Our suspicions mainly concern the two named in the form. One of them, Liam Fenners, died at the weekend in a house fire, along with his wife. We think it was arson.'

'You're talking possible murder, as well as this smuggling operation? Now that is serious.'

'Absolutely. I'd like to spend time going through what you've dug out, but I wonder if it would be possible for Jimmy here to go walkabout with someone from your team? If he could talk to some of the guys who'd been around at the same time as Fenners and Boulden that would be great.'

'I don't see a problem in that. I'll get one of my NCOs to take him to the canteen. A lot of the units will be starting to drift in for lunch. Then we can meet up with him there a bit later and grab a bite to eat ourselves. How does that sound?'

'Perfect.'

* * *

Jimmy Melsom was the ideal person to put off-duty soldiers at their ease. His engaging, man-on-the-street personality and his obsession with football and cricket meant that he had plenty of topics for conversation. His temporary host, Lance Corporal Jacqui Winter was a great help, she seemed to know most of the soldiers by their first name. She also knew those that would have been serving there at the same time as Fenners and Boulden.

Halfway through his pasty, she touched Jimmy's arm. 'There's a possible useful contact. He's been here yonks. It'll be worth chatting to him.'

They moved across to join a middle-aged man with a round face and grizzled hair, who'd just settled at a nearby table.

'Can we join you, sir?' Jacqui asked. 'I'd like you to meet Detective Constable Jimmy Melsom from Dorset. He's visiting the base as part of an ongoing inquiry. Jimmy, this is Sergeant Graham Dixon.'

The two men shook hands.

'Must be important if base security have got themselves involved,' Dixon said.

'We've left our bosses doing the important stuff,' Jacqui replied. 'Jimmy wanted to meet some ordinary squaddies, so I decided to bring him in here for lunch.'

'Nice place. Good people,' Jimmy said to Dixon.

'Yeah, I like it. Otherwise I wouldn't have stayed so long. I'm one of the permanent staff, in charge of the stores here. I'm probably too old to move on now and, to be honest, I've lost the wish to keep moving about. It might have suited me in my younger days, but I've put down roots around here, so I'm happy to stay put.'

'I've never been away from Dorset,' Jimmy said. 'Apart from holidays, that is. Lived there all my life, so I'm a real stay-at-home.'

'Nothing wrong with that. I wouldn't have agreed with you when I was your age, but I've changed my tune as I've got older.'

Jimmy took an instant liking to this man. He seemed shrewder than all the other soldiers Jacqui had introduced him to, who were keen to gossip about football and the current state of the premier league. He wondered how to start, but Jacqui did the job for him.

'Jimmy is interested in some people we had with us a few years ago, Graham. I think they may have created a few problems in their time. Fenners and Boulden? Do those names ring a bell?'

Dixon laughed. 'Why aren't I surprised that the police are here about those two? Real pair of scumbags, if you ask me. Do you want to know what they were thrown out for? Though it'll all be in the records anyway.'

'That's what my boss is doing at the moment, going through the paperwork with your security chief,' Jimmy said. 'I thought I'd try a different angle, speak to people who were here at the time, and try to get a feel for what they were like. Your comment about them's told me a lot already.'

'It wasn't just what they got cashiered for — filching stuff from the stores. They just weren't nice people. I never felt like I could trust them. They were the worst two I ever had working for me, particularly Fenners. He could be nasty.' He paused. 'Well, they were almost the worst.'

Jimmy's ears pricked up. He waited, but no further explanation was offered. Instead, Dixon changed tack.

'In one way, they did us a favour. We were forced to examine all of our store security procedures afterwards and tighten them up one hell of a lot. Then other logistics corps places copied our new system. Stuff's always gone missing from army stores, and always will, but it's mostly small things. What those two managed to do was steal stuff by the vanload by exploiting loopholes no one knew about.'

'I didn't realise it was that serious,' Jimmy said. 'Why didn't they end up in prison for it, rather than just being chucked out?'

Dixon shrugged. 'I asked myself that question all the time, and I could never come up with a sensible answer. It's a mad world, not a whole lot of fairness or justice in it.

Why are you interested in them, by the way? Still the same nasty, lying, cheating thieves?'

'Pretty much. I can't give you any details, since it's still an ongoing case. I'll tell my boss, though. She might get back to you.' He wondered how much he could safely tell Dixon. The information was already in the public domain, so how could it do any harm? 'Fenners is dead, by the way. He was killed in a house fire at the weekend, him and his wife. Luckily his two kids escaped. It was arson. Possibly deliberate murder.'

Jacqui Winter sat bolt upright in her seat. Graham Dixon whistled. 'Blimey. That is a shocking bit of news.' He was silent, frowning. Jimmy waited.

'There was a third man, though nothing ever stuck to him. He was only here briefly, and he was gone before we got started on the investigations, transferred to some other unit. I could never understand why we couldn't trace him, but he somehow slipped into the shadows. I always thought he was the ringleader. If the other two were bad, this guy was evil. Nastiest person I ever came across. Taylor. That was his name.'

'Right,' Jimmy said. 'Any other name?'

'Never knew his first name.'

'So he could still be in the army?' Jimmy asked.

Dixon shrugged. 'Anything's possible. If he's out now, it'll probably be because he decided to quit. The other two were stupid, but he always managed to escape trouble, often by the skin of his teeth. There was never any evidence to nail him.'

'Anything else we should know about him?' Jimmy asked.

'Well, if you ever have to confront him, you need to be prepared. He's a psychopath. I'm serious. He's just the kind of slime that would set fire to a house in order to kill whoever was inside, then stand and watch them burn.' He picked up his tray. 'I've probably said too much already. Good luck.' Then he was gone.

Chapter 31: Family Memories

Tuesday Morning

Kerry was tense and edgy, Rae could see. The teenager had been fine at breakfast, but as the morning wore on she'd become moody and irritable, snapping at anything Rae said. The latest cause of friction had been Kerry wanting to reply to a message on her phone asking where she was. She was sensible enough to show the message to Rae, but wasn't happy with her answer. Rae had said she could reply to the message but she wasn't to mention that she was still in Dorset.

'But it's not as though saying I'm in Dorset tells anyone where we are,' Kerry said. 'It's a big place. It wouldn't help anyone.'

'It would if someone had access to a list of police safe houses in Dorset,' Rae said. 'That's the problem. We think they have inside information.'

'In that case, wouldn't they guess that we were in one of them? They'd start checking them. It's obvious. Then they'll find us.' Rae was beginning to realise that Kerry was much brighter than she seemed.

'That's quick thinking, Kerry. And you'd be right, if we were in one of those places. But this house is special. Only a few people at county headquarters know it exists, and no one from Weymouth does. We want to keep it that way. We're worried about these tracking apps that can be installed on mobile phones. That's why yours was checked yesterday before we left the hospital. We can't afford to take any chances. Just tell your friend that you're okay, and so's Danny. I said earlier that your head teacher knows you're both safe and being looked after. She's happy as long as you keep doing the work your teachers send, and Danny keeps his music practice going.'

Kerry glared at Rae with a look of simmering distrust, but it didn't last long. Making sure that the two youngsters could overhear, Rae chatted with Charlie about his son-in-law.

'Did Liam ever talk about his time in the army, Charlie?'

Charlie took a sip of tea and settled back in his chair. 'He was in the army when he met my Sara,' he said. 'He was based somewhere well north of here, but was down for a couple of weeks doing something for the artillery at the Lulworth ranges. They met in a pub or club in Weymouth one weekend. He wasn't *in* the artillery, mind, he was in some kind of transport unit. He used to go all over the place. When they were first married, he and Sara had an army house up in Wiltshire. That's where these two were born.'

'Did he like the army?'

Charlie ran his fingers through his thinning hair. 'That's a hard one. It kept him busy, and he made reasonable money. And your mum used to work part-time in a local shop, didn't she, Kerry?'

The girl, who had indeed been listening intently, gave a slight smile. 'She bought sweets for us. It was great. Danny probably can't remember.'

Rae was intrigued by Kerry's change of mood. The smile softened her face and it lost its usual wary and pinched expression. She was very pretty then.

'So, why did he decide to leave the army? Do you know?' Rae was treading on eggshells here. She'd been asked to find out all she could about Liam and his background, and they needed this information as speedily as possible.

'They only got married because mum was pregnant with me. That's what I think,' Kerry interjected. 'It's obvious. You just got to look at the dates.'

'It wasn't like that, Kerry.' Charlie said quickly. 'I explained that to you. We never put pressure on your mum to get married. In the end, the choice was hers. We'd have supported her no matter what. I've told you that lots of times.'

'And with a baby they could get a better house. She told me that once,' Kerry retorted. 'It wasn't as if I was ever wanted. They never loved me. It's obvious.'

Rae listened. This explained a lot. No wonder the girl was so moody and aggressive if she had so little self-esteem.

'You're wrong again,' Charlie said. 'She doted on you when you were small. It was only when she started drinking that she got difficult. And that was after your dad left the army and was around a lot more. The two of them weren't really suited. They got on each other's nerves.' He turned back to Rae. 'As for why he quit the army, I never found out. But that's when all the trouble started — the arguments, the drinking. I think he fell in with a bad crowd. They came back to Weymouth, but I stopped seeing them. Babs, their gran,' he nodded towards the two children, 'she got ill, but Sara never came round to lend a hand. I gave up on her then, and just kept my eye on these two. I just couldn't understand why she never lifted a finger to help her own mother. I mean, her older brother and sister did. I still don't know why. That was the reason why the family split. And now, with both of them dead, there'll never be a reconciliation. It's tragic. I just keep thinking, could I have acted differently? It gnaws away at me.'

'Mr Bailey, you seem to me to be a kind and thoughtful person. I'm sure you're being too hard on yourself. And what you're doing now, and have been doing, for these two is fantastic.' She turned to the two youngsters. 'Isn't that right? Where would you two be without your grandfather?'

'Grandad,' Danny said with feeling, 'you're the best person in the world. Kerry thinks so too.'

Rae decided to leave it for now.

* * *

Rae was back at the safe house by late afternoon, in time to help prepare an evening meal. The sounds of Danny practising on his saxophone reverberated throughout the house. Rae was glad he felt able to resume such activities. Maybe things were settling down. She poked her head through the lounge door.

'Spaghetti Bolognese?' she asked. 'How does that sound?'

'I'm okay with it,' Charlie replied. 'How about you, Kerry?'

'Fine.' She didn't look up from the magazine she was reading.

'Do you feel like giving me a hand, Kerry?' Rae asked.

The girl looked up. 'What? Oh I get it — women's work, isn't it? Is that how you see it? Just like my dad?'

'No, I don't see it that way. My boyfriend's a better cook than me and he rules the kitchen. I'm too untidy for him. But I can cook a few things, and I'm always better with a bit of help. But if you don't want to, that's okay.'

Kerry rolled her eyes, stood up slowly and followed Rae to the kitchen where they searched the drawers for aprons.

'Spag Bol is messy stuff,' Rae said. 'Well, it is when I make it. It's safer to protect my clothes. Can you start by chopping an onion?'

They chatted about cooking for a few minutes, then, when Kerry seemed to have relaxed, Rae returned to the subject of Leary.

'Kerry, is there anything else you can tell us about this Tonto Leary character and how he got to know your dad?'

'I think they met in the army. We lived up in Wiltshire then, and I was younger. Dad left the army when I was about eight or nine. That's when we moved down here, and he got a job on the docks. But that horrible man has only been around for a few years, probably from when I was in year eight at school. I never liked him and Danny doesn't either.'

'Did he work on the docks as well?'

Kerry shook her head. 'No. I don't know what he did. He used to come round at all sorts of crazy times. Mum didn't like it, but she never said anything. I think they were both scared of him. Mum was anyway.'

'Did he live close to you?'

'I don't know. Look, I really don't know much about him. He gave me the creeps. I wasn't interested. I had better things to do. Danny was around a lot more than me.' She turned away and started to set the table.

Rae left Kerry and went in search of Danny. She found him in his bedroom, packing his saxophone away.

'What can you tell me about Tonto Leary, Danny? I need to know everything I can about him.'

Danny started talking immediately, his eyes averted.

'He's taller than dad. He works out so he's got big muscles. He's got a blotchy face and a bald head and he always looks angry. He always wears jeans and big work boots. He scares people. He swears a lot, even more than Dad did.'

'Fine, Danny. That's all very helpful. Do you know where he worked?'

The boy shook his head. 'No.'

'He didn't talk about work with your dad?'

'I never listened. I thought he was horrible. I didn't want to be there. I used to read in my room.' Danny stopped talking but, just as Rae was about to ask another question, he added, 'He used to have dust on his boots if he came to see Dad straight from work. Whitish dust. Once, Kerry got the Hoover out after he'd gone 'cause it was all over the carpet.'

* * *

'Charlie, do you remember why Liam left the army? Were you aware of a problem of some kind?' Rae had her hands in the washing up bowl, while Charlie wiped a damp saucepan with a dishtowel. The teenagers were in the lounge, watching TV.

'I never knew the details, just that something had happened that the authorities weren't best pleased about. I guessed he'd got thrown out, but thought it better not to pry. I wanted to stay in contact with the youngsters, and if I'd gone at it like a bull in a china shop, Liam would have cut contact. It was me that found them the house down here and sorted the first few months' rent. It meant they were close enough for me to build a relationship with Kerry and Danny. They both needed someone, but for different reasons. You'll have spotted that.'

'Well, yes. It's hard to miss Kerry's anger issues, and my boss spotted Danny's Asperger's when she first met him. It's fairly mild, though, isn't it? That's what she thought.'

'It just makes him a bit vulnerable. In some ways it's been good because Kerry's always had to look after him, and it's kept her feet on the ground. She's got a heart of gold, really, but she keeps it hidden away under that brash exterior. She started to come to her senses a week or two ago, though. I think it was when she fell through that big window in town. It scared her, I expect. I think she's started doing more work at school, so maybe the penny's dropped at last.'

'By the way, thanks for those old postcards. My boss is going through them. He called me earlier and said they'd helped to narrow down the search for the villa and I was to let you know.'

Chapter 32: Feeling Sick

Tuesday Afternoon

Simon Osman locked up his premises early. Outside, he glanced around nervously and hastened away in the direction of the police station. They had phoned to tell him that his car was ready for collection following its forensic examination, and Simon was sick with anxiety. They wouldn't have found traces of Andrea's presence in his car because he'd told the police the truth. He really hadn't used his car after leaving the wine bar the previous week. What he didn't say was that he'd led Andrea into a trap, and she'd been bundled into a waiting van as they passed some overgrown shrubbery close to his house. His job had been to get her out of the wine bar and into a quiet backstreet, and it had proved far easier than he'd expected. In fact, when he thought about it, Andrea had made most of the decisions herself. Weird. No, what made his stomach queasy was that he'd only just come to fully realise the implications of what had happened to her — and to the other recent victims. Had control been lost somewhere? Could the others be trusted now they had four murders under their belts? He'd never considered such an outcome, even as recently as a couple of weeks ago. What had really gone on and, even more worrying, did they trust him?

He remembered introducing Andrea to Bill. Bill had been wary at first, in case she was a plant. Simon knew that wasn't the case. Andrea just loved mixing with wealthy, influential people. It seemed to do wonders for her ego. She also had some pretty strong views on the immigrant problem, which meant she was useful in all sorts of ways. Added to which, she was a party girl who loved a good time. That's probably why she'd never made promotion above the rank of DC. From what he could tell, she didn't really work hard enough for anything more senior. Nevertheless, he'd always found her a useful contact to have in his dealings with the anti-immigrant group, and her inside knowledge had sometimes proved invaluable. Bill must have been similarly pleased with the information she gave him. Then, having supplied Bill with this very useful contact, he'd been side-lined. He knew that on several occasions, Bill had taken her away to the villa in Spain, and he assumed the relationship had become physical. Still, whatever the relationship, it had obviously soured of late. And the violence of the past two weeks was of real concern. What did it mean for the future? More importantly, what did it mean for *his* future?

He reached the police station and approached the reception desk, his heart pounding. He never reached the desk. The ginger-haired detective, the quiet one, suddenly appeared at his side.

'Good afternoon, Mr Osman. I can take you round to the car park to collect your car. Nothing's been done to it apart from a forensic sweep of the interior. That's all being analysed now, back at the labs.'

'You won't find anything. I meant what I said. I didn't give her a lift last week.' Osman could feel his heart thumping faster. Just stick to the script, he told himself. Don't say anything else.

'Well, it'll all come out in the wash,' the detective said. 'Not that there's anyone doing the washing. It's all totally automated these days. Any DNA traces get matched up against the database and eliminated. If what you say is true, there's no need to worry, is there? Unless, of course, you've had any criminals in your car and they're on the database. That could be a bit of a problem, couldn't it?' The detective walked back into the building.

Simon's heart nearly stopped beating. Christ. Who had ridden in his car during the past month or so? He tried to think back, but his brain was whirring. He didn't think that anyone had been who could get him into trouble. He forced himself to walk on towards his car, even more worried than before. He suspected that Bill was trying to manipulate him, just as he'd manipulated Andrea Ford. Andrea hadn't fully realised just what she'd got into. At first, she'd joined what she'd thought was a loose-knit group of anti-immigrant activists, trying to turn back the tide of multi-cultural influences. She had ended up becoming entangled in something far darker and more sinister. It was uncannily similar to his own situation.

Maybe he should just drive home, calm down and try to think things through. He needed a way out of this mess.

* * *

Back in the police station, Barry walked into the Operation Shadow incident room and made his way to the corner desk. Sophie was there with a technical support team.

'He's moving,' said one. 'Out of the car park and towards the town centre.'

'No surprise really', Sophie said. 'His house is in that direction. I don't think he'll do anything rash today.'

'If he's got any sense, he'll be extra careful over the next few days, ma'am. He must realise he's a top suspect, surely?' Barry was being his usual pragmatic self.

'Of course, Barry. But he might not be involved in the nasty stuff. If he's just a fringe player, he might panic. What I still don't understand is why we can't find anything on this Tonto Leary character. Surely he's got to be local, from what the Fenners kids tell us, and from the encounter with Lydia in Dorchester? And didn't George Warrander recognise the description and put him in Dorchester last weekend? We've got a name, a description, even some ideas about where he might work, but no one of that name seems to exist. Might it be an alias?'

'Well, it's happened before, ma'am. Maybe we need to concentrate on the information Rae supplied rather than the name. White powder on his boots? What could that mean?'

'I asked her to double check with the two youngsters,' Sophie said. 'White powder could mean a lot of things. Flour mill, cement works, plastering work. Even farm work, if it was insecticide or fertiliser powder. This area is full of workers who come into contact with white dust. Think of the quarries.'

Barry looked at her. 'That could be it, ma'am. A quarry worker. South Dorset is riddled with the things, right from Swanage in the east to along here at Portland. The powder would be grittier than other kinds of dust. Didn't the girl say it was bitty? I'll phone Rae to check.'

Sophie merely nodded, looking preoccupied. It was a few moments before she spoke. 'The other thing that bothers me is the fact that none of the people we've been tracking is a boat owner, or even shows any interest in boats. Yet we're pretty sure from the forensic report on Andrea's injuries, and the fact that she was found on the shoreline, that a boat was involved. And it wasn't hers. Hers hasn't been moved from its berth for weeks. So there's someone else who has a boat, and used it that night last week. And that someone is a violent psychopath, judging by what he did to her. It ties in neatly with the arson on the Fenners' house. So why can't we find him? It's so bloody frustrating.'

Barry didn't reply. He felt the same. Who was this Leary, and what was driving him?

* * *

Simon Osman poured himself a glass of scotch, sank into his favourite chair and closed his eyes. There really was no easy way out. If he broke rank and told the cops what he knew, he might pick up a lighter sentence, or even get off, but Leary would never forgive, or forget. He'd come looking for him once he got out of jail, and he dreaded to think what he might do. It would only work if he could get a new identity, and how easy would that be? But then if he didn't go to the cops, things might get worse and worse, and the whole thing would end up falling apart. And what then? He opened his eyes and took another gulp of whisky. He knew very well what would happen. He was a liability. He knew far too much. He'd end up going headfirst into the sea, like Andrea, with a couple of broken fingers, if not worse. Whichever way he looked at it, the prospect was dark.

He finished the glass of whisky, and a terrible thought struck him. What if someone was already planning to do away with him? What if they too realised that the writing was on the wall? Unlike him, they came from a background where violence was often the first option rather than the very last. They might already be debating the right time to do it.

Now he knew what he had to do. Strike the best deal he could with the police and tell them what they wanted to know. But he'd need to stay one step ahead of those thugs, and time it just right. He might well end up having to move away from the area, but he'd always been canny with his money, and his several bank accounts would see him through. After all, what use would his small accountancy business be to him once he was dead?

* * *

Late in the evening as the team were drifting away from the incident room, Sophie's mobile phone rang. Wondering who this unknown caller might be, she walked away from the noise and clatter of the main room and went into her office. At a nod from her, Barry followed.

'Where are you?' she asked.

She listened.

'But we can put you in a safe location, under protection,' she said, shaking her head slightly. 'I can understand your reasoning, but you'll still be at risk.'

She listened on, toying with a stray wisp of hair, a look of exasperation on her face.

'Well, okay. I guess I have to accept it, don't I? But I'm not particularly happy about it. I have your mobile number, so I can contact you for anything important. Please ring me in the morning, say about seven? I want to know that at least you're still safe. What name have you used to check in? Rodney Burgess? I suppose it's as good as any. Look, call me at any time if you feel threatened. But call 999 first. Okay? Is that clear?' The call ended.

She turned to Barry. 'That was bloody Simon Osman. He's done a runner and is holed up in a hotel somewhere, convinced that the baddies won't find him. He wants to talk but is trying to do some kind of deal with me before he'll open up. He's been watching far too many cop shows on the telly, if you ask me.'

'Did he say where he was?'

'No. He just said he'd left his car in the driveway and sneaked out across his back fence and down that house's drive to the street parallel to his.'

'So he got away with it?'

'It would appear so, but it won't take them long to find him.' She counted on her fingers. 'He hasn't taken the car, so he'll have gone by train. He's only five minutes from the station, after all. The service to Bristol is a bit hit-and-miss in the evenings, so I think he'll have taken the Waterloo train, but he'll have got off somewhere a bit more local than London. That would mean Poole, Bournemouth, Southampton or Winchester. I'm betting Winchester, because it takes him that bit further away from Weymouth. He won't want a taxi because the driver might remember him and be able to give a description, so he'll get a bus or walk. Buses in the evening are a bit erratic, so he'll have walked to wherever he's staying. So his hotel is within ten minutes' walk of Winchester station. Maybe five. Wanna bet on it?'

Barry grinned. 'You must be joking.'

Chapter 33: Feeding Fears

Wednesday Morning

'Hey, Barry, am I brilliant or what?' Sophie walked into the almost deserted incident room at seven thirty the next morning. Her second in command, having only just arrived himself, snapped awake.

'You're joking. You don't mean you got it exactly right?'

She grinned happily. 'Spot on, though I got one of the reasons wrong. He chose Winchester because he remembered it from when he was a boy. His grandparents lived there, apparently. He was totally spooked when I told him where I thought he was. I'm going across to collect him once we've had our briefing. Want to come?'

'You don't think he's at risk in the meantime? Shouldn't one of us go now?'

Sophie shook her head. 'I've been in touch with Jack Dunning in Southampton. He's arranging for a couple of local Hampshire officers to be on hand until we get there.'

'I'm sure I'll hear all about it from Gwen later when she calls. She might even volunteer to go herself if she's not too busy. I haven't seen her for days with all this going on.'

Sophie couldn't help but laugh at Barry's mournful expression. 'Life's so tough in the modern police service, isn't it, Barry? Weren't you warned at Hendon that romance and police work don't mix? And here you are, both of you hard-working detective sergeants, struggling to hold all that passion in check. My heart bleeds.' She ignored his scowl. 'By the way, I heard on the grapevine that a trace of DNA has put Liam Fenners inside the Quigley house at some time. I don't know the full details, but Dave Nash will be emailing them to me a bit later. Some of the guys in that gang will be getting jittery, surely? You can't just go bumping people off like that without causing others to wonder if they're next in line.'

'Should we put a bit of pressure on the other one, Luke Boulden?' Barry suggested.

'Well, it might be worth it. Let's think about the pros and cons before we act. And we'll need to bring Lydia in on it if we do.'

Rae arrived, carrying a laptop. 'I may have something. That CCTV footage from the pub in Dorchester, when Lydia ran into that gang? Well, you were right. Someone did get up and leave just after Lydia and Jimmy. You can just make him out.'

She opened the machine and ran the slightly grainy footage. It showed the confrontation between Lydia and the person they thought was probably Tonto Leary, then the arrival of Jimmy Melsom. The group of men drifted away a few minutes later, and then the footage showed Lydia and Jimmy talking to the bar staff. As soon as they left, a middle-aged man who'd been sitting at a side table reading a newspaper stood up and followed them outside.

'Can we do a screen grab of his head and shoulders?' Sophie asked. 'My guess is that he's about six foot tall, maybe slightly less, and of average build. Look at the way he stands so he's never facing the camera. Clever. And he's watchful as he leaves. Do you see how he pauses at the doorway and checks to see what's going on outside?'

'It could just be coincidence, ma'am, but when I saw it, I felt the same as you. Do you see that there's an empty glass on the table? He must have gone to the bar to get a drink earlier. I had a look at the bar camera and found this.'

This camera was focussed on the cash-till area, and the footage was clear. The man was probably in his late forties, with cropped hair and a wary expression. He bought a double scotch and retreated to the table shown in the other film. Once he'd moved away from the bar, the image was blurry, but he could still be seen. He sat reading his newspaper, showing no apparent interest when the group of a dozen or so men noisily arrived and ordered their lagers. When Lydia came in, he glanced up briefly but quickly returned to his paper.

'We need to find out who he is,' Sophie said. 'It might be entirely innocent of course, but we have to know. Maybe someone who lives around here might put a name to the face.'

The door to the incident room opened, and George Warrander walked in.

'Just about to start the morning shift, George?' Sophie asked.

He nodded, looking a little apprehensive. 'Yes, in a few minutes. Ma'am, I've called in because I've managed to find out a bit more about that gang you were interested in. You know, the ones I saw in Dorchester the weekend before last? You wondered why they might be there. I didn't know whether they were still of interest.'

'Oh, yes. Most certainly.'

'Well, I was in the town centre last night and I asked around some more, but, you know, keeping it low key. I found out that they'd hired a back room in one of the pubs that night for some kind of meeting. The thing is, the landlord of that particular pub is a notorious racist and I got the impression that he sometimes helps out groups that share his views.'

'Did you get the name of the pub?'

'The Highlander. It's an old coaching inn, just off the High Street. It used to be much larger than it is now, and straddled both sides of a carriage entry. Then one side got sold off to a hairdresser's.'

'That's really helpful, George.' She looked at Barry. 'I wonder if we should pay a quiet visit, maybe at lunchtime today, after we've lifted Boulden and rescued Osman? Just for a look see?'

* * *

Luke Boulden's arrest went without a hitch. Sophie wanted it done quietly, so the detectives timed their arrival to coincide with Boulden's departure for work. At eight fifteen exactly, he left his front door and strolled towards his car, parked on the driveway. There, he found his path blocked by Sophie, Barry and the intimidating figure of Greg Buller, the latter dressed in his usual black combats. Boulden was whisked away in a waiting squad car and driven to the police station. As expected, he refused to talk without his lawyer being present. Even then, progress was minimal.

'Maybe you don't realise the fix you're in, Mr Boulden,' Sophie said calmly. 'We have a murdered man, Tony Quigley, killed in his Dorchester home on Saturday, a week and a half ago.'

'Nothing to do with me,' Boulden said. He fixed her with a challenging stare. 'I wasn't there.' He sounded confident, but his eyes were wary.

'But you were in Dorchester earlier in the day. You've been positively identified by several witnesses as being in a town centre bar.'

'I didn't say I wasn't in Dorchester, just that I wasn't at that dead guy's house, this whatshisname. Never heard of him.' His right hand rested on the tabletop, little finger tapping the surface.

'You were very close friends with Liam Fenners, who died at the weekend.'

'What of it?'

'You served in the army together. Some of your fellow servicemen said the two of you were very close. According to witnesses, you were still close friends.'

'Yeah, we were mates, always have been. So what?' His eyes darted around the small interview room.

'Mr Fenners, along with his wife, was killed in a house fire that was started deliberately. We know that. Petrol was poured through their letter box and ignited. Fenners and his wife never stood a chance. How do you feel about that?'

'What do you mean, how do I feel? I said, we were mates. I feel sick about it. But what's it got to do with me?' He kept looking around, angrily.

'Where were you in the early hours of Monday morning?'

'At home, asleep. Don't try to fucking pin it on me, because it won't work.'

'Can someone vouch for that? Can anyone confirm that you were at home at the time?'

'No. But why would I want to kill Liam? I said we were mates.' He sounded puzzled.

'But someone did it, Mr Boulden. Quite deliberately. Someone wanted him dead and didn't mind who else died at the same time. His children escaped by the skin of their teeth, only just avoiding being burned alive like their parents. It takes someone very sick in the head to do that. Who do you know that's capable of doing such a thing?'

'Make your fucking mind up. First you say it was me, now you say it was someone I know. What's the point of this?'

'Because we think you're next, Mr Boulden. Think back through the list. Can't you see what's happening here? People are being rubbed out. Tell me something. Has anyone else vanished during the past couple of days? If so, what does that tell you?'

The lawyer interrupted. 'It would seem that you aren't going to charge my client with an offence. In that case, I must ask that you let him go.'

Sophie smiled thinly. 'He's free to leave if he wishes to. For the time being, at least.' She turned back to Boulden. 'But stay around, Mr Boulden. I'll want to talk to you again. And good luck. I wish you a long and happy life.'

* * *

'That was very clever, ma'am, feeding his fear like that. Do you think he knows about Osman?' Barry and Sophie were walking away from the interview room.

'Probably, though it hardly matters. If he doesn't know by now he soon will, and it will all help to feed his unease. All he'll find out is that Osman's disappeared. We know Osman's safe in Hampshire, but Boulden will think he's been neutralised like the others. If so, he'll be wondering why he hasn't been told about it. Why he's being kept in the dark. The thugs don't dare trust each other. It's always dog eat dog when you get to this level of criminality, the only thing holding them together is fear for their own skins. We'll leave him to stew for a while. He's not on a murder rap and I let him know it by switching from Quigley's murder to Fenners. Let's hope he's sharp enough to take the hint, once he's thought things through.'

Lydia Pillay had been watching the interview from the room next door. She came out to join them. 'What's the next move, ma'am?'

'We'll watch him like a hawk, obviously, if only to keep him safe. There's also a chance he might do something rash and lead us to his masters. If not, you and Jimmy can bring him in tomorrow in exactly the same way. Question him about his army days, and start dropping hints about the smuggling operation. But don't bring him here to Weymouth. Use Dorchester nick and pretend you're on a completely separate inquiry. Don't use Greg Buller as backup either, use someone else from his team. We want him to think that our right arm doesn't know what the left is doing. Does that all sound good?'

Lydia smiled. 'I love all this cloak and dagger stuff. Maybe I should have been a spy.'

Sophie looked at her watch. 'So, let's go and collect the esteemed Simon Osman from his luxury hotel room in Winchester. Do you want to come with us, Lydia?'

'Fine. He's in a nice hotel, is he?'

Sophie laughed. 'He's in a flea-ridden dump near the station. According to our Hampshire colleagues, it's a cross between a doss-house and a knocking shop. I wonder if he's started itching yet?'

Chapter 34: Into a Safe House

Wednesday Midday

Simon Osman's grand plan to negotiate with the police from a position of strength was falling apart. The detectives looked around his room at the peeling paint and the grubby furnishings. The so-called en-suite facilities consisted of a tiny cubicle containing a toilet and a wash basin, both appearing to date back to the nineteen eighties, judging by the sick-green colour and the number of cracks in the porcelain.

'Nice to find you in the lap of luxury, Mr Osman,' Sophie said. 'I think we should move you out, though. Even these fancy hotels can't keep out a determined assassin, despite the huge sums they invest in security.' She walked to the window and poked gently at the frame. A splinter of rotten wood fall to the ground. 'I'd prefer to keep you out of Dorset for the time being, though. Luckily, I'm on good terms with the CID here in Hampshire, and they have the ideal place for you to stay and be safe. It's a good bit further west than here, so it's easier for us to get to you. Dorset will be paying the bills, so in return we expect your unconditional help with our investigation. I'm sure you understand the deal.' She smiled at him breezily, ignoring his scowl. 'Shall we go?'

The safe house they'd been offered was in a tiny tree-lined cul-de-sac in the New Forest market town of Ringwood, almost on the border between Hampshire and Dorset. All the houses were small, with postage stamp front gardens, most of them neatly kept. Sophie guessed that most of the neighbours were elderly retired people. Inside the house, they settled down in the tiny sitting room, where Sophie introduced Lydia.

'According to what you said to Superintendent Allen here, you were never aware of any criminal activities on the part of these people, other than the anti-immigrant drive that you were involved with. But that isn't why I'm here, even though, as you can see, I'm from an ethnic minority. I need to get to the bottom of the other stuff, the things you say you know nothing of. My guess is that you do know some details, even if you're not aware that you do.'

Osman shook his head. 'I don't know what you're talking about.'

'Just listen, Mr Osman,' Sophie said. 'Let DS Pillay explain.'

'Think back to some of the conversations you might have overheard. Did anyone mention prisons at any time? Maybe Portland or Guys Marsh?'

Osman looked puzzled. 'No. Why should they? We want these immigrants chucked out of the country, not put in prison. Anyway, I never really went to any social events with them. Most of the others I only saw at a distance, when I was at a rally or something. I never knew they were involved in anything else. Do you think someone in my position would get involved with anything criminal?'

'So, you don't think stirring up racial tension is illegal?' Lydia fired back. 'You don't think issuing threats to people born and bred in this country breaks the law in any way? What kind of fantasy world do you live in, Mr Osman?

Not the real one, that's for sure. I do much more for this country than any of your racist friends. Just think about that.' She took a breath. 'Let's go back to my question. Was there anything you overheard that might give a clue as to what else they were up to?'

He shook his head. 'Not really. Once or twice I caught them chatting about money and how much some scheme was generating. And once, in the bar after the meeting, a small group of them were talking about getting hold of stuff, but they shut up when I joined them.'

Lydia leaned forward. 'What kind of stuff were they talking about?'

Osman shook his head. 'Mobile phones maybe? I can't be sure though. Come to think of it, someone mentioned the word "miniature," though I may have misheard.'

'Was there any indication that they were involved with drugs? Even legal highs like spice?'

He ran his fingers across the bald patch on the top of his head. 'There might have been some talk but, as I said, they shut up when I came within earshot. I never got to hear any details.'

'Let's go back to this chat about money you mentioned. Did it sound as though large sums were involved?'

'I got that impression, but I don't know for sure.'

'So, who were these people? The ones you overheard?'

'One was the guy who died in the fire at the weekend. Fenners? Was that his name? I just knew him as Liam. I wasn't sure about the others. The other main one might have been called Luke, but I could have misheard.'

'You must have been thinking things through overnight and this morning, Mr Osman. Is there anything else you can tell us about the activities of this group?'

Osman seemed to think, and then shook his head. 'No. That's it, from that angle. What bothers me more is what happened to Andrea.'

'What do you mean?' Sophie asked.

'Look, all I know is that I was asked to check out Andrea's whereabouts that night, which I did. I phoned with the information and was asked to get her outside. I did that too.'

'Who did you phone?' Sophie asked.

'My contact, Bill. I don't know much else about him. He asked me to do it because Andrea and he had fallen out. I introduced them a few years ago now, after which I got the cold shoulder from both of them. I'd served my purpose and wasn't needed any more. She even went on holiday with him. Lucky bugger.'

'To Spain?' Sophie asked.

'Yeah, I think so. She told me Bill owned a villa out there. After they met, I hardly ever saw either of them. Then, in the past few weeks, I kept seeing her around the town late at night, visiting some of her old haunts again, on her own. They'd obviously broken up. I chatted with her a few times, but she wasn't interested in me. Then Bill called me. He said he needed to see her again, but she was refusing to even speak to him. He wanted me to try to talk her into meeting him. I didn't get that far. She seemed depressed, then out of the blue she suggested we go back to my place.' He fell silent for a while. 'As I said, she'd never seemed particularly interested in me, so I was a bit surprised.'

'Did you pick up on any reason for her change of mind?'

He shook his head. 'Look, I haven't been in a relationship since my marriage broke up years ago. And this was Andrea, suggesting she might come home with me for the night. I mean, why would I question it? Maybe I didn't fancy her as a long-term partner, but a no-strings night of sex was on offer. If you must know, I jumped at the chance.' He sighed. 'And then she changed her mind, and decided to head off home. I left her outside the park.'

'Did you see anything unusual just after you separated? Any vehicles parked in the vicinity?'

'I think there was a white van nearby with its engine running, but I wasn't really paying much attention. But if it was Bill's people that grabbed her, why did they need to do it that way? Why involve me? They could have picked her up from her flat, couldn't they?'

Sophie looked at him. Was he really this stupid? 'Surely you can guess why. It meant you were the last person to be seen with her. It made you the obvious suspect for her murder. If they'd left you well alone in the days after her death, their plan might have worked, but we spotted someone keeping a watch on your house, and we wondered why they would feel the need to do that.'

Again, Osman looked mystified. 'I was always an outsider. I know now that they were using me. I suppose they were watching me to make sure I did what I was told.'

Sophie said nothing.

Finally, Osman broke the silence. 'So what kind of deal can I get? I wasn't involved in any of these deaths. I don't know what they're up to. I've told you all I know. So?'

Sophie looked at the man facing her — the perspiration dotting his brow, the tired, almost pleading look in his eyes — and said harshly, 'I don't do deals, Mr Osman. You were involved with setting a trap for Andrea Ford. You lured her out of that bar and she was shoved into a van before being killed out at sea. It was you who identified her and got her outside, so you're an accessory to the deliberate murder of a serving police officer. It'll all come down to the evidence and the decision of the CPS when we go through it with them. They'll listen to my opinions.' She leant back in her chair. 'I still think there's a lot you haven't told us. Your relationship with this man, Bill, for starters. Well? I'm all ears.'

'There's not much to tell. I met him at a political rally opposing an Amnesty International march. We got talking and he asked me if I'd help his group. I said I was willing to do what I could, as long as it wasn't anything illegal. We swapped phone numbers, and he said he'd be in touch. And that's what happened. The only thing I had to do was look out for business contacts of mine who looked as if they were in tune with us and might want to help financially. Any who showed interest, I pointed in his direction.'

'You gave them his phone number?'

'Oh no. I'd pass their contact details on to him and he'd do the rest.'

'And how many people do you think you recruited in this way?'

'Probably about half a dozen or so. Look, I didn't know about anything else going on. As far as I was concerned, that part of it was all legit. And that's where Andrea's information came in useful.'

'You'll need to explain.'

'She passed over some useful contacts.'

'Did you meet regularly?'

'Not me, but I heard that there was a group of them that met to plan marches and stuff. Bill organised that, along with a few others.'

'When and where did they meet?' Sophie was intrigued. Did it coincide with Andrea's work pattern?

'I think it was at a bar in Dorchester on Wednesday afternoons.'

Bingo. She didn't push him for the location. An idea was already forming in her head.

'What's this guy Bill's surname?'

Osman shook his head. 'I don't know for sure. It might be Mapps or something like that.'

'So, the only definite things you know about him are his name, Bill, and the phone number?'

'Even that I had to memorise. I wasn't supposed to write it down anywhere or put it in my phone.'

'Remember it for me now, please.'

Osman recited it.

'Do you have a photo of him? Even at home?'

'Why would I?' Osman said.

'Could you describe him for us?'

'He's about the same age as me, maybe a bit younger. Average height and build. Hair starting to turn grey. That's all I can say, really.'

'Exactly what are we meant to do with that, Mr Osman? It doesn't tell us a thing. I'm really interested in your advice here.'

Osman looked puzzled. 'You're the detectives, not me. Surely you can trace him somehow? Then you can arrest him before he finds me.'

'You'd think that might be possible, wouldn't you? Tell you what, I'll ponder on it. Meanwhile you stay here, safe and sound under the watchful eyes of CID. Shame we couldn't offer the same service to Andrea, isn't it? Did you know they crushed some of her fingers before dumping her overboard a mile or two out to sea? In January. You've been mixing with some dangerous people, in case you hadn't realised.'

She got up and stalked out, followed by Barry and Lydia.

'He's not to be trusted,' Sophie said once they were outside. 'He's still holding back, I can feel it.' She looked at her watch. 'I think there's just about time to visit that pub in Dorchester on our way back. I could do with something to eat, I'm starving. Pub lunch anybody?'

* * *

Most of the pubs in Dorchester are bright, attractive places. Not so the Highlander. Its traditional coaching inn entrance leading to a yard at the rear showed that in times past it had probably been a building of historic importance. It had once had a bar or sitting room each side of the narrow alley with bedrooms above but, as George Warrander said, one half had been sold and converted into a hairdressing salon. With a lick of paint and a well-maintained flower display, the old inn could easily have been turned into a tourist trap, but now the building looked half derelict. Barry opened the door to the bar and led the way inside. The shoddy interior was little better than the outside.

'Do we really want to get food in this place?' he whispered.

His question was resolved by the appearance of a heavily built man wearing a grubby T-shirt. 'No food today. Kitchen's out of order. Sorry. But can I get you some drinks?'

Sophie looked at the beers on offer. 'No cask ale?'

The man shook his head. 'Don't get enough call for it, not in winter.'

'Are you the landlord?' she asked.

He nodded.

'Trade good?'

'We get by.' He yawned and rested his palms on the counter, showing the tattoos running up his arms.

'I'm looking for somewhere to hold a regular monthly social group meeting. Do you have a room that would do?'

'Yeah. The room at the back. It used to be a second lounge, but it's empty most of the time. When would you want it?'

'First Wednesday afternoon of each month?'

He frowned. 'It's already taken on Wednesdays. Pretty well any other day's okay though. Can you switch?'

'Not really, no. Maybe we'll look elsewhere. Thanks.' Sophie made for the door, and the other two followed her out.

'Eugh. What a tip. I wouldn't want to eat in there or even have a drink. Let's get some sandwiches and head back to the incident room.'

Chapter 35: The Junk Shop

Wednesday Afternoon

Back in the incident room, Lydia went to join Jimmy and Rae, who were ploughing through a pile of documents relating to incidences of prison smuggling. Some, but not all, of the prison staff had made detailed records of the items they'd discovered during their snap searches: the serial numbers on the miniature mobile phones, barely legible, identifying marks on packets of "legal highs," manufacturers' batch numbers on small packets of razor blades. These were consistent across the whole region, giving weight to Lydia's suggestion that a single gang was responsible. Why else would goods seized at Portland prison share batch numbers with items confiscated from Winchester and Devizes? The pattern was too obvious, clear evidence that a single gang was supplying much of this stuff. Who were these people?

Rae had been contacting suppliers, starting with the mobile phones. It hadn't been difficult, whereas trying to trace the supply chain for the drugs had been like attempting to pin jelly to the wall. The people involved were as slippery as eels. Nevertheless, some details had emerged, and the pieces of the jigsaw were beginning to form a picture. A Weymouth company called Dorset Service Supplies seemed to have been involved with many of the orders.

'They've got a registered office that doesn't exist,' Rae told Lydia. 'I think it's just a convenient forwarding address. We've been trying to trace the company directors but we think they're all aliases. They might have made one slip up, though. There used to be a company called Wessex Regional Supplies that's been operating in the Weymouth area for ten years or more. I had a look at the description in the Companies House archives because they had a director called William Mapps. I think it's written by the same person who did the entry for Dorset Trading Supplies. The text is almost identical, as if it's been cut and pasted, then a few words altered. The line of business is the same in both cases — office supplies and general trading. I think it's worth looking into.'

Lydia was impressed. She thought back to the time when she'd served in Sophie's Violent Crime Unit, trying to track down the rogue company behind the trafficking of young women into the country. It had taken her and Barry days of brain-numbing searching through a labyrinth of false trails. Pity they hadn't had Rae on the team then.

'That's fantastic,' she said. 'We came across the name Bill Mapps just this morning. It helps to confirm things.'

'Jimmy did most of the groundwork,' Rae said. 'I had a few spare hours late yesterday while I was at the safe house with the teenagers, so I did some extra checking.'

Lydia smiled. 'Leave it with us. And thanks. How are you getting on with the boss, by the way? You've been with her a couple of years now, haven't you?'

'I can't believe how things have worked out. Sometimes I have to pinch myself. It's the little things that make the difference. She wrote to one of my neighbours a month or two ago. I'd let slip about an incident at home where this woman, who's a bit transphobic, had totally misinterpreted something I'd done. She slapped me across the face and called me a pervert. The boss wrote a really nice letter explaining what had really happened. The woman was round like a shot to apologise.'

'That's her. She really looks after the people who work for her. I think that's why she's so upset about Andrea Ford's death. It would never have happened under her watch. Kevin's the same. Sometimes I feel he fusses a bit too much, but they're two of a kind. They both take their responsibilities towards their staff very seriously.'

'I get the impression that she always regrets you leaving.' Rae said tentatively, her eyebrows raised.

'That's why I had to leave. Well, one of the reasons anyway. It was getting too claustrophobic.'

Rae looked puzzled. 'What do you mean?'

'You haven't guessed? Maybe it's because of your transgender background, and the fact that you're in a happy relationship with your boyfriend. You obviously haven't spotted it.'

'Spotted what?'

Lydia sighed. 'I'm a lesbian, Rae. I can pick up the signals from others, even if they don't fully realise it themselves. Even if they think they're totally straight. Enough said?'

* * *

Just as Rae had surmised, Dorset Trading Supplies wasn't a real company. When Lydia and Jimmy arrived at the registered address, on a side street of terraced houses and the occasional run-down shop, they found a down-at-heel premises belonging to a company called Wyke Trading that offered all kinds of small-scale financial and administrative services: promotional printing, storage lockers for rent, used office equipment for sale, key cutting, and mail-forwarding. A slim, freckled young woman, whose badge proclaimed her to be Millie Prince, seemed to be in charge of the small shop, which was crammed with slightly shabby office equipment. She greeted the two detectives with a smile which turned wary when they introduced themselves as police officers. She confirmed that mail for the trading company was held there but not forwarded on. Someone from Dorset Trading Supplies collected it every week.

'Do you know the person's name?' Lydia asked.

Millie Prince shook her tight, carroty curls vigorously. Lydia noticed a small butterfly tattoo on her right shoulder. 'No. My boss takes care of that. I'm only here part-time. Some of the mail-forwarding customers ask for extra security, and Dorset Trading is one of those.'

'Can we see your boss, then?' Lydia asked. 'We need some information about the company.'

Millie Prince shook those curls again. 'He's not here. Hang on a sec, I'll phone him and see if he can pop across. He'll be in one of his other places. You can ask him, but he'll probably tell you that we offer all our clients total discretion, and we assure them that their details will be kept secure. He might not agree, not without a warrant.'

Lydia was growing exasperated. 'Look, I'm on a high-level investigation into organised crime. Just phone and tell him what I want and that I'm not happy with anyone who tries to hold up the case.'

Millie held up her hands. 'Okay, okay. I'll do what I can.'

She went into a small inner office and closed the door firmly behind her. Lydia indicated to Jimmy that he should move closer and try to catch some of what was being said, while she sidled across to a rickety table on which a pile of opened letters were balanced, some of the contents spilling out. She flipped through the pile, glancing at the names and addresses, until Jimmy signalled that the phone conversation was coming to an end. Millie came back into the room, smiling cheerfully.

'Mr Brown should be here in about twenty minutes. He's in Dorchester at the moment, just finishing off a meeting, so it shouldn't take him long.'

'You explained why we were here?' Lydia said.

'Oh yes. I thought I'd better, so he can try and remember the terms of the contract with Dorset Trading. It shouldn't be a problem. If you don't mind, I need to get back to work.'

Her work consisted of collecting up the letters and papers that Lydia had gone through and carrying them through into the tiny inner office. She came back out and closed the door firmly behind her, turning the key in the lock for good measure. She then proceeded to pick up a cloth and polish some of the items on display. Lydia and Jimmy sat down on a couple of old office chairs.

'Have you worked here long?' Lydia asked.

'No. I'm only part-time, as I said. I do Monday and Wednesday afternoons, and Saturday mornings. I'm at college and Mr M . . . I mean, I chose the times that would fit with my timetable and he said he'd adapt to suit me.'

'Who said, Millie?' Lydia asked.

'The owner, Mr Brown.'

'What are you studying?'

'Secretarial. I'll see how I get on with the end of year exams, then decide what I'll do next. Either look for a permanent job or, if I do well, try for a degree course in business studies.'

'You wouldn't want to work here permanently, then?'

The look on Millie's face was answer enough. 'No, I don't think so.'

She turned her back on them and energetically continued to wipe the dust from the old filing cabinets. They would probably never be sold. Who would want them?

While they waited, a couple of people drifted in, looked around in a desultory way and left. No one else came in.

'It seems quiet,' Lydia said. 'Is this normal?'

'We sell most of the stuff via the web,' Millie said. 'We don't get many sales from people popping in on the off-chance. It's usually busier than this, though.'

A few minutes later, a middle-aged, crop-haired man came into the shop. He approached the two detectives warily, folded his arms and stood facing them, feet apart. It was him — the man in the pub who'd been in the background when Lydia had her altercation with the racist gang, who'd sat by himself and left soon after the troublemakers. She decided to say nothing, but surely he'd recognise her?

'What is it you want exactly?' he asked.

'Good morning, Mr, er, Brown? Is that right?' Lydia showed him her warrant card. 'I'm DS Lydia Pillay and this is my colleague, DC Jimmy Melsom. We're on an investigation, and the name Dorset Trading Supplies has come up as being of interest. This is their registered address.'

'Yes, but we act as a forwarding agency for lots of different people. It's a common practice.' He smiled condescendingly.

His attitude caused Lydia's hackles to rise. 'I'm aware of that. Apparently mail comes here and you keep it until someone comes and collects it. I'd like the details of who collects it, and when. Apparently they have a special contract with you, and Millie doesn't have the clearance to give us that information. But presumably you do.'

'Yeah, but I'm not going to. Not without a warrant. All our contracts would be worth shit if people found out I was giving out information. They'd take their business away and I'd go to the wall.'

'I know how to run fraud cases, Mr Brown. We're not some jumped-up street cops with big mouths. I control all the information, no one else. It stays with me. It'd save time and effort if you were just to tell us what we want to know now. Think of the benefits. You'd be in our good books.'

'The answer's still no. That's it. I've got work to do, so good morning to you.' He turned and marched into the tiny inner office.

'Sorry,' mouthed Millie, and returned to her cleaning.

Lydia looked at Jimmy. 'Okay, if that's the way he wants it. Let's head back and consult the boss.'

* * *

'So, you don't think his name is Brown?' Sophie asked, and leant back in her chair.

'No. He made a couple of slips that gave it away. The main thing though, apart from the fact he was that guy in the CCTV footage, was the post I glanced through. It had a few items addressed to a Mr William Mapps. That's when I thought, "Bingo! We've really got something here."' Sophie looked puzzled. 'I'd better explain. William Mapps was a name that Rae dug up. Two of the companies that we might be interested in have him as director, and the young woman working there told us he had other premises. I wonder if he's actually the top guy, the one we're after.'

Sophie tapped the desktop. 'Well, it's worth considering. We know from Simon Osman's abridged version of events that his contact's name is Bill Mapps.' She fell silent for a while. 'We haven't done anything with that phone number he gave us yet. He'll be cleaning up the place as we speak, but that doesn't matter too much, particularly since you had that rummage through his post. We'll pay him another visit late afternoon with the warrant, and Barry can phone that number while we're there. If we're in luck, they'll answer. If it's him, we'll have the connection we need. How does that sound?'

Lydia smiled. 'Killing two birds. I like it, ma'am.'

'You don't mind me tagging along? I promise I'll stay in the background. We'll take Jimmy and Rae, and I'll rustle up a couple of forensic people.'

'Sounds good.'

It took Sophie just an hour to organise the warrant, which Lydia thought must be a record. She'd had some misgivings about her former boss's recent promotion, although she wasn't sure why she felt that way. Well, this was one of the undoubted benefits, along with the speed with which Sophie could "borrow" two members of the county's forensic team. That afternoon, the seven of them drove to the dingy shop.

* * *

Millie looked up, startled, as Lydia pushed open the door. 'He's not here at the moment. He went out just after you left. He said he'd be back in an hour or two. Can you wait while I phone him?'

'Sorry, we can't wait. I have the warrant here. You can check it if you want, but everything's in order, I assure you.' She handed it to Millie. 'Feel free to phone your boss, but we're taking over in here from now on.'

When the other members of the team came in, Millie looked aghast. 'He said you wouldn't be back till tomorrow, and that's one of my days off. I don't know what to do.'

'Just phone him,' Lydia said. 'There's nothing else you can do. Then put the kettle on and make yourself a tea or coffee. We'll have one too, if you've got enough cups. Find a quiet corner and sit down and relax. This doesn't really involve you, not unless you know more than you've let on.'

Millie shook her head vigorously. 'No, honestly.'

She tried to contact her boss but there was no reply, so she perched on a stool in the corner of the shop and watched the action unfold. As far as she could tell, the search team consisted of three groups of two. The two detectives who'd visited earlier, two grey-clad people who she guessed were forensic workers because they'd brought cases of technical equipment, and two other women who she thought might also be detectives. One of the forensic people asked to take her fingerprints. "For elimination purposes," he explained.

This could well mean the end of her part-time job here, Millie realised. The place was conveniently close to her home and the hours were ideal. What would she do for money now? Mr Mapps, her boss, frightened her a bit, and now she wondered just what he was mixed up in. Why had he told her to lie about his name if any strangers came into the shop?

She realised that the older woman detective was watching her.

'Are you okay?' the woman asked. 'You don't look very well.'

Millie shook her head. 'I don't feel well. He's bound to have a go at me, and I'll probably lose my job. And it's unfair because I don't think I've done anything wrong.' She began to cry.

'Have you worked here long?'

Millie shook her head. 'Just since the summer. I started here at about the same time as I started at college. I live just around the corner so it's really good. And I like organising the place. It's the first time I've ever been in charge of anything. I'm here on my own quite a bit. It'll be awful if I get the sack or it closes.'

'Do you have to find your rent yourself, or do you share?'

'I live with my mum, but she struggles a bit 'cause she's disabled. She's got a part-time job at the supermarket, and between us we just about get by. If he sacks me, I'll have to find somewhere else pretty quick.' She sniffed and blew her nose. 'I s'pose I knew it was gonna happen. He's been looking grim for the past week or so, muttering about closing up. Most of the stuff we have is junk, and we're just not selling much. I wouldn't buy it. I s'pose it's his other businesses that keep him going. I can't see how this place has ever made him any money, not while I've been here anyway.' She looked at the woman. 'But I never knew there was illegal stuff going on. It can't be that bad, can it? It's only old office equipment that's worth nothing. Why are so many of you here for junk like this?' She squinted at the woman's neck badge. 'I mean, you're a superintendent. Isn't that one of the high-ups? Why are you interested in total crap like this?' She waved her arm at the collection of outdated printers, photocopiers and old laptops.

'Because it's possible he isn't who he claims to be, and this place is just a front. That's all I can tell you about it at the moment, Millie. But there is something you can tell me. Have you met anyone else since you've worked here? He must have other people for the days you're at college.'

'Yeah, but we don't ever meet. They must be part-time as well. There was one guy who I took over from. He stopped because he was getting ill and couldn't work anymore. It was him that showed me round when I first started, and I never saw him after that. He told me he used to work in the prison over at Portland till he retired because of his health. He only did a day or so here as a favour to Mr, er, Brown.'

At this, the woman seemed almost to jump. 'Did he tell you his name, this man?'

'Tony, I think. He never told me his last name.'

The superintendent woman was silent. It looked like she was thinking.

'Did anyone ever talk about holidays in Spain?'

Millie wondered if she should be talking to the police like this, telling them stuff she'd found out during her days here. But it wasn't to do with the business, was it? What harm could it do? 'Yeah. He's got a villa out there.'

'Who? Your Mr Brown?'

'Yeah. He said if I played my cards right, I could have it for free, take a week's holiday. No chance of that now, is there?'

* * *

"Mr Brown" arrived some ten minutes later and stood in the doorway, his mouth agape.

'What the fuck?' was his first comment. He turned on Millie. 'Why didn't you let me know, you stupid cretin?'

'I tried to. You didn't answer your phone.' Her voice quavered.

'Oh, for fuck's sake.'

Lydia intervened. 'Here's the search warrant, Mr, er, Brown. You'll see everything's in order. No need for you to harangue your staff.'

On the other side of the room, Sophie sent a text message to Barry Marsh, who was waiting in the incident room with a communications technician. The single word, "Now!"

When it rang, the shop owner already had his phone out, and was jabbing furiously at the buttons. He looked at it in surprise and pressed answer, seemingly unaware that the room had fallen silent.

'Yeah?' he said, and listened. 'Yeah, but I can't talk just now. Things are hectic. Call me again later on. Who are you?'

Still listening, he wheeled slowly around to face Sophie Allen, who was moving towards him.

'What? Who?'

He lowered the phone and stared from it to her.

'William Mapps, I'm arresting you on suspicion of involvement in the murder of Detective Constable Andrea Ford. You do not have to say anything, but it may harm your defence if you do not mention when questioned something which you later rely on in court. Anything you do say may be given in evidence.'

He stared for a moment longer, open-mouthed, then made a dash for the door. Lydia and Jimmy were ready and waiting. Lydia, a martial arts enthusiast, looped her arm around his neck and forced him to the floor in an arm lock, ready for Jimmy to clip the handcuffs on.

Chapter 36: Bluster

Wednesday Afternoon

In addition to Wyke Trading, William Mapps owned two other businesses in the West Dorset area: Chesil Procurement, a specialist supplies company, and a security agency operating under the name of Picketline Security. The first claimed to be leading experts in sourcing unorthodox items in a hurry. "You Need It? We'll Source It!" was the company motto on its publicity material and website. The company office was half a mile away from the Wyke Trading shop.

Picketline Security operated out of a small office on the outskirts of Weymouth. Its expertise was extensive, if the company flyers were to be believed. It offered advice across a range of security needs and employed security personnel on short or long term hire.

Both were of great interest to the police team. The first was exactly what Lydia was seeking in her investigation into prison smuggling: expertise in procurement and supply. And the second? Those intimidating characters she'd been faced with in the

Bournemouth bar a couple of weeks ago were exactly the type some organisations would want as security personnel — people who would quell any potential trouble just with their appearance and manner.

In addition to his three local companies, Mapps was also involved in the running of Dorset Trading Supplies, the company that had first aroused their interest. It quickly became apparent that the company was just another front for Chesil Procurement. Both businesses shared the same trading address. The whole operation was a labyrinth of interlocking connections. It would take several days to search through the paperwork at the three sets of premises, although they found very little at the Wyke Trading shop, and the team finished there within two hours of Mapps's arrest. The shop had been left in the care of the forensic team, and Millie was sent home, having been forewarned by Lydia that she'd be needed later for a formal interview and to make a statement.

The police team split into three. Lydia, along with Rose Simons and George Warrander, visited the procurement agency, while Jimmy and Rae moved to the Picketline Security premises. Matt Silver was to visit Mapps's home, along with a forensic team. Matt, now a senior DCS, was relishing this rare opportunity to take part in some action, something he hadn't been able to do for years. His and Sophie's unease about how far the rot had spread within the local CID unit meant that they couldn't use any local detectives, so Rose and George had been co-opted. Local detectives were still being sent out to visit boatyards and marinas in the search for the boat used in Andrea Ford's murder. They interviewed neighbours, and followed up lines of enquiry from previous statements. They were also given the task of checking whether Mapps kept a boat anywhere.

Sophie and Barry interviewed Mapps, and at first they got nowhere.

'This is outrageous,' Mapps's solicitor blustered. 'It's ridiculous bringing in my client like this for a few book-keeping errors. As to your allegation of involvement in murder, that's just laughable.'

Sophie looked across the table at the red-faced, corpulent lawyer. 'I'm not laughing, Mr Simpson, nor is anyone on this team. Murder is the tragic and unwarranted ending of someone's life in a ruthlessly premeditated way. In this particular instance, one of my officers was tortured before being killed. We have a witness to her abduction. We have a phone number for one of the people involved, someone with the name of Bill. We rang that number and your client replied, confirming that the number was his. We have other evidence of his involvement. No, nobody is laughing, as you so insultingly put it. Stick to your role, Mr Simpson, and stop acting. The situation doesn't warrant it. The best advice you can offer your client is to come clean and tell us everything he knows.'

The lawyer sank back into his chair, his brief moment of drama brought to an end. Sophie knew this type of lawyer well, and they rarely caused much concern. They were full of superficial bluster with little substance. The more effective ones knew their stuff and kept quiet. They were the ones to watch.

'So, where were you on the evening of the Monday before last, the eighteenth, Mr Mapps?'

'I was having a meal in the New World Bistro with a friend. We were there until almost eleven, discussing business. He'll vouch for me.'

'What's his name?'

'Osman. Simon Osman.'

Sophie struggled to keep her expression impassive. So this was the scheme. The two suspects would give each other an alibi. Too bad that Osman had turned his back on his erstwhile comrades and gone to the police. Clearly Mapps didn't know about it yet.

'Is that the same wine bar that DC Ford visited just before she vanished?'

'I couldn't say. I don't know her. All I can tell you is that Simon chatted to a blonde middle-aged woman for a few moments on his way to the bar. She was sitting in an alcove by herself. Could that have been her? He told me her name when he returned to our table, but I can't remember what he said.'

'What did you both eat?' Sophie asked.

Mapps looked vague. 'Chicken, I think. We shared a bottle of wine.'

'How did you pay for the meal, Mr Mapps?'

'Cash. I gave my half to Simon and he paid the bill. I think he paid the whole lot by cash.'

'What did you do when you left?'

'I dropped into the Highland Bar to see if any of my friends were there, but they weren't. I had one drink then went home. I got in at about midnight.'

'Can anyone vouch for any of this?'

'Not once we left the New World. Simon can vouch for me there.' He sounded confident.

Sophie looked him in the eye. 'No, Mr Mapps, Mr Osman hasn't vouched for you. The exact opposite in fact. There is absolutely no evidence that you were in the wine bar that evening. However, we have several reliable witnesses to the fact that Mr Osman was there, as was Andrea Ford. We also have witnesses to the fact that they left just before ten. Just the two of them, together. That was verified by the staff on duty. No one can recall seeing you there. It was a cold Monday in January and a quiet night. I have a complete list of everyone who was in the wine bar that evening and every sale that went through the till. There were no men sharing a meal and a bottle of wine, just couples. As I said, we know Simon Osman was there but he only bought two rounds of drinks, each of two double brandies. One for him and one for Andrea Ford. No food, though. They chatted for nearly an hour before leaving. Those facts check out with the statements from staff and other witnesses, and with the till transactions. Your story is exactly that. A story. Complete fabrication. So tell me the truth.'

Mapps looked shocked. 'I have nothing further to say.'

'In that case, we'll end this interview now and resume in a few hours when you've had time to mull things over.' She turned to the lawyer. 'Mr Simpson, I suggest you keep yourself available. More evidence is accumulating as we speak.'

* * *

Sophie had been somewhat optimistic when she'd made that last comment to Mapps's lawyer. But damning material did indeed turn up at one of the search locations.

The first person to phone in was Lydia, at the Chesil Procurement office. After they finished with the office's legitimate business records, they moved to a cabinet half hidden in a dingy, locked cupboard. There they struck gold. The contents were exactly what Lydia would have expected to find in her prison investigation: orders for the kind of miniaturised phones, tools and weapons that could be hidden easily once inside a prison. In a separate drawer, Rose Simons had found a contact list, made up of unknown names along with telephone and bank account numbers.

'Drug suppliers,' she'd said at once. 'I bet that's who they contact for their supplies of spice and all the other junky stuff. Look at the coded nicknames. Just the kind of thing these creeps use.' She jabbed her finger at one of the names. 'Snakebite. I lifted him last week, in Dorchester. That's his number. What a result.'

'I thought they only dealt in cash,' Lydia said.

'The ones who deal to individuals do,' Rose said. 'But cash means you need to meet the person face to face, and that's always a risk. The advantage with using internet banking is that you never have to even see the nasties you're supplying the stuff to. You make a payment online, the dealer drops the goods at a prearranged drop-spot — done.'

'So, these bank account details could be gold dust? We can hand them over to the drug unit once we've finished?' Lydia said.

Rose smiled at her. 'Exactly. But choose your moment. Don't share too soon because you don't want their big boots stomping all over your neat and tidy investigation. I never said that, by the way.' She winked at Lydia.

Chapter 37: Quarry

Thursday Morning

The following day was cold and blustery, with squally showers driving in from the west. Lydia climbed out of her car and stood beside Jimmy, who was carefully scanning the quarry. This was the third such site they'd visited this morning. None of the others employed anyone with the name Leary, nor did the staff they'd spoken to know anyone of that name in Portland, either in the quarries or anywhere else. Despite the lack of progress, Lydia had decided that they should carry on working their way down the list. There were, after all, only another two to visit. Maybe their assumptions had been wrong and their man worked in a completely different industry — a flour mill or cement works? It was just that in this area of Dorset the quarry option seemed the most obvious one to start with. Quarrying of Portland and Purbeck stone was an important part of the local economy.

She joined Jimmy at the quarry edge. Bare sheets of rock, with occasional tufts of greenery, vehicle tracks across the quarry floor, a single parked truck, but no one in sight. They tramped towards the small huddle of portakabins near the entrance, their shoes already covered with a film of dirty grey residue, although there was little dust. The rain that had been falling on and off since the night before had turned it into a slimy grey mud. They climbed the few steps to the closest cabin, the one most likely to be an office or sales desk. It certainly looked the part, but there was no one about, even though a light was on, a jacket hung on the back of one of the chairs and several documents were spread across a desktop.

'Well, there's someone around somewhere,' Lydia said. 'Maybe they're out at the workface. Shall we have a look in the other cabins?'

The second building appeared to be a storage shed and was also empty. The last looked to be a small toilet block.

'I wonder if we should visit the last quarry on our list and then come back to this one,' Lydia said.

'Okay. But I'll need to use the loo before we set off. I'm bursting. It's that second coffee I had in the last place.' Jimmy opened the door to the toilet building and went inside.

Lydia looked around at the desolate scene. She began to feel increasingly uneasy. Why was there no one in sight? Here, in the bowels of the quarry, she couldn't be seen from the road. Even their car would be hidden from view. Yet anyone standing up on the edge of the quarry would be able to see her easily. Nothing moved up there apart from a few birds, scudding across the grey sky. She turned up her coat collar and stamped her feet. Why was Jimmy taking so long? She walked back to the small office building and went inside, deciding that she might as well wait in relative warmth. A large week-to-view calendar was pinned to the wall, with a few scribbled notes in today's box. Someone called Jane was at a doctor's appointment from mid-morning, due back at noon. Another note stated that Paul would be collecting a new van this morning from a dealer in Dorchester. No wonder the place seemed deserted. But surely there should be others about? Lydia glanced at some of the documents on the desktop. The topmost one seemed to be a covering letter for an invoice from the stores manager, ready to be signed. The name on the bottom was E Taylor. That sounded familiar, but from where? Lydia frowned. She moved to the window, thinking hard and, as a particularly hard flurry of raindrops hit the glass, she remembered. Taylor was the third name that had been mentioned at the army barracks. She looked out at the other two cabins, now really worried. Where on earth was Jimmy? He was taking forever in that toilet block. She hurried to the door and stepped outside. As she did, an indistinct shadow just at the periphery of her vision began moving towards her. She lurched sideways and so avoided the worst of the heavy blow that came her way. Instead of hitting her head, the crowbar caught her on the shoulder, and she stumbled against the waist-high balustrade at the top of the steps. Instinctively, she lashed out hard with her left leg and felt it connect with her assailant's body. With luck she'd given herself a few vital seconds. Despite the blazing pain in her upper arm she half-jumped, half-toppled across the timber safety rail, and hit the ground running, dropping her bag in the process. In order to escape whoever had attacked her, she was forced to run away from the car, away from the buildings, away from Jimmy and into the depths of the quarry. She glanced back. It was him, and he was only a few yards away. Mr Angry from two weeks ago in the pub, Tonto Leary, suspected psychopath and extreme racist thug. Holding a crowbar in one hand, he limped after her, his face distorted in pain and rage. She turned and ran, ignoring the phone ringing in her pocket. Her Taser was still in her bag, dropped at the portakabin.

* * *

Back in the incident room, Sophie had finished discussing with Barry and Rae the possible connections between Mapps, Boulden, Osman and the late Liam Fenners. Where did Tonto Leary fit into it all, and why wasn't his name turning up anywhere? Moreover, why hadn't they come across any mention of the other suspect in the army pilfering operation? What had been his name? Taylor? Sophie made herself a coffee and returned to her desk to look again at the list of names. Why would anyone be called Tonto? Clearly it was a nickname, and had stuck with the man for some reason. His real name would be something else entirely. But what if his surname was also a handle? Her mind ran over some of her past cases where false names had been used. And then she realised. Tonto Leary was an anagram of Eton Taylor. Eton Taylor was the man who'd served with Fenners and Boulden in the logistics corps but who'd managed to avoid being caught thieving. How had the officer who'd spoken to Lydia described him? A psychopath of the first order?

Sophie called to Rae and told her what she'd discovered. 'See if you can find out if anyone with this name works or lives in Portland.'

It took Rae precisely four minutes. 'Both. He lives in a small terraced house in the town and he works as stores manager at the Greenjack Quarry.'

Sophie turned pale. 'Christ. That was the next one on Lydia's list. They'll be there now.' She called to Barry. 'Grab your coat. Quick. Lydia and Jimmy could be in danger!'

The three detectives ran down the stairs and out to the cars, Sophie frantically punching in numbers on her phone. She tossed her keys at Barry. 'You drive. I'll call for a support unit to meet us there. Shit, why isn't Lydia answering her phone?'

Chapter 38: The Chase

Thursday Morning

The cars slewed to a halt behind Lydia's abandoned vehicle. They looked around them, at the walls of rock rising sheer above the slimy surface of the quarry floor. The place seemed deserted. Each of the three detectives ran to one of the three portakabins. It was Barry who found Jimmy Melsom, slumped on the floor in the toilet block with blood oozing from a head wound. He checked for a pulse, finding it steady, although Jimmy's breathing was shallow. Barry called for an ambulance and went outside to tell the other two. Rae was sent back in to stay with Jimmy, to await the arrival of the medical team and ask for a second backup unit to be despatched. Meanwhile, Sophie and Barry and the two uniformed officers from the squad car descended into the quarry to search for Lydia. They carried no weapons, except for their Tasers.

The rain had stopped, though the sky was still overcast. Once they rounded the first corner of the quarry complex the wind dropped, although they could see a few sparse bushes at the top of the rock faces moving in the breeze. Where would Lydia have gone? Sophie had to assume that she was being pursued, she would not have abandoned Jimmy otherwise. They followed a meandering track which seemed to head east, in the direction of the coast, probably made by generations of quarriers bringing the stone to the surface. Rounding a corner, Sophie noticed a narrow path heading up a slope to their left, probably a route up to the top of the cliff face. It snaked around numerous large boulders on its way up the slope, and in several spots it was hidden from view. Had Lydia followed it? After all, if she'd remained on the quarry floor she'd have been trapped. Sophie pointed to the path, and Barry nodded. They sent two uniformed constables to scout the rest of the quarry floor, and then follow her and Barry. Then they sprinted across to the bottom of the slope and started up the steep track, finally emerging onto rough moorland at the top of the quarry, with Weymouth Bay about half a mile in front of them. They stopped to listen, breathing hard. The track ran straight on, away from the quarry complex and towards the coastline. Further on, it disappeared beneath a large tangled clump of gorse bushes. Was that a noise? What was it? She jabbed Barry's arm and pointed. He nodded.

'I can hear something too,' he gasped. 'I can't make it out. The wind's too strong.'

They started running again, following the track, and both began to shout Lydia's name. They heard the sound of breaking foliage as they grew nearer, and a thickset man emerged from the far side of the shrubs, glanced back and then ran towards the clifftop. Sophie and Barry made for the spot, and began pushing through the spiny branches. They heard the whimpering before they spotted Lydia. She was in the middle of a dense pocket of bushes that had been partly flattened by something heavy. The broken and torn branches were evidence of the attack's ferocity. Lydia lay curled into a ball, her arms hugging her body and her legs drawn up into her chest. Her clothes were soaked in blood, and blood oozed from several deep cuts on her head.

Sophie bent down and touched her gently.

'Lydia? Can you hear me? Can you say anything?'

But Lydia just whimpered. What damage had that thug done? Sophie felt for her pulse. Thank God. It was still strong, and her breathing was regular, though it rasped.

'Call back. Tell them we'll need the air ambulance up here, right now. Get another squad here, along that lane across there. You stay here until the other two catch up. I'm going after him.'

'Leave it, Sophie,' Barry said. 'He's trapped. We can wait till they get here. He's done enough damage already. You'll be in danger of getting the same treatment. I'll go after him if one of us really needs to.'

Sophie shook her head. 'One of us has to stay here, and I'm ordering you to do that. I'm not going to put myself at risk, don't worry, but I need to spot where's he's heading. This place is like a rabbit warren, and he'll know it like the back of his hand. We could lose him. I've had a few walks here, and I know the terrain.'

Without waiting for a reply, she switched her phone to silent and set off at a fast trot across the open heathland after the rapidly disappearing figure. She pulled her Taser from its holster and looked around. The man had vanished. Here, the rough, rocky land fell away towards the coastal clifftop area. Where had he gone? Sophie suspected that he'd dodged behind one of the large boulders. She decided not to follow him but to circle around to the south, taking her time and keeping low to the ground. This might prove to be a waiting game if he'd found somewhere to hide. She moved slowly and carefully around the outside edge of the rock formation, constantly scanning in all directions. She didn't think he'd had time to get across the open ground and reach the coast path that lay ahead on the clifftop. He was holed up somewhere in this outcrop, she was sure of it. And had he been limping? If so, he wouldn't be able to get much further.

Sophie worked her way up a low mound on the coastal side of the rough ground, keeping below the line of boulders that lay scattered on its surface. She spotted the arrival of the two squad car officers at the gorse thicket, and Barry emerging, setting out to follow the track she'd taken across the heath. There was a dense area of rocks in front of her, in the shadow of a small clump of spindly gorse bushes — the ideal place for the assailant to hide. Was that a low gully running towards it from the coast path? That might be the direction he'd take if he were disturbed. She picked up a stone and threw it hard across the rocks, to where she'd have been if she'd kept to the path and not circled around. Nothing happened. Maybe he'd be expecting a stunt like that. He was an ex-army man, after all, and it might be difficult to trick him. She pulled out her phone, logged her position and sent a text to Barry. She could see him in the distance, checking his own phone. As she put her phone away she heard the faint sound of sirens and spotted two police vehicles in the distance, approaching along the narrow lane. What would happen now? She didn't have long to wait. Her target suddenly appeared from the shadows beneath the rock outcrop and, stooping low, ran along the gully. He had a crowbar in his hand. Sophie stood and looked down at the path he was following. He would surely see her.

'Taser!' she shouted. 'Primed Taser. Stop now.'

He looked up and shouted something but kept running, now heading straight for her. She fired the Taser, but he veered to the side just as she pulled the trigger. Only one of the darts hit home and Sophie wasn't sure how deeply it had penetrated his clothes. He stared at her, sneering. He lifted the iron bar.

'You're fucked now.'

Sophie fired the second chamber and this time both lines lodged in his chest, dead centre. He crashed to the ground like a felled log.

'No. You are,' she said. 'We changed to two-chamber Tasers last year. Unlucky for you.'

She doubted whether he'd heard. His body was in spasm. She walked forward and stood over him a moment, and then rolled him roughly onto his front, scraping his face against some protruding rocks. Wrenching his arms behind his back, she put cuffs on his wrists. Sick with fury, she had an overwhelming urge to kick him in the face, on and on, until his features were mashed to a pulp. Then Barry arrived, closely followed by a group of officers from the second backup team.

'Get this animal out of my sight,' she snarled, panting, 'before I try to kill him with my bare hands. Jesus Christ, why does it have to be like this?'

She turned and ran back along the track to where they'd left Lydia, now in the care of the other two officers. She bent down and cradled Lydia's head in her arms, resting it against her chest. She patted her brow with a tissue and whispered in her ear.

'Lydia, sweetheart, it's me, Sophie. Hold on. There's an ambulance on its way. You'll make it. Just hang on, please.'

Barry arrived, having supervised the transfer of Leary to a police secure van. 'Any news of Jimmy?' she asked him anxiously.

'He's come round, but he's probably got concussion from that head wound. An ambulance has just arrived.'

They heard the chatter of a helicopter just above them. Would they be in time to save Lydia?

Chapter 39: A Great Little Earner

Late Thursday Afternoon

Sophie escorted the chief constable out of the hospital building and returned to the intensive care room, where she rejoined Kevin McGreedie at the observation window.

'I'll be heading off myself in a few minutes,' he said. 'Is there anything I ought to know that you didn't mention in front of the boss? You were a bit tight-lipped. I got the feeling you were holding something back, but maybe I was reading too much into it.'

Sophie chewed her lip. 'I think there's more,' she said at last. 'We've got them all in custody now, but it still doesn't seem right somehow. I keep thinking how apt our name is for this whole tangled mess — Operation Shadow. I think something, or someone, is missing, still out there lurking in the shadows. I just need time to think things through.' She looked through the glass panel. Lydia was unrecognisable beneath the swathe of dressings that covered her. She was surrounded by monitoring machines, with sensors and drips looping across to various points on her body.

'I still can't believe this has happened. I feel so bloody useless,' Sophie said. 'Just look at her. I keep asking myself, how did it get so violent so quickly? What could we have done differently? As well as my guilt over what's happened to Lydia, I feel I've let you down, Kevin. You loan me two detectives, and look what's happened to them. I feel sick about it.'

'We can't blame ourselves,' he said, 'either of us. You heard what the chief said. They've checked the logs, and everything was done by the book. No one could have expected this to happen during a routine investigation. Look, they were members of my team, but you seem to be taking it harder than me.'

Sophie bit her lip. She couldn't tell Kevin how deeply she felt about Lydia. The young woman had been like another daughter to her. And look at her now — bloody, bruised and in an induced coma, her life hanging by a thread. She nodded slowly. 'She's one of the best I've ever come across, and it wasn't easy for her. When she started she was a shy young woman from the Asian community who wouldn't say boo to a goose, but I could see her potential. I met her parents once, and they made me promise to look after her. They'll be here shortly. God knows what I can say to them.'

'In that case, I'll stay a bit longer and help you out. Good to see Jimmy on the mend so quickly. Does he know about Lydia?'

Sophie shook her head. 'The doctors suggested we hold back on telling him until they're assured of his recovery. He'll be devastated.'

The two of them fell silent. What else was there to say?

* * *

As Sophie had explained to the chief constable, all the obvious culprits were now in custody. Tonto Leary, or Eton Taylor as he was better known, remained silent. He exuded an intense, contemptuous hatred towards anyone who interviewed him. Neither Sophie nor Barry had made any attempt to do so — their feelings were too raw. Instead, they watched on a screen in Sophie's office. Sophie was hopeful that his attitude would change once he realised the mess he was in. Anyway, did it really matter whether he talked or not? The evidence against him was overwhelming.

The other two, Luke Boulden and Bill Mapps, were beginning to cooperate, both had obviously realised the strength of the case against them. They'd been told of Leary's attempted murder of a police officer and his serious assault of a second. So, they were asked, did they want to be associated with those crimes in addition to the ones already filed against them? Both were adamant that they hadn't been involved in the murder of Andrea Ford.

Luke Boulden showed the most unease, despite his taciturn manner. Sophie and Barry both noticed the anxiety in his eyes when they interviewed him. They had no direct evidence of his involvement in any of the deaths, and no traces of his DNA had, as yet, been identified at any of the crime scenes, but he was clearly guilty of conspiracy. He denied any involvement in the abduction of Andrea Ford, but his body language said otherwise. The detectives explained the seriousness of his predicament and left him to stew.

Mapps looked the more likely to have been involved, particularly in Andrea's abduction and murder. The problem with the prison smuggling operation, in which Mapps was clearly implicated, was that the two detectives with the most knowledge were both lying in hospital beds, with Lydia, the head of that investigation, in intensive care. Although the Violent Crime Unit team had been working closely with Lydia and Jimmy, they didn't know all the finer details. Wading through the volume of material that Lydia had amassed, Sophie again began to have doubts about the brains behind the whole thing. Was Mapps capable of leading the operation? But if not him, then who? Certainly not Fenners or Boulden. They were the foot-soldiers, along with Leary, who also supplied the violence, something he clearly relished. The smuggling operation had been running like a well-oiled machine, and she was sure that those three lacked the brains to orchestrate it. So was it Mapps?

She decided to interview Luke Boulden again. He'd had time to think his position through, maybe he'd decide to spill at least a few of the beans.

* * *

'I wasn't there,' he said. 'and that's the truth. My sister was taken ill in Bristol that day and I went across to visit her in the evening. You can check. I spent the night with them and drove back here early the next morning.'

'What about the others?' Sophie said. 'You can't all have been visiting sick relatives.'

'Liam told me he didn't know they were gonna kill your woman, Andrea. They asked him to drive the van instead of me but didn't say nothin' else about what they planned to do with her — that's what he said anyway. I knew they were going for her, they'd been on for days about how much she knew, but that's all. I thought they were just gonna put the frighteners on her.'

'When did you find out she was dead?' Barry asked.

'When it was on the news, and some of the guys at work talked about it.' He rested his hands on the table, palms up.

'Take us through what Liam told you about that night's events,' Sophie said.

'Tonto arrived at his place and said they had a job on and he had a van ready. It was about the middle of the evening. He told Liam he was gonna be the driver. They parked up and went to a pub and Bill met them there. They waited until Bill got a message on his phone. Liam said he drove to where Tonto told him, in a side street.

They got out but left the side door open. They stood chatting and when she came along with some bloke they grabbed her and pushed her into the van and drove off.'

'Who was the man she was with?'

'I dunno. Liam didn't say.'

'What happened then?'

'Bill told Liam to drive down to the quayside at Portland. He wouldn't tell me anything else. He was a bit sick about it, I could tell.'

'Did he say anything about the van?' Barry asked.

Boulden shook his head. 'Nah. And I never asked. Tonto always got them for us when we needed one.'

Sophie looked at Barry. Could it have belonged to the quarry? They'd need to follow it up.

'So, you don't know the details of what happened to DC Ford?'

'No.'

'Didn't you ask? I'd have thought you'd have wanted to know, out of simple curiosity.'

'You don't know Tonto. You don't ask that bloke questions. And Liam went quiet on me. He was worried about something.'

Sophie decided to change tack. 'Did you know the man who was found dead a few days before? Tony Quigley? He lived in Dorchester.'

Boulden nodded, wary.

'We need an explanation, Mr Boulden. How did you know him?'

'He was with Bill a couple of times when we met for a few pints. He used to be a screw at Portland, but that was before I met him.'

'What do you know about his death?'

Boulden shrugged.

'I'll repeat what we said earlier. It's in your interest to tell us what you know. We're in the process of putting the charges together for these crimes, and let me stress that they are serious ones. Murder, attempted murder, conspiracy, the lot. We'll be charging you very soon, but what we charge you with depends largely on what you tell us now. So it's decision time for you, Luke Boulden.'

For almost a minute, Boulden was silent, his thin face twisted with anxiety and unease.

He sighed. 'Quigley was useful. He supplied the gen about the prison layout and other stuff. I reckon he helped a lot more than that, but they never told me. I was just the driver whenever they did a run. Quigley was taking money for helping the operation. That's all I know. Then Tonto reckoned he was starting to talk to the cops, especially that Ford woman. That was weird, 'cause I'm pretty sure she was in on some of it. She was cosy with Bill for a long time, but then they fell out. I dunno anything else about what was going on. It was all beyond me and Liam. We just did what we was told.'

'So you were taking material to the prisons and finding ways of getting it smuggled inside? What methods did you use?'

'Anything. Visitors, drones, the lot. Some of the staff are open to a bit of extra dosh, like Quigley used to be, I s'pose. We used drones a lot until the screws got wind of it. They've started fixing up wires and netting, so we've stopped using them as much unless it's an open bit of ground like a recreation field. We've even just chucked stuff over a fence or wall if it's been arranged in advance. We got paid by their families. Bill sorted out the money, and it was always up front. If there was any trouble with anyone not paying, Tonto sorted it. Liam and me, we were the experts at finding ways to get the stuff inside.'

'How did you make contact with these people, and their families outside?' Barry asked.

'We started off contacting a few people and letting them know what we could supply. After that, it was all word of mouth. The families on the outside all know each other and pass on any news. Once they realised we did what we said we would, we never had any problems. We never had to do any work to get the jobs. They contacted us.'

'And you started in Portland, then moved on to other prisons? Guys Marsh? Then out to nearby counties?' Barry said.

'Yeah. That's about it. It was a great little earner.' Boulden smiled to himself. 'Maybe we should've kept it local. It's when we started spreading out to Winchester, Devizes and the like that the arguments started. It got too big and we all got uptight with each other. Someone was trying to turn it into a full-time business. That's what Liam thought. He complained about it, maybe he complained once too often. That was the trouble with Liam, he didn't know when to keep his mouth shut.'

Sophie looked at him. 'Who was trying to expand it, Mr Boulden? Bill Mapps?'

Boulden shrugged. 'Dunno. Prob'ly, but we wasn't told. I didn't see him all that much. He looked after all the paperwork and ordered the stuff through his businesses. But I dunno who made the decisions, not for sure. Who else could it have been?'

Sophie decided to change tack again. 'There was an incident in a local bar, two weeks ago. Saturday lunchtime. Tonto Leary threatened one of my officers. What was that about?'

'I dunno. Tonto runs this group trying to stop migrant spongers getting into the country. We want to get all these foreign crappers out. We meet up for a few beers and go to rallies. It's a free country. Anyway, that's what we were doing.'

'Who organised the group that day?'

'Tonto, I reckon. I dunno why he went for her either. He's never done that before. I tried to calm him down. Then I spotted Bill, sitting in a corner. Least I thought it was him. Tonto wouldn't tell me when I asked him, and we left pretty quick after. Didn't have a clue she was a cop until she showed her card. Something was going on, but I didn't know what it was. Dunno why Bill was there, if it was 'im. It got me worried, Liam too.'

'Do you know why Liam was killed, Mr Boulden?' Sophie asked. 'We know it was deliberate, and we're pretty sure it was your friend Leary. Why would he have done that?'

Boulden's face took on a haunted expression. 'I dunno. I've been thinking about it ever since it happened. I just dunno.' He sat, shaking his head slowly.

* * *

The two detectives were in the corridor sipping coffee.

'What do you think, Barry?'

'It's what we've been saying for some time. His story holds up. We have no evidence that he was involved in any of the murders, and we know he managed to restrain Leary in that bar incident with Lydia. I tend to believe him, but we'll need to check his alibi for that night. And if we can trace the van, we can check it for DNA. That would tell us who was in the van and involved in Andrea's murder. So where do we go from here, ma'am?'

'Onwards and upwards. It's time to talk to Mapps again. Maybe he's seen some sense, though I don't hold out any great hopes. He can't seem to see the seriousness of the position he's in, God knows why. His lawyer should be back here by now.'

Mapps had lost some of his composure of the previous day. He was jittery and looked tired.

'You said yesterday that you'd see me again in a few hours,' he complained. 'I've been stuck in this place overnight. Those cells are a bloody disgrace.'

'Don't complain to me, Mr Mapps. Your great friend Eton Taylor, or Tonto Leary as he prefers to be known, assaulted one of my officers with a crowbar yesterday near the quarry where he works. She's still in intensive care. As you can imagine, I've been very busy. He's in another of our cells, hopefully thinking about his future. We'll be charging him with attempted murder on top of the other crimes. These violent incidents keep mounting up, don't they? I thought you should know in case it helps you make up your mind to come clean about all this.'

'I haven't killed anyone. I haven't assaulted anyone. What they do when I'm not around is nothing to do with me. Don't try to pin any of that stuff onto me. It won't work.'

'But you were involved, Mr Mapps. We think you were a member of the group that pushed Andrea Ford into a van and drove her down to the quayside. If a decision had already been made to kill her, and we believe that to be the case, then that makes you complicit in her murder. The same goes for Tony Quigley's death. Both of them had holidays at your villa in Spain at your expense. We have evidence to prove it, it's all in your business records.'

'Andrea and I had a thing going a few years ago,' Mapps said. 'I took her to Spain because that's the kind of thing people do when they're in a relationship. They go away together. It's fucking stupid to use that to say I was involved in killing her.'

'The holidays were one of the rewards for services rendered. In Andrea's case, she kept your operations off the police radar. And Tony Quigley? He was a key player in your smuggling operation. His help was indispensable, and you made sure he was well rewarded. Then, when they'd had enough and your demands began to escalate, they both wanted out. They ended up dead instead.'

'You've got it all wrong. That's all I'm gonna say. All wrong.'

Mapps refused to say anything else, and he was taken back to his cell.

Rae, who'd made a quick visit to Taylor's home with the forensic team, met them as they left the interview room.

'Eton Taylor has a boat. He keeps it in Portland marina, in the furthest corner.'

'Well, what are we waiting for? Let's go and have a look.'

* * *

'The one we're looking for is along here at the end of this pontoon,' Rae said. 'It's called Lone Ranger.' They made their way along the timber walkway.

'Would you believe it?' Sophie replied. 'Just like the old TV series.'

'You'll have to explain, ma'am,' Barry said. 'Doesn't mean a thing to me.'

'It's a really old western series that my mum watched when she was a girl. I think it was made into a film about ten years ago. The Lone Ranger supposedly fought for truth and justice. He wore a facemask, which I always found a bit creepy. His loyal helper was an Indian tracker by the name of Tonto. It all makes sense now, doesn't it?'

Barry and Rae continued to look bemused.

They reached the boat, a beautiful, thirty foot sailing yacht, its white hull glinting in the afternoon sun. They climbed aboard and peered into the cabin through the portholes. Barry lifted the canvas cover off the cockpit and the three of them stepped down into the open area. They examined the varnished timber edgings to the cockpit, looking for signs of damage. Barry spotted it, at the rear port corner. On such a perfectly maintained boat, the marks stood out. The layer of shiny varnish had been damaged in several places, consistent with a hard blow with a hammer or something similar. In one spot the timber had been damaged, it's surface no longer smooth and shiny.

'This is it,' Sophie said. 'Problem solved. Let's get a forensic team in. They can match it up with the fragments found in Andrea's fingertips, though there's not much doubt, is there? Those marks could be blood, though someone's wiped the surface down by the looks of it.' She looked around at the marina. 'Maybe someone saw something that night. We might find a witness.'

'How likely is that, ma'am? It was a cold Monday night in January.'

'Boat enthusiasts can be strange people, Barry. There's no predicting when they might be down here doing some maintenance work on their boat, or even just sleeping off a hangover. Some of these cabins can be nice and cosy. Maybe there's a record of this boat being taken out last Monday night. Let's go and pay the harbour master a visit. I wonder why they didn't report it when we asked a few days ago?'

'We didn't know the name Eton Taylor then, ma'am,' Rae said.

They spoke to an assistant manager. 'If the boat went out late in the evening and returned a few hours later, there wouldn't be a record. Even during daylight hours, small boats come and go as the owners please. We're not funded for that degree of record keeping. What you're hinting at is a bit big-brother-ish, isn't it? Do we really want that level of snooping, just in case it might provide useful information to the police?'

Sophie sighed. 'You're right, of course. It's just that we could do with some hard evidence about that boat's recent movements.'

'Well, there isn't any.' She still sounded critical. 'The only CCTV we have is scanning our land entrance, recording who comes in and out on foot or by car. That's where the trouble lies from our point of view — thieves and vandals.'

'Would you still have the recording for Monday night of last week?' Barry asked. 'That might be all we need.'

The woman remained indignant. 'Of course. We have a state of the art system here, not some tacky device that uses the same tape over and over again. What do you take us for?'

'Can we see it, please?' Barry said, smiling slightly.

They were led to an inner office, where the woman switched on a computer screen and navigated her way to the footage for the night in question. Barry spotted what he was looking for: the arrival of a plain white van at ten fifty in the evening. Eton Taylor was seen to climb out of the vehicle and unlock the security gate.

'There's someone else in the passenger seat,' Sophie said. 'I can't make out the features. Could it be Bill Mapps?'

Barry shook his head. 'It's too dim to tell. As it is, it could be anyone.'

'Blast. It helps to nail our friend Tonto, but not the people with him.'

They watched the van disappear from view.

'It'll give the view from the other side of the van when it leaves,' Rae suggested. 'Maybe we'll get a clearer view then.'

'Good thinking, Rae. Why didn't I think of that? Am I getting too old? And don't answer that, either of you, on pain of dismissal.'

Rae had been right. The return of the van, at four fifteen in the morning, clearly showed Liam Fenners in the passenger seat, peering through the window as the van drove slowly through the entrance. It was Liam who climbed out to close the gate once the van had passed through.

Sophie frowned. 'It doesn't really help, does it? Was there anybody else in that van, other than Taylor, Fenners and Andrea Ford? That's the key question. According to Boulden, Mapps was there, but this footage doesn't show him, or anyone else. And the problem is that Boulden's version of events is second hand. He says he wasn't there, and we've no evidence to the contrary. We need to find the van. A detailed forensic examination might tell us all we need to know. And why wasn't Fenners still driving on the return? Maybe they'd had an argument? It's still too tangled up for my liking.'

Barry and Rae looked at her, puzzled. This evidence nailed Eton Taylor. It put him and Fenners directly in the frame as Andrea's killers. They already knew that DNA evidence from Quigley's house had placed Fenners there at some time. Maybe Eton Taylor had been there too and his DNA would show up now that he'd given a sample. It also explained why Taylor killed Fenners a few days later. His death removed possibly the only witness to the events, particularly what happened on the boat that Monday night. Why did the boss seem so ill at ease? Why so dissatisfied?

Chapter 40: Witness

Thursday Evening

Rose Simons and George Warrander had been carrying out house-to-house inquiries near the New World wine bar but had drawn a blank. None of the residents of the flats above the shops and cafes could remember seeing anything unusual on the night when Andrea had been abducted.

'Not surprising really,' Rose said. 'It's January, for God's sake. Who in their right mind is going to be spending their late evenings peering out at a cold, damp street when they could be tucked up in bed, sipping a mug of rum-laced cocoa? I ask you.' She looked at her watch. 'Time's ticking on, Georgie boy. Let's hoof it round the corner to the spot where the delightful Andrea was reported to have been pushed into that van. Maybe we'll strike it lucky there.'

They found a terrace of rather grand Victorian houses with small front gardens facing a small park on the opposite side of the street. The shrubs and hedges along the boundary were held in check by black railings. They could see clumps of trees and scattered flowerbeds, although these were largely bare at this time of year. Most of the houses had been converted into flats, so it would take them some time to visit them all.

Rose sighed deeply. 'There's a pub at the other end and we'll have finished our shift by the time we get there. Mine's a double scotch and a packet of cheese and onion crisps. You'll be driving us back to the station, so I can only allow you half a pint of piss-weak lager. Think of the health benefits, though.'

To Rose's astonishment, they found their witness in the third house, an elderly man who'd been drawing his front curtains just as Andrea and Simon Osman approached on the opposite side of the road.

'It was a few minutes before eleven,' Bob Hughes said. 'The news had finished on the TV. I watched the weather forecast and a few minutes of the next programme but it was rubbish, so I decided to go to bed. I was pulling the curtains and I saw them walking along just opposite. The woman looked as if she was in a right state. She was really wobbly on her feet and only stayed up because the man was holding her. She was leaning into him and he was supporting her with his arm around her back and under her armpit. It was odd because she was smartly dressed, and she wasn't a youngster. That's why I carried on watching.'

'What happened to them?'

'A bit odd really. There was a van parked a bit further along with its engine running. The couple disappeared behind it, so I couldn't see them. Then the van drove off. When it had gone there was no one there.'

'No one there? Had they moved on and disappeared from view?'

'I didn't see anyone. But the entrance to the park is about there, so maybe they went in. She might have wanted to be sick for all I know. Or they'd speeded up for some reason and were past where I could see by the time the van moved off.'

George took a note of his contact details, thanked him for his help and they walked back to their car.

'I know for a fact that the gate is locked at six sharp,' Rose said. 'I've had to rescue people who've got stuck on the railings trying to get in or out at night. So what does that tell us, Georgie? A bit suspicious, don't you think? Let's hot-foot it across to your favourite 'tec and report it. Maybe she'll pay for our drinks as a thank you.'

* * *

It was mid-evening before the three detectives were able to visit Eton Taylor's small, end-of-terrace house in the old part of Portland. Local detectives had been there for some time but had been ordered to stand back and wait for the arrival of the forensic unit. Its members had been there for several hours before Sophie and her team arrived.

'Anything for us, Dave?' she asked the county forensic chief.

'Most definitely yes,' he said. 'Lots of what I call thug-stuff. A collection of knives that are definitely not the kind you find in your average kitchen. Several baseball bats. Combat-style clothes. Balaclavas. Books and magazines about citizen armies and self-defence. Photos of a few well-known extreme nationalists. Exactly what you might expect from an extremist hoodlum. We haven't finished yet, so just use your usual caution. There's a mad dog, by the way. We've tied it up outside. It's been snarling and spitting at anyone who goes near it. I don't really know what to do with it. I've called the local RSPCA but I'm not sure they'll want to take it when they see what it's like.'

'We're not expecting it to be a crime scene, not as far as we know. I doubt whether Andrea was ever brought here, or anyone else to be honest. It just gives us an idea of the type of person he is.'

They had a quick look round the gloomy interior. Posters of men in combat gear lined some of the walls. A pin board in the kitchen held photos of British politicians from different ethnic groups, all defaced with an inked bullet wound in the middle of their foreheads. Pride of place went to a photo of Barack Obama, with a neatly drawn cleaver embedded in his skull.

Rae shook her head slowly. 'God, this is sick. Really sick.'

'The forensic people will find more than this, Rae,' Barry said. 'There'll be far nastier stuff on his computer.'

They left the forensic squad to do their work and returned to the station. Sophie steeled herself to interview Eton Taylor. This was the man who had attacked Lydia with a crowbar. Could she control her anger?

* * *

Taylor was exactly as Danny Fenners had described him. Sophie could see why the young, nervous boy had been so scared of this man. He sat leaning back on the plastic chair, narrowed eyes moving slowly around the room, observing the people who had just entered. Eton Taylor, or Tonto Leary as the Fenners children knew him, oozed intimidation like poisonous liquid slime.

Sophie spoke in a measured tone. 'We've just visited your house, Mr Taylor, and we've left a forensic team there. We've also examined your boat, particularly some marks on the cockpit edging, and a forensic unit have taken samples. The game's up. It's time for you to start talking. We want some explanations. Let's start with where you were just under two weeks ago, on the Saturday. You visited the Baldwin Bar in Bournemouth. Why were you and your friends there?'

'We can go where we want. It's a free country.'

'I don't dispute that. But you instigated an incident that was clearly motivated by racial hatred. Why?'

He shrugged. 'I don't like foreigner leeches. I said that to the bitch who came into the bar. I didn't know she was one of yours.'

'Oh, but we think you did know. The evidence from the bar's CCTV and the statements from witnesses lead us strongly to that conclusion.'

'You can't prove that.'

'Where did you go when you left the bar?'

'We split up, if you must know. We'd had enough hassle from your lot. Bloody police state.'

Sophie looked at him coldly. 'You've avoided answering my question.'

He laughed. 'No comment.'

'When did you first meet Tony Quigley?'

'No comment. Look, I've had enough of this. It's fucking pointless. If you think you know it all, go ahead and prove it. I'm not gonna give you any help. You can forget it.'

'What's your dog's name, Mr Taylor?'

There was a short silence. Taylor looked straight at her for the first time. 'Skipper. Where is he?'

'The RSPCA are trying to find someone to take it in but it isn't easy. It snarls and lunges at anyone who comes near.'

'Skipper isn't an it. He's a he. He's a fucking good dog. Totally loyal. Totally.' Taylor sat up.

'Well, its future is in doubt. If it's impossible to find someone, it will have to be put down,' Sophie said indifferently.

'I fucking told you, Skipper's a he.' Taylor was getting angry.

'It's only a dog, for goodness sake. And a bloody nuisance, if you ask me. You're not likely to see it again, so why should you care?'

Taylor looked down at the faded plastic of the tabletop. Sophie watched carefully.

He spoke in a low voice. 'I love that dog. If I tell you about Quigley, will you see he's looked after?'

'I want the truth about Andrea as well.'

Chapter 41: When a Plan Comes Together

Friday morning

Like its neighbours, the stylish, detached house was quiet. Unlike them, it had been unoccupied for several days. Two cats, fresh from a night's hunting, eyed the three detectives as they approached the front porch. Sophie took a key from her bag and opened the door.

'So where do we start, ma'am?' Barry asked. 'I'm still not sure what we're looking for.'

Sophie shrugged. 'Nor am I. Let's get our bearings by taking a look around the front sitting room. It'll be familiar to us. And let's stay together. We can talk while we're searching.'

They entered the sitting room, with its brown leather suite staged around the open fireplace, a stack of logs neatly arranged in the hearth. There were several pieces of artwork on the walls, all originals by the look of them, possibly by local artists.

Rae looked through the magazine rack while Sophie and Barry examined the shelves of a small unit. Nothing seemed out of place or out of the ordinary.

'We need to find the study or office, or wherever he keeps his documents. I want to piece together his history and get an idea of what type of man he is.'

Barry found what they were looking for on the first floor, a room, once a bedroom, that had been tastefully converted into a functional, comfortable office. A desk was placed close to a bay window, at an angle so that it wouldn't receive direct sunlight.

'Isn't this lovely?' Sophie said, but her two juniors were already moving towards the storage units standing side by side against a wall. Sophie started to sift through the desk drawers. Where would he keep personal material? In the end, she found it in the bottom drawer of the desk. It was the only drawer that was locked, but the key was conveniently kept in a small leather container in the top drawer. A ring-binder contained a sheaf of certificates, diplomas and personal papers, all in chronological order. She turned the pages with increasing interest.

'He was in the army,' she said. 'That's where he got all of these qualifications.'

The other two came and looked over her shoulder.

'He was a major. Would you believe it? Doesn't it all make sense now? Look. He was in the SPS branch.'

'What's that, ma'am?' Rae asked.

'Staff and personnel support. It used to be known as the Pay Corps. This is fantastic. Let's keep looking.'

Barry turned up the next item, something totally unexpected. A list of properties he owned and with it documents that showed clearly that the Highlander Bar in Dorchester, the apparent centre of racist activity in the region, belonged to him. He turned over a few more pages. The Villa Rosina near Malaga in Spain.

'Ma'am, time to break open the bubbly. You need to see what's in this folder.'

* * *

'Hello, my hunky man.' Barry's fiancé, Gwen, a detective sergeant with Hampshire police, greeted them at the door. 'Bet you didn't expect me.'

The look on Barry's face was priceless. Sophie couldn't help but laugh. 'I didn't tell him. I thought it would be a nice surprise. What with this case being so complicated, who knows when you two last managed to see each other. I can leave him with you, if you want, Gwen. We're just about wrapped up. We won't start the admin stuff until Monday, so we can all afford some time off to relax this weekend. How does that grab you, Barry?'

'I might have known,' he replied. 'I should have guessed you were up to something with that last phone call. But I appreciate it. I've been running on near-empty for a couple of days now.'

'Haven't we all,' Sophie said. 'It only occurred to me when Jack mentioned that Gwen was on duty across here. But I do love it when a plan comes together. Who said that, by the way?'

Barry and Rae looked blank, but Gwen answered immediately. 'Hannibal Smith in the A Team. My dad was a total addict of that show. He had a T-shirt with that very quote on it. It was his pride and joy and he nearly cried when the cat was sick on it while it was in the laundry basket. He claimed he could smell cat vomit ever afterwards, despite mum washing it over and over again. He wouldn't throw it out, though.'

'Well, this is all well and good, but we're here for a reason,' Sophie said. 'I suppose we'd better get on with it.'

The group of detectives moved into the hallway. 'He's in the lounge, reading,' Gwen said.

Simon Osman looked up as the team entered the room. He put down his book and gave Sophie a wary smile. She didn't return it.

'Good morning, Mr Osman. You've obviously been well looked after and well protected during your few days here. That will be coming to an end, as of now.'

'Thank goodness,' he replied. 'So, you've got them all? And I can go home quite safely?'

Sophie folded her arms as Barry moved around the room to stand beside the seated man. 'Yes, we have them all safely in custody, along with lots of evidence. And that evidence is growing by the hour, in all kinds of unexpected ways. We have new witnesses, we have documents and at long last I feel that I can safely say that the end is in sight. Over to you, Barry.'

Barry cleared his throat. 'Simon Brian Osman, I'm arresting you for the murder of Andrea Ford. You do not have to say anything, but it may harm your defence if you do not mention when questioned something which you later rely on in court. Anything you do say may be given in evidence.'

He clipped the handcuffs onto Osman's wrists.

'DNA, Mr Osman,' Sophie said. 'On the damaged gunwale timber on Taylor's boat. It looks very much as if it was you who held her hands down while your sick friend hit her with the hammer. And we have a witness who saw you earlier that night as she was bundled into the van. And, of course, there's all the army stuff in your house. You never told us you were the financial administrator for the same signals regiment the other three served in. Or that you were the joint owner, along with your friend Bill Mapps, of the Highlander Bar in Dorchester and that villa in Spain. And there you were, trying to act the innocent when we interviewed you earlier. I can't begin to tell you what I think of you, Mr Osman. You and Tonto Leary, as he likes to be known, that sick, barbaric man. Well, you're right there in the gutter with him. I can't find words for the utter disgust I feel.' She turned to Barry. 'Let's get him back to the station and put him where he belongs. In a cell.'

* * *

At midnight, in Dorchester Hospital's intensive care unit, a light on a monitoring unit beside Lydia's bed began to flash, while a repetitive warning beep sounded at the nurses' monitoring station out in the corridor. Several nurses ran into the small room, followed quickly by a doctor. A group of anxious-looking staff surrounded the bed, knowing they only had seconds to decide on the best course of action.

Outside, in the skies above Dorset, the moon shone, cold and bright, its silvery light glinting on the waves lapping the shoreline, onto the bleak heathland, throwing clumps of gorse and heather into stark silhouettes, and down onto the deserted country roads and lanes, causing deep shadows to mottle their surfaces. All was quiet.

Chapter 42: Concert

Saturday Evening

As arranged, a few minutes before seven, Sophie called at Charlie Bailey's neat little house in a quiet backstreet in Weymouth. The door was opened almost immediately, and the excited face of Danny Fenners greeted her.

'We're all ready,' he said. 'We've just got to get our coats.'

'Rae should be there already. She's planning to bring her boyfriend,' Sophie said. 'I think a couple of the others will try to get in as well. I hope there are tickets left. We're all really looking forward to it. My husband's going too. I never told you that, did I?'

Danny looked puzzled. 'Why would he want to come along?'

'Well, I don't think I ever told you that one of our daughters plays in the Dorset senior band, and they're on after your group, in the second half. She plays alto, like you, but I think I did mention that.'

He frowned. 'Yeah, but not that she'd be in my concert. Which one's she?'

'Tall? Dark hair? She's eighteen now. She's in her last year at school, up at Wareham, where we live. She's got a couple of solos to play.'

'Oh, wow. I know who she is. She's great. I didn't see the seniors until the dress rehearsal this morning. Is she really your daughter?'

Sophie nodded solemnly, just as Kerry and Charlie appeared.

'Let's go,' Charlie said. 'Got your music, Danny?'

The local concert hall was buzzing with excitement while youngsters of all ages found their places in various bands, and family members hunted for their seats. A silence descended on the auditorium as the first conductor appeared, and a junior band of enthusiastic eleven and twelve-year-olds launched into their opening number.

Rae's boyfriend, Craig, leant across to speak to Martin Allen. 'This was me, fifteen years ago, but across in Winchester, where I grew up. Me and my trumpet, making a lot of squeaky noises. It's great. I love it.'

'That's music for you. It starts with little kids making all kinds of weird sounds on their instruments and ends up with Elton John and Mozart. It's just fantastic. And that's a mathematician talking.'

At the other end of their row, Kerry was hugging her grandfather's arm. Sophie glanced across. Was it too early to think that this troubled girl had turned a corner? The shock of her parents' deaths seemed to have shifted her from her previous self-destructive path, but it was early days yet.

The time soon came for Danny's intermediate level band to play their numbers. Danny himself played his short solo in the middle of one of their tunes. He made only one slight mistake, which was far better than most of his friends.

'He's been practising for ages,' Kerry said, her eyes shining. 'Wasn't he good? We're so proud of him, aren't we, Gramps?'

* * *

Once the concert was over, the group gathered in the foyer before making their way home. Jade walked across to them, carrying her saxophone case.

'Is there room in your car for me, Mum? It'll give me a chance to chat to my fellow superstar here.' She grinned widely at Danny, who smiled sheepishly back.

'I want to play like you one day,' he said. 'That was awesome.'

Kerry, too, was interested in this tall, elegant eighteen-year-old who'd managed to captivate the audience with a moody solo in the middle of a Duke Ellington number. Kerry tilted her head and looked at the older girl through narrowed eyes.

'Are you gonna study music when you leave school?' she asked.

Jade shook her head. 'Nope. I've got a place to do medicine. That's if I get the results they want. It was a hard choice between the two, though. My older sister's an actress, and Dad always says that having one prima donna in the family is quite enough.' She paused. 'What about you?'

All the adults pricked their ears up and tried not to look at Kerry.

'I dunno really. I think I'll stay on at school after my GCSEs and see what it's like. What's history like? Do you know anyone doing it?'

'Oh yeah,' Jade said. 'One of my closest friends. She's got it down as her first choice for university. She loves it. I think she's mad. But we're all different, aren't we?'

Charlie put his hand through his granddaughter's arm. 'That we are. And it's a bloody good thing, if you ask me. Wouldn't things be boring if we were all the same?'

Sophie switched her phone back on and found a text message from Kevin McGreedie. She leaned back against the wall, tears running down her face.

'Thank God,' she whispered. 'Lydia's pulled through.'

ACKNOWLEDGEMENTS

This is a work of fiction, and none of the characters and situations described in this novel bear any resemblance to real persons or events.

I must thank many people for their help, support and continued friendship during the writing of this novel. Firstly, the staff at Joffe Books. My thanks to the editorial team, particularly Anne Derges, the crime editor, who is an expert at sharpening up my slightly rambling original text to make it fit for people to read.

Next, to the friends, particularly Sylvie and Becky, who help me to keep my sanity intact by accompanying me to noisy pub-gig nights. I must also mention my friend Patricia Davies, now 91 years young, still a jazz fan and still going strong!

Finally, and most importantly, a mention of my nearest and dearest. To my sons, Stephen, Malcolm and David, and their families. Above all, to my wonderful wife, Margaret.

Thank you for reading this book. If you enjoyed it please leave feedback on Amazon, and if there is anything we missed or you have a question about then please get in touch. The author and publishing team appreciate your feedback and time reading this book.

Our email is office@joffebooks.com

www.joffebooks.com

More about Michael Hambling:

www.michaelhambling.co.uk

ALSO BY MICHAEL HAMBLING

DARK CRIMES
DEADLY CRIMES
SECRET CRIMES
BURIED CRIMES
TWISTED CRIMES
EVIL CRIMES
SHADOW CRIMES

Printed in Great Britain
by Amazon

35058659R00163